Books by Gwen Mayo and Sarah E. Glenn

Murder at the Million Dollar Pier

Murder on the Mullet Express

Books by Gwen Mayo

Concealed in Ash

Circle of Dishonor

Books by Sarah E. Glenn

All This and Family Too

The Strangely Funny Anthologies

Murder at the
Million Dollar
Pier

Gwen Mayo
and
Sarah E. Glenn

MURDER AT THE MILLION DOLLAR PIER

A Three Snowbirds Mystery
Copyright© 2019
Gwen Mayo and Sarah E. Glenn

Edited by Sarah E. Glenn
Cover designed by Patty G. Henderson
at Boulevard Photografica
Published by
Mystery and Horror, LLC
Clearwater, FL

ISBN-13: 978-1-949281-08-8

This is a work of fiction. Historical persons and events depicted in this book are carefully researched. The authors have tried to remain true to the known facts, but our primary concern is in telling a compelling story. Any resemblance to any actual person living or dead, or to any known event or location is included only where it is relative to the setting and history.

This book is dedicated to Christy Mayo McMillen. When I think of strong, courageous women doing whatever is necessary to take care of others, I think of you.

ACKNOWLEDGMENTS

The first person I need to thank for her support is Kathy Glenn. She is always the first to purchase copies, get our book into her local library, and generally acts as our number one cheerleader.

We need to thank the staff of the Vinoy for providing us with information about and access to the hotel. Thank you, St. Petersburg, for preserving many of the unique features of the city that make it a wonderful setting for a book. During the writing of *Murder at the Million Dollar Pier* we have explored the parks and historic buildings, dug through library archives, and read copies of the 1926 *St Petersburg Times* and *The Evening Independent* newspapers.

As always, we want to thank our Sisters in Crime for their support, assistance, and wide range of knowledge. Whenever we needed an answer, one of you was there to help us find it. Over the years, Sarah and I have belonged to several chapters and found wonderful friends in each of them. A special thank you goes to Cheryl Hollon, author of the Webb's Glass Shop Mysteries, for taking time out of her busy schedule to read and review the book.

There are always people that I forget to mention in this section of the book. To all of you, I am sorry. I tend to remember who answered questions, provided help, or listened to me whine the day after the book goes to press. So, THANK YOU and please accept my humble apology for failing to include your name.

Murder
at the
Million Dollar
Pier

CHAPTER ONE

"Teddy! Put that jar away before you get us arrested." Cornelia looked back to see if the sheriff's car they had just passed was turning around.

"I have my prescription with me," Teddy cheerfully replied.

"That's for a bottle of medicinal alcohol, not Mr. Scroggins' hooch. What happens when they find out you have a whole suitcase full of illegal booze?"

"It's not full—anymore."

If she had not been driving, Cornelia would have planted her face in her palms. "You're incorrigible."

The belly laughs from the rear of the Dodge Brothers Touring Sedan didn't help. Her uncle was laughing so hard that his face, above the snowy beard, was beet red and tears had formed in the corners of his eyes. Her traveling companions were impossible, both of them.

She sighed, shifted the gears of the car, and turned onto the paved road.

The road into the heart of Saint Petersburg was broad and lined with restaurants and stores. "Civilization at last!" Teddy sighed, silver curls glinting in the afternoon light. "We've left the jungle."

"I must say," Cornelia replied, "that even I am glad to be back on paved roads. It's easier on the tires."

"And one's backside," Uncle Percival added from the back seat, jammed between suitcases. "Makes it difficult to nap."

Cornelia shifted to a gear better suited to city traffic. "No more need to nap or trade off driving, Uncle. We've arrived."

The conversation died when Cornelia turned off Central Avenue onto the street that paralleled the waterfront. A wide ribbon of grass bordered a yacht basin filled with pleasure craft. Their tall masts reached for the heavens. Beyond, they could see an expanse of brilliant waters in shades of turquoise, green, and blue sparkling in the sunlight. Tampa Bay was even more beautiful than when she first saw it some thirty years before, en route to San Juan. The car ahead of them lingered for a better look at the toys of the wealthy, and Cornelia veered around it. The view of the bay opened before them, and the pale shades of shallow water gave way to dark blue under an azure sky dotted with cotton ball clouds. At least a dozen sailboats glided along the horizon. Cornelia couldn't help smiling as she breathed in the salty sea air.

"Look at the palm trees lining the road," Teddy said. "So stately."

"I thought you were happy to be leaving the jungle," Cornelia teased. "We've seen plenty of palms for the past couple of weeks. They grow all along the highway."

"But these are decorative palms. There's a difference."

"If you say so, dear."

"There's the Pier," Cornelia's uncle announced, with excitement in his voice. "I can hardly wait to walk it. Do you think we have time to speak to the workers?"

The women in the front seat didn't reply. They were staring at the enormous hotel facing the water. Its brilliant pink wings opened from a rosy façade with columns and frescos.

"Is that the Vinoy?" Teddy asked, never caught without words for long. "It's marvelous."

Uncle Percival shifted his view. "It is an impressive structure, although I think the local builders are overly enamored with flamingo colors. I've never seen so much pink."

"I love it," Teddy asserted.

"Of course you do," Cornelia said.

Their friend Mitch, a reporter with the Saint Petersburg Times, had told them that a meal at the Vinoy would cost him a week's pay. Cornelia believed it; the scrollwork and carved details on the front entrance alone told her the hotel was not intended for ordinary travelers. In her experience, graceful lines and beautiful architecture amounted to a pretty penny on the final bill.

She pulled into the circular drive, and a uniformed valet rushed to the side of her car. His eyebrows rose when he saw a woman at the wheel. The surprised look vanished in an instant.

Cornelia was impressed with how fast his smile returned.

"Welcome to the Vinoy, ma'am. How may I help you?"

"My uncle"—she indicated the elderly man in the back—"has booked rooms for a few days."

The valet eyed the embroidered curtains Teddy had added to the rear passenger windows. Hardly standard issue. "Very good, ma'am. We'll handle your vehicle and luggage while you register."

Cornelia climbed out of the Dodge and handed it over to the young man. Her first deed was straightening her suit jacket—an ingrained habit after decades with the military—followed by donning her broad-brimmed hat.

On the other side of the vehicle, a bellboy assisted Teddy and her uncle to the curb. He and the valet began emptying the back seat of its luggage. This was no easy task; between Teddy's steamer trunk and her uncle's camera equipment, it had been difficult for Cornelia to squeeze a single carpetbag in for herself. Her clothes were probably crushed again; she made a mental note to inquire about laundry service at the front desk.

The valet was standing at her side, looking expectant. She reached into her bag and gave him the tip he openly expected. He glanced at the change she'd given him before thanking her.

He looks disappointed, she thought. *He's probably used to wads of bills from the swells and swank businessmen.*

3

Well, she'd given him a fair price for what he'd done. It was the bellboy who was going to deserve the bigger tip.

The line of registrants stretched out the double doors and down the stairs. If it was this busy on a Wednesday, the weekend would be frightful. They were in for a long wait.

Her uncle repeated his name for the concierge, more loudly this time. The echoing chatter in the lobby would challenge any ear. "No, I'm not part of the group from Portland. Professor Percival Pettijohn, retired. I engaged a suite with an adjoining room for my nieces."

The young man flipped through the pages of hotel reservations. "Certainly, sir, but it may take me a moment to sift through the state of Maine. Oh, there you are. You were supposed to arrive last week. It says here that you were delayed."

Being jailed on suspicion of murder counts as a delay, I suppose, Cornelia mused. She had enjoyed bird-watching in Homosassa, but there were moments in their visit she could have done without.

"Indeed we were," Uncle Percival replied, without losing the twinkle in his smile. "You were so kind to accommodate the change on short notice. I hope you can still grant us the suite arrangement. If not, we need two rooms close together."

"Of course, sir." He checked the reservation. "Yes, they have you listed with a bay view suite, and an adjoining room with a private bath for your nieces."

Technically, Teddy wasn't a niece, but the claim made traveling arrangements easier. Cornelia glanced around the lobby, with its vaulted ceiling, large cypress wood beams, and heavy chandeliers. A beautiful place, but how much was this stay costing her uncle?

Her gaze returned to ground level, and she saw that Teddy was speaking with two attractive young women. Both had bobbed hair and wore the long strands of beads currently in fashion. Their dresses were the latest style, with long waists and skirts shorter than the ones the French girls wore during the Great War.

4

As usual, Teddy was already making friends. Or was she on the search for a swell party? Honestly, the woman was a dowsing rod for booze.

When Uncle Percival was ready to go to their rooms, though, Teddy was all a-chatter about the short hairstyles and the hotel salon instead.

Their room was enormous; large enough for two full sized beds, a dresser, a wardrobe, and a private bath. There was even a space with two chairs by the window, which overlooked a spacious lawn. In the distance, the azure waters beckoned.

Teddy had the bellboy arrange their suitcases on the luggage racks before dismissing him. She tipped him well for his trouble. Once he was gone, she plopped on one of the mattresses and grinned.

"Big beds, plump pillows, a lovely view, and we don't have to share the bath," she said. "This is the life!"

Cornelia removed her jacket and began hanging things in the wardrobe. "It definitely beats the nurse quarters in the Philippines, but I'm worried about the cost. Uncle's money isn't endless."

"No, but I don't think you need to fret. I've noticed that your uncle always keeps a close eye on his finances. This was supposed to be his birthday treat, remember? Although it's an odd one—visiting a pier that's still under construction doesn't sound like fun."

"It's the engineer in him," Cornelia said, smiling at last. "He's retired from teaching, but not from his curiosity. You're right about his views on money, though—no one in our family was ever frivolous. My late grandfather may roust from the grave and tan Uncle Percy's backside for wasting so much money on one hotel stay."

"I intend to be frivolous enough to make up for the two of you," Teddy said. "When you're visiting the pier with your uncle, I'm going to go make myself beautiful at the salon."

"You're already beautiful. What makes you think I'm going to follow my uncle to the pier instead of going to the salon with you?"

"Easy," she replied. "He's going to expect you to lug that tripod around so he can film the construction. If he spent his time studying people instead of projects, he'd be another Cecil B. DeMille."

They dressed for dinner. The professor wore a more formal jacket and tie than he usually chose, and Cornelia donned her black silk gown. It was getting a lot of use on this trip; tomorrow, she would have it properly laundered.

Teddy, of course, was the flashy one. Her evening dress was embroidered voile over an aquamarine slip. She had foregone her usual bandeau for a rhinestone-studded comb at one temple.

"I shall be the envy of everyone tonight," Uncle Percival said. "A beautiful woman on each arm."

"They'll think you're a real sugar daddy," Teddy replied. "We'll need to beat the shebas off you."

Cornelia smiled at the mental picture. Her uncle was charming, but no ladies' man.

Her father told her that Percival had been engaged once, but when she'd asked what happened, he'd shrugged and said his brother never told him. As they waited for the elevator, she remembered all the tragic reasons she'd conjured to explain why Uncle Percival never married. Most of them were worthy of the worst sort of radio drama. At some point, she'd concluded that his intended must have realized that his greatest devotion was reserved for the miracles of engineering. No woman wanted to be second fiddle to a chunk of metal.

The entrance to the dining room was broad, opening into a space filled with linen-covered tables. Open archways flanked each side. Dark-suited men sat with their jeweled companions, talking, laughing, and eating.

They were escorted to one of the tables and left to study the menu. Cornelia looked for an option that wouldn't bankrupt her uncle and discovered there were no prices on her menu. "How are we supposed to know what this meal is costing?" she grumbled.

"Our stay is on the American plan, dear," her uncle said. "Unless you want the meal delivered to your room, there are no additional charges."

She frowned as she read through descriptions of entrees. Did rich people really care that their roasted turkey was from rice-fed birds? How would they even know the claim was true? She sighed, decided on the red snapper, and laid the menu aside.

Teddy was more interested in the deep red and blue murals on the walls than ordering dinner. "I think they've gone for a Roman theme," she said. "Everywhere you look, there's a new detail to enjoy."

Their meal was excellent and, Cornelia suspected, very expensive. She was glad that she could get her fish sans Mornay sauce. It was tender, flaky, and baked to perfection.

The professor was so excited about the pier that he wouldn't have noticed if his short ribs were replaced with sawdust. He spent most of the meal discussing his plans for visiting the construction site in the morning. The concierge hadn't been sure whom to contact for permission, so the Professor had tasked the youth to identify the construction company from their equipment. This evening, he would settle for examining the design from the mezzanine terrace through Cornelia's field glasses. She wasn't planning to use them, was she?

"Did the concierge find the right person?" Teddy asked.

"I don't know," the professor said. "He was off duty when I stopped by later."

"So, your visit's been delayed," Cornelia said.

Uncle Percival reached for his water. "No, I intend to go down there tomorrow morning."

"What if they say that you haven't gone through proper channels?"

"I'll tell them that I'm too old to go through proper channels. Bureaucracy is a curse on mankind. By the way, Cornelia, I'll need you on camera duty. I must get this on film. I'm sure the engineering department at the university would be thrilled to see a project of this magnitude being constructed."

Teddy laughed and started to say something to Cornelia—probably "I told you so"—when a strange voice broke in.

"Nurse Teddy! Is that you?"

A young man stood at the empty side of the table. He was blond and square-built. He looked familiar, but Cornelia had met many young men during the Great War.

Teddy immediately recognized him. "Mac! How delightful to see you!" She turned to Cornelia's uncle. "Professor, this is Mac Stevens. He was a flying ace during the war. He spent some time in our hospital after a dogfight that sent a Fokker Eindecker down in flames."

Now Cornelia remembered him. The haphazardly landed airplane, the bleeding young man, then, later, sitting beside him in the back of the ambulance. "You're looking well, Mac."

"Thank you, Miss Petticoat—Pettijohn. Sorry, I misspoke."

"No, you didn't," Cornelia said. "You flyboys didn't come up with that nickname. Soldiers were calling me the Iron Petticoat before you were born."

"You make an impression, ma'am."

Uncle Percival stood and shook Mac's hand. "Pleased to meet you. I am Percival Pettijohn, Cornelia's uncle."

"It's good to meet you too, sir."

The professor returned to his seat. "And you're a pilot. Fascinating. When I served with the Union, we surveyed the battlefield with balloons of heated air. True flight must be much more exciting."

"I loved it," Mac confessed, "except for the time I was wounded. I spent many hours in the ward talking to Nurse Teddy."

"That sounds like Nurse Teddy," Cornelia said, and received a swat from her companion. "Are you also visiting Florida, or do you live here?"

"I have a place in town, but my parents are staying at the hotel. My father is involved with the construction in Saint Petersburg, so they're spending the winter here. It may be a permanent move if he continues to get so much business." He hesitated, then added, "My family is at a nearby table. Would you like to meet them?"

"I would love to," Teddy said. She and Cornelia followed the young man back to his family's table, which was a large one. "This is my mother, Florence," he said, gesturing to a plump woman with a dark blonde coiffure. "I was right; these are the nurses who took care of me in France. This is Nurse Teddy, and this is Nurse Pettijohn."

The woman smiled and clasped Teddy's hand. "Thank you for being there. You must be such brave women."

"Oh, no, he was the brave one," Teddy said. "We were there to help boys like him."

"Where's Father?" the young man asked.

"He went off to smoke," Florence said. "You know how he is."

Mac sighed. "He would be gone when I have someone important here. Ladies, these are my sisters, Evelyn and Violet."

Evelyn was a younger, blonder version of her mother. She was smartly dressed, with a gold sautoir that ended in sparkling beaded tassels. Violet, the youngest child, was the odd one out with jet black curls.

The man beside Evelyn, who had risen at their arrival, offered his hand. "Pleased to meet you, ladies. I'm Arthur Downs, Evelyn's fiancé." He was well-tanned, with hair kissed by the sun. Like Mac, he had a military bearing. He'd probably served in the Great War, too; he looked to be several years older than his prospective bride.

"So, Mac, what have you been doing since you left the service?" Teddy asked. "Are you flying again?"

Mac started to answer, then stopped. "Good, he's back. Father, I'd like you to meet the nurses who took care of me in France."

Cornelia turned around and saw a middle-aged man, dark-haired with white at the temples. Like his daughter, he appeared to be fond of gold: cufflinks, cigarette case, even a pinky ring. He began to smile, then froze, staring at something behind her.

That something was Teddy. Her face was now pale except for the powdered blush on her cheekbones, and her dark-rimmed eyes were wide. She stared back.

Then, she lunged past Cornelia and slapped Mac's father hard. "You—you scoundrel! You out-and-out rotter! You misbegotten—"

"Teddy!" Cornelia couldn't believe her eyes. Should she intervene? But no, her companion was stepping back, breathing hard from emotion.

Teddy turned, almost reeling, to Florence. "Mrs. Stevens. Mac. I'm sorry you had to see this," she said, trembling. "I hope—I hope he has been kind to you. I'll go back to my table now, if you don't mind."

Strangers gaped as Teddy lurched away like a wounded butterfly, hair comb taking flight from her tresses. It flashed in the air, then disappeared under one of the chairs. Cornelia started to go after it but was stopped by the head waiter.

"*Madame*, we cannot have this disturbance. The governor of Maine is here tonight!"

"She didn't slap *him*," she retorted, more sharply than she intended. "I'll hold her back if she goes for a rematch."

"Do you think she will?" the poor man asked in a worried voice.

"I don't." She pushed him aside. "Let me go to her."

Teddy sat at their table with her arms wrapped around herself. Uncle Percival was patting her shoulder solicitously. His expression was dour, but his eyes were alive with questions. She couldn't blame him. In all the years they had been together she had never seen Teddy have an outburst like this, not even when she was more than a little drunk.

"What was that about?" Cornelia demanded. "I assume that you know Mac's father."

"Know him? I was supposed to marry him." Teddy's body still shook, but her voice was firm. "I don't want to discuss it here."

Cornelia had shared many confidences with Teddy during their years together as army nurses, but this was a complete flabbergast. Questions pricked her mind, but none found exit through words. Teddy was right. A public restaurant was no place for this kind of discussion.

"Should we take you back to our rooms, then?" the professor asked, then added, "To recover, of course."

Teddy straightened in her seat and detangled her bangles. "No, I don't intend to allow him to ruin our visit. I'm going to finish my squab *au cresson* and soldier on."

"Good girl," Uncle Percival said, crestfallen.

Arthur's prospective father-in-law took his seat, rubbing his jaw.

Mrs. Stevens raised a well-shaped eyebrow. "That was *her*, wasn't it?"

"Not now," Stevens snapped.

Her? Arthur leaned close to Evelyn, inhaling the scent she usually wore, musky with a hint of tobacco. It wasn't unpleasant, but who wanted a wife that smelled like a fine smoke? He'd purchased some Shalimar to give her on Sunday, Valentine's Day. It was all the rage, according to his secretary, and a floral scent fit better with his business. "Who was that?"

"I don't know," she whispered. "Now shush, Daddy will hear."

Arthur looked from face to face. Violet was gazing directly down into her plate, picking at the food but not eating it. Mac had a dismayed expression on his face, as if the woman's explosion had somehow been his fault. It certainly wasn't; she'd seemed as surprised as the old man when they saw one another.

But, in the aftermath of the incident, Florence Stevens wasn't flustered at all. Arthur didn't find it a surprise, either, given Stevens' temperament, but the incident was interesting. He'd known a few military nurses in the navy. They didn't rattle in the face of mortar fire. It must have been some hullabaloo to cause that much anger.

CHAPTER TWO

After dinner, Cornelia found the words to go with her questions. She and Teddy were back in their room, and the professor had been shooed away. He'd urgently whispered to his niece that he expected an intelligence report on the situation in the morning. Cornelia had whispered back that no such report would be given.

She sat down on the edge of one of the beds. "Tell me about this man. You were engaged to him?"

Teddy, now wearing a kimono dressing gown, took a Ball jar out of her 'medicine' case and poured herself a stiff drink. After swallowing a hearty belt, she sunk into one of the easy chairs. "For a short time, yes."

The strong scent of the moonshine wafted through their room. Cornelia's nose wrinkled as she spoke.

"I can't imagine you marrying a man. You were in love?"

Teddy let out an exaggerated sigh. "No, not really, but I didn't know my own mind then."

"I've always found you to be quite opinionated."

Teddy's mouth, softer without the lipstick, curved. "I had a somewhat sheltered upbringing. At seventeen, I was indecisive and still biddable by my parents ... at least, in matters I had no knowledge of. Men were one of those."

"They chose a husband for you?"

"They didn't put it that way." She stretched out in the chair and dangled a slipper from one foot. "They said they wanted me to be well cared for after finishing school, and Ansel's father was successful. They encouraged me to meet him and see how things went." She swung the foot.

Cornelia eyed the slipper, clinging to a foot full of nervous energy. "So, you agreed to marry him?"

"Not immediately," Teddy replied. "We attended several social functions together, and events went swimmingly. He was well-spoken, intelligent, and an excellent dancer to boot."

"The dancing part must have been persuasive." Cornelia was only half teasing. There were few things Theodora Lawless liked to do more than dance, even now after being injured in the war.

"It was a strong selling point. He was handsome and charming. My friends were all envious of the attention he lavished on me. My parents pointed out daily what an excellent match we were. So, when Ansel asked me to marry him, I thought my confused emotions were normal for a young woman. I agreed because it seemed the proper thing to do."

"You, proper? I never met this Teddy."

"She died young," her companion said caustically. The foot with the slipper bounced. "The preparations began. My mother ordered Venetian lace for my gown. Can you imagine it?"

Teddy had been a dark-haired beauty when Cornelia met her. "I can picture you in the gown."

"I could, too." Teddy chuckled. "I might have married him for the dress alone." Her foot kicked hard, and the slipper flew.

Cornelia caught it. "But you didn't marry him. Why, if you didn't know any better?"

Teddy pressed her lips together and looked up at the ceiling. She did this when she was searching for the best way to put something. Cornelia suspected there wasn't a good way to tell her what happened.

She finally found the words. "Close to the wedding, he began talking more about how we would live—except he wasn't consulting me for my opinion. And you know I..." she faltered, "I always have one."

Cornelia handed Teddy her handkerchief. "Naturally. This was your future together."

"I realized that the life he was describing wasn't one I liked. So, I tried to tell him what I really wanted. To learn something more important than flatware placement for a formal dinner. To travel. To do something...of meaning. He was getting angry, but I kept going. I had to make him listen."

She stopped, and Cornelia kept quiet. After a moment, Teddy drew in a great breath.

"Well ..." she continued, "he heard me, because he exploded. He shook me, shouting that I was his wife, and this was his household we were talking about. I was angry and told him that I was not his wife yet, and I didn't think I wanted to be his wife any more. He slapped me, so I punched him. Then he really thrashed me. God, I had been spoiled and indulged my entire life, and I discovered how powerless I really was that night. Finally, I lied and told him that of course he was right, and I would do what he wanted."

"Oh, Teddy ..."

"There was no way to conceal the injuries I had when I got home. At first, they assumed Ansel had forced himself on me. But he hadn't, and they then considered my condition less frightening. I told them that I had no intention of marrying the man, and they told me that wed him I would. It was too late to back out, simply because I'd gotten the worse end of a quarrel I started. Arrangements had been made, invitations had been sent, and," her mouth twisted into a smile, "business alliances had been formed. I was afraid of what Ansel would do to me once we were married and alone in his house."

"So, you fled," Cornelia said.

"Like those Filipino rats when they caught sight of my slingshot."

"Oh, Teddy." She didn't know if she would laugh or cry.

"I took the train to my grandmother's house in New York. She kept me there in secret and paid to enroll me in nursing school at Bellevue."

They'd visited the grandmother together a few years before she passed. The woman had doted on Teddy; Cornelia wasn't surprised that she would provide sanctuary. "So, you were safe. That doesn't explain your reaction."

"It's what he did after I left!" Her face and chest flushed. "He told everyone that he had broken the engagement, because I was with child by another man. That I

15

had fled to Europe to clandestinely give birth and dispose of the baby."

If Stevens had been in the room, Cornelia would have socked him herself. "And they believed that flapdoodle?"

"He was there; I'd flown the coop. You know what an unspeakable sin having a child out of wedlock is, and it was more so back then. People love repeating a scandalous story. My father lost several customers and couldn't acquire new ones. It took years for him to rebuild the trade he lost." Teddy's hands clenched. "He never spoke to me again, even when he learned where I was, and my mother told me not to come to his funeral. I was disinherited."

Disinherited? Cornelia was confused. "But—but you have an inheritance."

"It was from my grandmother. She left her money to me, which is another reason my mother and I don't speak. But that's my story, sordid as it is."

"It *is* sordid. I can't believe everyone believed him, and you had to suffer."

One corner of Teddy's mouth turned up. "That slap was thirty-five years too late. I pity his wife."

"Mac seems to have turned out well."

"I'm sure that's of his mother's making, not Ansel's." She took another gulp from her glass.

"It does create an awkward situation, though. Should I ask my uncle if we could move to a different hotel?"

Teddy waved a hand and shook her curly head vigorously. "No. No, don't do that. This is his special treat, and he should enjoy it. Especially after that mess in Homosassa. Besides, I'm not a frightened girl anymore. Ansel isn't going to get the satisfaction of bullying me into leaving. I think we can find plenty to do that doesn't involve bumping into him at the hotel. Although I may see his wife in the salon. I'm sure we can politely ignore one another."

She sprung up and took off the kimono. "I need to get out of here. I'm in a mood."

"Really, Teddy, I'm sure Uncle Percival could be persuaded to change hotels tomorrow morning—after he films the pier construction, of course."

"No!" Teddy was already at the wardrobe, riffling through her dresses. "I'm not running away again," she said. "I'll be hanged if I'll let him spoil our vacation."

Cornelia was pleasantly surprised. "That's the spirit. We're going to the Palm Room?" She'd seen a sign advertising the Paul Whiteman Orchestra. Teddy always turned up the volume on the home radio when one of its songs played.

"No, that rat might still be downstairs. I have another place in mind. I learned that there's dancing every night at the Coliseum. It's not that far from here, although we'll need the car."

"What about Uncle Percival?"

"If he wants to go with us, he can." Teddy opened her makeup case. "You can ask while I freshen my face."

Cornelia was about to enter her uncle's suite when she saw a suspicious black square retreat from beneath the adjoining door. She kicked the door hard and was rewarded with a groan from the other side. Perhaps the old coot would resist future temptations to listen in on other people's conversations. Her kick must have sounded thunderous when amplified by his hearing device.

The professor gave her a sheepish grin when he opened the door.

Cornelia's face softened. Neither of them mentioned the eavesdropping. It was impossible for her to scold him for snooping. Teddy would have done the same, had the situation been reversed. She knew; she'd seen her press a water glass to closed doors often enough.

He declined their invitation to go out; he wanted to be well-rested for his visit to the Pier the following morning. They bid their farewells and headed for the lobby. Once again, it was packed—this time, by spillover from the ballroom. There were no valets in sight.

Teddy walked up to the front desk, where two clerks dashed from customer to customer. She dinged the bell until she got service. "We need our car, please. Could you ring a valet for us?"

"They're all busy pulling cars out for the Governor and his party," the harried young man said, "I apologize, ma'am, but even if one of them were free, your vehicle would still be boxed in. The street and driveways are blocked."

"I see. Thank you." Teddy put some change on the counter and headed for the double doors.

Cornelia rushed to keep up. She asked, with a bit of suspicion, "What are we doing?"

"We're getting a ride. Don't say anything; just look your most formidable."

The desk clerk was right; large cars and trucks jammed the area between the hotel and the marina. Teddy strode to the first car at the edge of the makeshift parking lot with swift assurance. Cornelia brought up the rear, forming her face into hard disapproving lines.

The driver, who had been taking a smoke, looked surprised. He tossed his cigarette aside.

"Drive-uh, take us to the Coliseum," said Teddy in an authoritative voice.

Cornelia's surprise almost ruined her grimace. Teddy's impression of Sergeant Allen was dead on.

The man shook his head. "These cars are reserved for the Governor and his entourage. They're making several stops tonight."

"Ayuh, that's exactly why we're hee-uh," Teddy said. "We're due at the Coliseum in fifteen minutes. Please take us they-uh immediately."

"The ... the Coliseum?" The man checked his ledger. "That's not on the schedule."

"It's on his dotter's schedule," she snapped. "We-uh the chaperones. Now take us they-uh before some disreputable mash-uh spikes the punch."

The driver looked from her to Cornelia. He nodded at the latter's scowl. "Get in, ladies."

It was hard for Cornelia not to smile.

Even at this late hour, traffic was heavy on the downtown streets. It slowed to a crawl on Fourth. Everything from flivvers to luxury vehicles jammed the road ahead.

Finally, their car stopped. Their driver got out and opened the back door. "Here you are, ladies. Sorry we didn't get here sooner."

Teddy mock-sighed. "It will have to do. Hee-ah, young man, take this for your trouble." She pressed a crisp bill into his hand.

"Ma'am, you don't have to—" But they were already walking away.

Once the women were out of earshot of the car, both burst into laughter.

"You haven't lost your gift for bamboozle," Cornelia said. "I hope he doesn't get into too much trouble."

"If he does, the money should assuage his pain," Teddy replied. "He'll probably make it back to the hotel in good time to perform his assigned duty. Politicians love long speeches."

The Coliseum, a tall stucco building, rose like a pale castle above the palm trees. At its base, people swarmed round. The ladies joined the line for entry and were swept into a grand ballroom with a barrel-like ceiling. It reminded Cornelia of the inside of an aircraft hangar, if an aircraft hangar had been lit with chandeliers and had a stage for a live band.

"This is wonderful." Teddy raised her voice to be heard above the music. "Just what I need."

Cornelia could see why; merriment surrounded them. Couples danced on the ballroom floor in swirls of fringed dresses and dark suits. Headdresses bobbed. Knots of young men and women eyed one another from the sidelines. *There must be no Hard-Shell Baptists in Florida.*

"You go have fun," she told Teddy. "I'll find a seat."

Her companion fluttered away in her peacock-colored dress, a fairy godmother among the flappers. Cornelia, wearing her black gown, felt more like the bad fairy who wasn't invited to christenings. She headed towards the chairs near the wall, then spotted a concession stand. Knowing Teddy's penchant for overdoing it, she purchased two drinks before choosing a chair.

Six minutes later, her companion, now puffing from exertion, plopped into the seat next to her. Cornelia handed her a cup.

"Thank you," Teddy gasped, before taking a gulp. She sank back in the chair. "I can't believe someone hasn't laced the punch."

"Perhaps they thought I was Mrs. Grundy and didn't offer."

"I did claim we were chaperones," Teddy said, "so I probably jinxed us."

In a short time, she was up and off to dance again. Cornelia got in line for more punch.

She was almost to the front when a shout of pain from the dance floor made her turn. It made many people turn.

Ansel Stevens teetered on one foot, clutching the other in his hand. He looked like a crane, if cranes wore pants with satin stripes. A red-haired girl with a too-short skirt steadied him.

Teddy stood nearby with one hand on her hip, and the other shaking a finger.

"You should be ashamed of yourself!" she cried. "A married man with grown children, and this is how you carry on?"

The redhead straightened. Her eyes narrowed in a way even the fashionable waves in her hair couldn't soften. "Married?"

"Yes! I met his wife and family earlier tonight."

"Ignore her, Shirley," Ansel said. "She's still mad about my breaking our engagement twenty years ago."

The fairy godmother of the flappers kicked him in the shin of his good leg, and he howled.

"*You* didn't break it, you liar!"

Cornelia noted that Teddy didn't correct him about the number of years; she wasn't going to do that with an audience. And she did have an audience. The musicians had halted, and the youngsters were enjoying the spectacle.

Time to stop this scene. She moved forward, muscling between the gawkers. "Teddy! Stop that before you get us thrown out."

"Me, stop? It's not my fault!"

Cornelia took her wrist and led her away from Ansel, who was cursing under his breath. Shirley was no longer by his side.

"Yes, take that harridan away!" he bellowed after them. "Miss Sour Grapes ..."

"Applesauce!" Teddy retorted, and Cornelia pulled harder on the wrist.

"You're going to embarrass yourself if you keep on," she said, getting her arm around her infuriated companion's shoulders and herding her away.

"I just wanted to go out, so I could get away from him," Teddy whined.

Cornelia wondered if Ansel was thinking the same thing.

They took a taxi back to the Vinoy. Teddy was slumped against her side of the vehicle, muttering insults.

Cornelia had never seen her like this before. Happy, sad, and yes, angry, but never muttering in a corner. "How much did you drink before we left?"

"Not enough."

"I think I should ask Uncle to change hotels."

"No!" She sat up. "No, don't deny the poor dear his fun. I don't think the rat will be dancing for a while. I got him right in the Achilles tendon."

Calculating while infuriated. Well, that was closer to normal.

CHAPTER THREE

Cornelia awoke to brilliant light filling the room. She usually didn't sleep in, even on vacation. She pulled the curtain aside and stared out at the water, lambent in the morning light, and the yachts neatly arranged in their slips, sails packed, their naked masts rising to greet the sun. She settled into one of the chairs near the window and read the last few chapters of her book while Teddy slept. Now and then, she gazed out at the seascape for a moment before turning the page.

They had breakfast in their siting room. Cornelia appreciated the small luxury; this was going to be a busy day. There would be a good deal of manual labor, carrying her uncle's camera to and from locations. She wondered what he was going to do when she returned to Colorado. The novelty of creating motion pictures would wear off quickly if he had to tote his own camera gear around.

She was filling out the laundry form for her black dress, when Teddy told her that she shouldn't bother.

"You've worn that dress so often during this trip, I think I should burn it."

"Then I hope you like the one I'm wearing, because this, my uniform, and my travel suit are all I packed. You and Uncle didn't leave me much room."

Her companion plucked a bottle of Lily of the Valley perfume from her cosmetics case. "We need to get you some new clothes."

"That's an interesting thought. Unfortunately, it must remain a thought. There's no room in the car for new clothes, and this trip is already straining my resources."

"We'll find a place to put them," Teddy said, dabbing the fluid behind the ears. "I intend to visit the shops this afternoon. It will be the best thing to take my mind off last night. And I'll pay for your new gown."

Cornelia relented. "Very well. But you may be burning more than one dress when we leave Florida."

The workmen at the pier stolidly bore the professor filming them from a distance, but grew hostile when he, trailed by Cornelia, trod upon the unfinished walkway.

The foreman was the one to confront them. "Step back, sir. You too, ma'am. It's not safe."

"I've been on many a construction site, young man," the professor said, "and I assure you that I know how to be careful. As for my niece, she faced far more danger during the Great War and emerged with aplomb."

Their adversary, who seemed puzzled by being addressed as 'young man', was not swayed by Uncle Percival's words. "I don't care who she merged with. This is off limits to tourists."

Cornelia stood by as her uncle took the man aside. "I'm not only a tourist, I'm a retired engineer. I realize that I'm imposing upon you, and perhaps I could compensate you for your time and trouble."

They negotiated briefly, and the foreman agreed to a short tour. "But walk where I tell you to, and don't wander. That goes double for the lady. Women don't belong at a construction site. My men's language gets salty."

He led them across the boards and away from the shore. Steam cranes from nearby boats quickly surrounded them. Trucks rolled past, carrying equipment and supplies. The wind of their passing pelted her with flying sand and tugged at the brim of her hat, making Cornelia grateful that she'd tied it securely under her chin instead of relying on a hatpin to hold it in place.

"Stand here," their new guide said. "This should give you a good view of the pier construction without getting into the crew's hair. We got a timetable, and I won't fall behind so you can take pictures."

"I understand, completely," Uncle Percival said. "I wouldn't dream of disrupting your schedule."

Cornelia's self-control was taxed as she tried to keep from laughing at the idea of Percival Pettijohn causing a delay. Her uncle's obsession with punctuality was legendary. She could still remember the shame he heaped upon himself the day his steam buggy stalled on the railroad tracks in downtown Lexington, putting half a dozen trains behind schedule. In his mind, being late was a mortal sin. She pushed the thought from her mind and focused on the task at hand.

As her uncle and the foreman talked about specifics of the project, Cornelia set up the tripod and recorded the men's labor.

While she cranked the handle for the camera, Cornelia considered the short time she had left before her leave ended. Like it or not, she would soon be headed back to the Army hospital in Colorado. Should Teddy go with her, or should she return to Kentucky with Uncle Percival? He was over the pneumonia he'd caught late last year, but Cornelia still worried. She would have appreciated Teddy watching over her uncle, but Teddy hadn't been herself since running into her former fiancé, the lout. Men who hit women were no better than vermin.

Perhaps shopping would help her forget Ansel for a while. And with any luck, they would find a new place to move to before any more clashes took place. Her uncle was too thrifty to stay in the Vinoy for long, good view notwithstanding. That is, if you called this clamor of construction a good view.

A steam whistle blew on the largest floating crane, and several workmen stopped what they were doing to rush to the edge of the pier. Seconds later, thick chains rattled, and a cloud of rust showered down on them as an enormous steel beam rose from the shore and crept over the bay. Inch by inch, the heavy beam was moved into position atop concrete and steel foundation.

With one last scrape of metal on stone, the waiting workmen leapt into action.

Cornelia cranked away with the camera as a man in leather overalls used long-handled metal tongs to pull a red-hot rivet from a large steaming bucket and slide it into a pre-drilled hole. The bucket boy moved down the row of workmen. One man would place the hot bolt and his waiting partner would hammer the base of the rivet into a second head before it could cool enough to lose its red-orange glow. Their hammers beat out a deafening rhythm as bits of metal sheared off the rivets and burned through whatever it touched. There was indeed salty language when bits seared men's flesh.

Her uncle blushed on her behalf. He came over to ask if she would like to return to the hotel.

It was a nice gesture. She could see how much he was enjoying the being in the middle of the construction. He hadn't even removed his hearing device from his ear. To him, the racket of a dozen hammers pounding in unison was a symphony. She wouldn't take him away from the pier for anything. "I've heard much worse," she assured him.

Arthur dropped in at the Stevens' office downtown to pick his fiancée up for lunch. It meant time away from his own business, but a man should be permitted a few indulgences when he was newly engaged—especially to someone who hadn't given him the time of day the winter before. There were plenty of other girls who were more than happy to have his company. He wanted more than that. The moment he met Evelyn he'd realized that she was exactly what he was looking for: smart, sophisticated, ambitious, and beautiful. She was solid, the kind of woman who would be an asset in the social circles he was entering. While all of that was true, it wasn't the real reason he had persevered in his suit. He was head over heels for her from the first day she and her father had walked into his garden shop.

Unfortunately, Evelyn was busy helping the old man in the office. They seemed to be holding down the fort alone. Mac was not there, which was predictable. His head was always in the clouds. The secretary was busy collecting estimates from vendors. He looked around for Evelyn's sister, but she was nowhere to be seen.

When his fiancée popped out of the office, arms full of files, he inquired, "Where's Violet?"

"Downstairs getting her curls refreshed," his beloved said, plopping the folders down on her desk.

"So, you don't get time to eat?"

Evelyn checked the clock. "She should have returned by now. Why don't you be a dear and hurry her along? And get a wiggle on; I think I deserve a longer lunch today."

Sufficiently motivated, Arthur hied himself to the Movie Star Gallery, which was one of several shops on the first floor of the Stevens Building. The place was buzzing with young women; it took him a few moments to locate Violet.

"May I help you, sir?" the woman at the counter inquired.

"I need to speak to the girl back there." He pointed. "Her sister sent me."

He was granted entry to the feminine domain. He took a tentative step forward. Until today, he had assumed beauty shops were little more than barber shops with prettier decorations. Odd chemical odors assaulted his nose and eyes as we walked deeper into the room. He wanted to appear nonchalant, but Arthur couldn't help gawking at the strange devices women used in the effort to be beautiful. The eyes of other clients swept over him as he passed, making him feel like an intruder.

"He lives on his yacht," Violet was telling the stylist, who was busy teasing out a multitude of curls on her head. "He can sail from job to job without leaving home."

"How romantic!" the stylist replied. Arthur thought the woman was anything but a romantic: her hair was as short as a man's. Kohl-rimmed eyes and diamante earrings were her only nods to femininity. She looked familiar, though; where had he seen her before?

Violet noticed him staring. "Arthur! What are you doing here?"

He returned to the present. "Evelyn sent me. She'd like to have lunch before dinnertime."

"Oh, I'm so sorry. It took longer to get done than I expected it to. This is Lucy. Are we close to done, Lucy?"

"We'll be through in a minute," the stylist said, looking up at him. Recognition lit her eyes, and she stood. "Arthur Downs!" she exclaimed. "How have you been?"

She smiled, and he saw the small gap between her front teeth. It triggered his memory; he'd gone to school with her. She'd had a fuzzy cloud of brown curls then; now it was short, wispy, and peroxide blonde.

"I've been fine," he said. "How are you doing?"

She gestured around her. "I am mistress of all I survey."

"This is your salon?" It was a long way from their rural childhood.

Lucy laughed, a deep bubbling sound. "It's mine. Are you still working for your father?"

"He passed away a few years ago. I'm running the business now."

His former classmate began to offer her condolences, but was interrupted by Violet, who sat up from the styling chair and poked Arthur. "Look!" she whispered to him. "There she is again!"

The woman who had slapped old Stevens was standing at the door, scanning the room with either intensity or nearsightedness. She leaned on her cane, ignoring the woman at the counter trying to invite her forward.

"Who is it?" the salon owner asked. "Pretty stylish for someone her age."

"She slapped my father last night," Violet said. "At the Vinoy. Mother said that she was engaged to Father once, and he dumped her."

Lucy chuckled. "Spitfire turned silver, huh?"

"She's leaving," Arthur said. "She must have spotted us."

"Better than casting a kitten here," Lucy said. "All right, doll. You're finished."

CHAPTER FOUR

When Cornelia and Uncle Percival returned to the Vinoy, they found a surprise in their suite. The young redhead who had been Ansel's companion the previous night sat in one of the chairs, leafing through a magazine.

A different Teddy greeted them. "I hope you had fun," she said, fingering her newly shorn curls. A few wisps surrounded her face, but the hair in the back had been cut very, very short. "What do you think? They call it a shingle bob."

"The barbering trade has changed since my days," the professor said. "They didn't name haircuts; just asked what size bowl they should use."

They all laughed before Teddy continued.

"I didn't have to use the barber shop. I went directly to the salon and ran into Shirley. Shirley Wheeler, this is Cornelia Pettijohn, and this is her uncle, Percival."

Shirley put aside the magazine and got up. Her too-red lips opened into a beautiful smile. "Right pleased to meet you."

The professor took her hand with a flourish and bent over it. "Charmed to meet you as well. Do I detect the lilt of Tennessee in your voice?"

The young woman giggled. "You do."

Seen in the light of day, Cornelia placed her age in the early twenties. That was perhaps a third of Ansel's years. What a goat he'd turned out to be. "Pleased to make your acquaintance. So, Teddy, you met again in the salon?"

"Yes. I asked the concierge where I could get the best finger curls, and there she was. We discussed mutual dislikes, then found out we had some interests in common."

"I see that," Cornelia said, eyeing the two glasses on the nearby table with an empty Ball jar between them.

"I try to be a gracious hostess," Teddy replied. "Besides, she's given me some excellent advice on where to shop. I invited her to join us."

Cornelia had forgotten the planned shopping trip. She'd spent the morning tromping around the construction site loaded down with her uncle's camera equipment. It took all her willpower to smile at the prospect of an afternoon of carrying Teddy's purchases.

The shopping began on Central Avenue, not far from the hotel, and continued onto First Street. Cornelia hadn't seen so many clothing stores since the time she'd been stationed in San Francisco. Above them, a plane hummed through the sky, trailing smoke that eventually, between their entries and exits of shops, succeeded in spelling out "Lucky Strike." It reminded her of Mac, whom they'd seen striding towards the hotel as they pulled out of the entrance. Poor lad, he was caught in the middle between Teddy and his father.

The professor had excused himself from this expedition. Cornelia wished she had that option. Few things bored her more than looking for new clothes. Naturally, it was one of Teddy's favorite activities.

They sat down on one of the benches outside of McCrory's to rest their feet. Teddy and her new friend cooed over the colorful dresses and costume jewelry in the shop windows while Cornelia enjoyed sitting, if only for a short time.

Suddenly, she realized that Teddy was talking to her. "I'm sorry. Could you repeat that, please?"

"I want to go to a new place tonight. There was an ad about a Club San Remo in the newspaper, but Shirley tells me it's booked solid till next week. Instead, she wants me to visit this marvelous nightclub out in the jungle," Teddy said.

"Not in the jungle, at the Jungle Prada," their new friend said. "The place is called the Gangplank. It's the berries. They have everything you could want—music, dancing, and plenty of refreshments. It's near the new hotel."

Cornelia didn't know what 'the new hotel' was—they all looked new to her—but she had a good idea what "refreshments" meant. "I take it we're going there tonight?"

"Well, I'm planning to," Teddy said. "I hope you'll come along. It sounds like fun. I need to lift my spirits."

Lift *some* spirits was probably more accurate. Cornelia looked at Shirley. "What are the chances that the cad from last night will be there?"

"Absolutely zilch," she said. "That sap thinks he's a real sharpie, but he don't know nothing I don't tell him."

"We need to get you a new dress for this evening," Teddy said, taking her hand. "Come along."

"I don't have room in my bag," Cornelia said. "And you're not burning my black dress."

"We'll put it in my trunk, then."

"There's not going to be room in the trunk for anything if you buy more clothes."

"I'm sure we could fit it in. I'll give some of my frocks to the poor if I have to."

Shirley interrupted. "Why don't you ship some of them back north?"

Cornelia stopped mid-refusal. "What?"

"Mother and I discovered that our clothes were too warm for the climate here. We sent some of them by post back to family. Do you have someone who could use them, or keep them for you?"

"That's brilliant!" Teddy cried. "We could contact Mr. Scroggins to pick them up." She turned to Shirley. "Mr. Scroggins raises corn on Cornelia's farm and does odd jobs for us."

"This would be an odder job than most," Cornelia grumbled.

Cornelia finally chose a silver-gray gown that was reasonably comfortable and met Teddy's standards of proper evening attire. It was also cooler than the black dress; Shirley was right about the climate difference requiring a change in wardrobe. Florida was definitely too warm and humid for the civilian clothing she wore in Colorado. She could have done without the dropped waist that was all the rage, though—God had given women a natural waistline; why did fashion have to meddle with it?

"Oh, Teddy!" Shirley exclaimed. "How daring! I love it!"

Cornelia turned to see which frock was 'daring' and gasped at the half-naked swim dress her companion was wearing. The skirt was short enough to see not only the pale calves, but the knees as well. It was sleeveless and low-cut enough to reveal the collarbone. Quickly, she moved to block Teddy from view of the other shoppers and pushed her back into the dressing room.

Teddy collapsed in laughter. "You look so shocked!"

How could she find this funny? "Theodora Lawless, you could be arrested in a getup like that! Especially with so little to get up!"

"It's the twentieth century," Teddy said, stifling a giggle. "And it's only two inches above the knee, well within the legal limit here."

Cornelia ground her teeth. Teddy liked wearing the same outfits the young girls did, but it was so inappropriate.

Shirley knocked on the wall from outside. "Hold your ground! You look like the cat's pajamas in that."

Inside, Cornelia made her own case. "Everyone will stare," she began, then realized that was probably the desired result of the short blue suit. "Please don't make me endure walking through the crowd on the beach with you in that shred of fabric. You know I don't like people staring at me."

"I noticed how shy and retiring you were with the soldiers during the war," Teddy joked, then softened her smile. "Perhaps I could wear a robe over it when I'm not in the water. You won't be as embarrassed, and I won't get as sunburnt."

Cornelia grumbled before nodding her head.

"Now," Teddy cooed, "what swimsuit shall we get you?"

Shirley departed after the shopping expedition. She would meet them later for the promised visit to the Gangplank, but she needed to help her mother close the salon for the day. Teddy was amused by Cornelia's surprised expression; she, too, had been startled to find the young woman with the impressive finger curls and half-moon manicure standing behind a chair instead of sitting in it.

She'd located Shirley in the fourth salon she checked. It was a horrible thing to admit, even to herself, but Teddy wanted to learn more about Ansel. A deep blistering emotion had crouched inside her chest since their encounter in the restaurant, and she wanted to get the dirt on what he'd done with his life. Her prayers that his business was on the edge of failure and the law was on his heels had been unanswered. He was now in charge of his father's development business and enjoying more than modest success building in Florida. Life was filled with injustice.

The three women set out from the Vinoy after dinner, Cornelia at the wheel of the Dodge Touring Car.

"Oh, look, there's Mac!" Teddy waved at the young man entering the hotel, but he was turned the other way, walking with purpose. "Poor boy, to have such a father. And he's so nice."

Cornelia wasn't eager to revisit the subject of Ansel Stevens. "Perhaps his mother was a good influence. Now, Shirley, where do I turn?"

They followed the trolley route along Ninth Avenue to the west. Their surroundings became less urban, but not quite rural. They drove through swaths of darkness where new construction had ended for the day, and through the well-lit glow of finished neighborhoods.

The palms and pines grew thicker ahead of them.

Teddy twisted in the front passenger seat towards Shirley, sitting in the back. "I thought you said this place wasn't in the jungle."

"It's not. Just wait."

Ahead, Cornelia saw a set of lights from another vehicle. She pressed harder on the gas pedal, moving closer. More lights formed a train in the dark. The trees parted, revealing a group of large buildings.

"Turn right up here. That's the Country Club Hotel," their Tennessean tour guide said, pointing. "There's a golf course nearby, and even an air strip."

"This is more like it!" Teddy exclaimed. "And the club?"

"A little further up the road," Shirley said.

The Jungle Prada was a complex of stores adjacent to a gasoline station. *All the comforts of home.* Cars matching different tiers of income packed the parking lot. They quickly gave up on the paved area and crept along the rows of vehicles parked among the trees, which had thick interlaced limbs that defied the encroachment of civilization. Cornelia finally wedged the Dodge between a Ford Runabout and a Duesenberg. The trio piled out and walked towards the stores.

"Our car should be safe back there," Teddy said. "If thieves want something low-key, there's the Runabout, and if they want a high-ticket number, there's the Duesenberg."

"I hope they brought a machete to cut it out of the underbrush," Cornelia muttered.

The other women laughed.

The Jungle Prada buildings were long and roofed with Spanish tile. Their creamy walls and cool trellises gleamed in the streetlights. A restaurant beckoned to them with enticing aromas of steak and chicken. Music and laughter drifted through stucco Moroccan arches. The Gangplank was at the end of the complex. Its patio, covered by brightly colored terrazzo, provided a wide view of the bay. The edge pointing towards the ocean was the bandstand, buttressed by two cement ship prows. A sign identified the entertainment as "Earl Gresh's Gangplank Orchestra." The musicians, dressed in colorful pirate costumes, were still in the process of setting up.

Couples gathered under the awnings of the terrace and the live oaks in the spillover area, chattering happily. A mob of young people surrounded an outdoor station serving drinks. The glasses handed out to the customers looked like they held punch and soda, but the crowd was a little too enthusiastic. Cornelia bet they had been juiced.

Nearby, a line of men waited at the entrance for tables, their politeness assured by the presence of large bouncers on either side of the doors. The terrace crowd was largely male as well.

"This must be the hottest joint in town," Teddy said. "At least for going stag."

"Ab-so-lute-ly," Shirley replied. "The club has an act where this woman dances in a tiger costume. The strap broke on the dress once, and"—the redhead lowered her voice—"she didn't have anything on under it. Those mugs are hoping it will happen again."

"I could do without the gawkers," Cornelia said. "Or the noise." She scanned the crowded tables. "Are there any open seats out here?"

"One way to find out." Teddy approached one of the large men at the door and spoke to him politely. A bill was clutched in her hand. Shortly thereafter, the bouncer bellowed to someone inside. A busboy emerged, carrying a small table. He set it down at the end of a row of crowded tables, then returned to fetch chairs.

"No mean trick, that," Shirley said once they sat down. "Do you have a printing press in your bag?"

Teddy laughed. "The first lesson I learned from the soldiers—always bring the right ammo."

As they sat, Shirley crossed her legs and hiked her skirt. Cornelia believed the girl had skinned her knees until she identified the coloring as rouge. Were injured legs considered more attractive?

She didn't have much time to wonder. Cornelia was deputized to get the beverages, due to her superior height and forbidding demeanor. Even so, she had to put a few line breakers in their place.

Her guess about the drinks was correct: they were juiced. It wasn't as classy as the wine in France, but it would do. Teddy and Shirley were both pleased with the club's brand of refreshments.

The notes of "Farewell Blues" flowed from the bandstand, softening the chatter of the crowd. Cornelia sat and sipped her drink while her companions discussed the fashion choices of the women around them. Fine, as long as they didn't make her shop again. Her feet had suffered enough for one day. The line into the club shortened. A short distance from the patio, the lights across Boca Ciega Bay glistened on the water and reflected upwards on the limbs of the trees. A night heron sat on the short pier, its plumage glimmering in the lights from the terrace. Brand new houses and restaurants were springing up everywhere, it seemed, but nature still had a presence in this place.

Teddy tapped her arm, breaking her reverie. "Look over there, near the little palm. Is that Ansel's daughter?"

Cornelia reluctantly shifted her gaze from the pier. The girl under the palm was pale, black-haired ... it could be Violet Stevens, although she'd only had a brief glance at the Stevens' offspring before Teddy made a scene. A young man, olive-skinned, stood close to her, and they were having an intimate conversation. He was stylishly dressed, but his large ears rendered him more endearing than handsome.

"He's touching her hand," Teddy said. "Love under the Spanish Moss."

"Are you sure it's her? We only saw her the one time."

"I'm sure. She looks like him, even from here. Uh-oh." Teddy turned away and suddenly appeared engrossed in the nearest trellis. "She saw me, didn't she?"

"I'd say so," Shirley said. "She and her sheik made tracks into the club. The bouncers must be off for a smoke."

Teddy scrambled to her feet and headed for the door. Cornelia muttered a curse under her breath and followed. *What now?*

The terrace was merely busy. The interior of the club was jam-packed. The tables were full, of course, but men also leaned on the walls and clustered around the bar. Teddy slid between them, murmuring "Thank you," as she passed. Cornelia, nowhere near as slender or flexible, issued apologies instead as she jostled them aside. When Teddy did stop, Cornelia collided with her.

"Ooof! You should have given me more warning."

"Sorry." Teddy stood on tiptoe. "It *is* her. They're going into the smaller room."

"They who?"

Teddy was already giving chase. "Ansel's daughter and her young man."

Cornelia had to jostle more club patrons out of the way to follow. Shirley hadn't followed; smart girl. "What are you going to do when you catch them?"

"I wasn't planning to catch them. I wanted to see what they were doing."

The man behind Cornelia shifted position, and his elbow poked into her back. She poked back with her own elbow. "They came here to be alone together. Which you're not letting them do."

"Nonsense, this is a public place with an enormous crowd. Someone was going to bother them."

"Why does it have to be us?" Cornelia replied.

The music stopped then. A dapper man with a slick center part called for silence.

"And now, presenting Pierre and Paige. The tigers of the Jungle Prada!" He signaled the drummer who started playing a Latin rhythm, the beat picking up as horns joined the lively tune. The bandleader bowed to the crowd and stepped back, ceding the floor to the brightly costumed pair.

Teddy's toes tapped as they watched the floor show. "A rumba," she said. "How exciting."

In the spotlight, a young man in black satin pants and a sequined tiger-striped shirt glided over the dance floor. The tiger theme was repeated in his partner's dress, if it could be called a dress. Cornelia thought her own slip had to be less revealing than the shimmering gown that clung to the dancer's body. The gown was supported by a single strap, not much wider than the black fringe that swayed at its hem. "Exciting," wasn't the word that popped into her mind as she watched the suggestive movement of their hips. The sensual intimacy of the dance made her face color. She knew she should look away, but her eyes refused to obey.

Suddenly, Teddy poked her and pointed to a light above the bar. "It's flashing. We've got to get out of here!"

The two women were shoved back and forth by patrons eager to escape, mostly men younger and stronger than they were. Chivalry was no custom of the modern generation, at least not when the police were storming the gates of the castle.

Officers now blocked the main entrance. "Stay where you are!" one officer ordered. "No one is to leave the premises." He said more, but it was drowned out by howls of dismay and the crash of the mob changing directions.

These young men might lose a night of freedom, but Cornelia had more to lose. *I could be court-martialed. I could be discharged, even lose my pension.* It was one thing for Teddy or Shirley to be caught, but why had she ever been persuaded to take the risk herself? Cornelia grabbed Teddy's hand and used her shoulder to bull through the throng. No, there were police at that exit, too. *Where now?*

Teddy was pulling at her arm now. "This way!" She gestured towards the fireplace, and Cornelia saw that the bartender and one of the bouncers were ducking into it— *through* it, in fact. Teddy ran after them, her companion close behind, and they found themselves in a tunnel. A secret escape which had to have been added during construction. How clever of them.

They emerged in the trees surrounding the club. The men they'd followed were nearby. The bartender turned. "Who are you? You had no business chasing after us."

"You're quite right," Teddy said, "but it was any port in a storm."

Cornelia didn't like the man's expression. "The police are here," she reminded him, taking Teddy's hand again. "Run!"

The women fled into the brush, heading away from the brilliant lights and cries surrounding the Gangplank. There were no sounds of chase behind them; the man had gotten the point about the police being the people to worry about.

Eventually, it seemed safe enough to circle back. When they got back to the car, Shirley was waiting for them.

"I'm glad to see you!" she said. "I was afraid they'd nabbed you with the others. They got that sheba you were chasing, and her guy, too. They were loaded into different wagons, boys versus girls."

"We took a service exit," Cornelia said. "Sorry we abandoned you."

"Oh, no problem," Shirley said. "Some sheiks came over to chat me up when they saw I was alone."

"How considerate of them to do that," Teddy said. "after your chaperones left you high and dry."

The girl grinned.

CHAPTER FIVE

"We need to get out of here," the professor remarked.

Cornelia set her fork down. "May we finish breakfast first, or is this an emergency?"

"We can finish breakfast, but we need to leave if we're going to travel today," he said, folding the newspaper. "This is the last day the Maine delegation is in town. They will be coming here for a farewell luncheon."

"And you prefer not to deal with the crowds again. A sensible choice. What are we going to do today?"

"I didn't have a plan," he said, "but we should probably develop one quickly."

"We could shop," Teddy said.

"No," the Pettijohns replied simultaneously.

"Let me see that paper," Teddy said. "Hmm. There's a picnic for all former residents of Iowa. Plus, tonight, there's all sorts of things planned for people from New Hampshire, New Jersey, South Carolina ... the states all seem to have clubs here."

"I have yet to see a Kentucky club," the professor said. "I saw something you might like, Teddy, but we would be better off going there tonight. Tarpon Springs is holding a Venetian Festival, and most of the events are scheduled for the afternoon and evening. Our friends from Down East will be visiting it during the day, which leaves us with the evening. There will be art exhibits, music, and a floating stage in Spring Bayou."

"You're right, that does sound like something I would enjoy."

"Meanwhile ... there's the alligator farm. The advertisement says they have one nineteen feet long."

"Uncle Percy, didn't we see enough alligators in Homosassa?"

"I didn't see one that big, but I'll concede the point. I understand that there is a gentleman not far from here who has a spectacular garden and nursery. He drained a shallow lake on his property and filled it with fruit trees and flowers."

"And your agrarian sensitivities were piqued," Teddy said.

"You always put things so nicely," he said. "It should make a fair exchange—gardens for me, a festival for you."

"Well, put that way ..."

When Arthur dropped by Stevens' office on First Street to take his intended to lunch again, he discovered that a crisis had arisen overnight. Instead of Stevens at the helm, he found Evelyn handling the calls from suppliers and developers herself. Meanwhile, the secretary was buried under her work and Violet's.

He waited while she finished speaking to a lumber contractor, all poise and polish. It was one of the things he admired in her; they would be a formidable team once they were married. When she set the phone aside, he spoke. "What's wrong? Is your father ill? And where is your sister?"

"Close the door," she said.

He obliged her, then sat on the corner of the desk. Evelyn sunk into her father's padded chair, hands grasping the armrests.

"Father got woken up by a call last night," she said. "Violet was arrested at the Gangplank during a raid."

"*Our* little Violet?"

"The same. She was with a man Daddy doesn't like, either. He's fit to be tied."

"I imagine he was. So, she's at the hotel, trying to get back into his good graces?"

Evelyn gave him a sardonic lift of the eyebrow. "More like house arrest. He has ordered her to stay with me in my room until they head back north."

"Doesn't she live with Mac?"

"Yes," Evelyn said, straightening up in the seat. She began gathering the sheets of paper strewn over the desk. "Daddy caught him trying to bail her out of jail before he got there. Turns out she called Mac instead of him, so he was extra mad."

"So, who called him, then?"

She poked his hip. "Stand up." He obliged, and she swept the papers he'd been sitting on into the pile. "One of his business associates was at the station. I don't imagine he was there to buy tickets for the Policeman's Ball."

"Probably not. So now Mac's in the doghouse, too. Speaking of the devil, where is he? Why isn't he here helping you and the secretary?"

Evelyn chuckled. "He's touring the job sites. He figures a moving target is harder to hit."

Mac tended to avoid the office anyway, Arthur thought. Always tinkering with his plane and his engines. Once the old man was gone, the Florida office would be largely run not by Mac, but by his sisters. "Once again, you are the golden child."

"And my prize is a new roommate. We haven't shared a bed since we were little girls. At least the suite we're in is bigger than the one we had at the Princess Martha."

He took one of her hands. "Perhaps we should move up the wedding date and get you out of there. It's getting crowded."

"Down, boy." She withdrew the hand. "All things in due time. First comes lunch and a few errands."

The ladies relaxed on the veranda after the morning's trek through exotic gardens, followed by a long conversation about irrigation between Cornelia's uncle and the owner of said gardens. The discussion left Cornelia plenty of time to enjoy the birds. They were quite accustomed to people and didn't even pay attention to the camera. A pair of pastel pink spoonbills wandered within a few feet of where she and Teddy shared a bench. She could have spent the entire morning listening to the buzz of hummingbird wings as they flittered from one blossom to another.

She had no complaints about where they were now, though. Memories of this long, shaded veranda with its rocking chairs and magnificent view would provide warmth on those cold spring mornings in Colorado. Cornelia spent the rest of her morning engrossed in her book, while Teddy worked on embroidering more curtains for Mr. Scroggins' house, which she considered too spartan to be a real home.

The professor came to fetch them shortly after noon. He'd had a nap and was ready to play. Wherever they went, Cornelia prayed it would not be on foot.

Her prayers were not answered. The professor wanted to film the ocean. It was too late for the beach, so after a negotiation they agreed on the park next to the hotel, which wasn't that far. Teddy changed shoes and applied more Hinds cream to her face before they left.

"I really should have gotten a new hat while we were at the store; the ones I packed are more practical and less suited to these upscale surroundings," she said.

"Perhaps you could look for a new one tomorrow while Uncle and I are playing golf," Cornelia replied. They'd invited Teddy to join them, but she'd declined, saying she was a flower that bloomed best in the afternoon.

"An excellent idea."

Vinoy Park had broad, paved paths that led to the sea wall. The wind was cool and would probably become cold at sunset. Clusters of newly-planted palm trees dotted the landscape, with a sparkling band of blue as the backdrop. Despite her tiredness, Teddy felt excitement and awe at the sight.

She waited with the professor while Cornelia caught up to her with the camera. It was unfair that Cornelia was the designated Sherpa, but she had been overprotective of her uncle since his bout with pneumonia, and he was happy to let his niece stay that way if it benefited him.

"Where do you want to set up?" Cornelia asked her uncle, and they wandered off into the grass together.

Teddy parked herself on one of the green benches provided and stared out across the waves. Watching the shifting colors, cool and jewel-toned, eased the pain inside. A group of pelicans skimmed low over the water, looking for a meal.

Nearby, an artist sketched at an easel. Well, the beautiful setting should inspire the creative spirit. Teddy visualized how the scene would translate to needlepoint. Along the horizon would be the deepest blue, a navy perhaps. Closer to shore, the colors became more azure, taking on hints of aqua. She leaned forward, studying the play of light and shadow. How many shades of blue did she have in her sewing tin?

Arthur couldn't believe how prudish Stevens was with his youngest child. Becoming angry when your daughter was arrested was normal, but the 'crime' was a peccadillo with few real consequences. Instead, he occupied a central location in the suite, surly and radiating hostility.

Evelyn had not helped matters by getting a bob so short that she looked like a boy. He'd delivered her to Lucy's salon and went to call on some local businesses, since women's beauty talk bored him. When he returned, he'd thought the slender figure approaching his car was a stranger. He tried to hide his surprise, but she sensed it anyway.

"Don't worry, dear, it will grow out before the wedding. We can do me in ringlets then, if you like. I just wanted a change."

Arthur accepted it with her caveat, but Stevens hadn't. He was still angry with his youngest daughter, and when Evelyn took off her cloche, he'd exploded. He was wroth with fury, as the saying went.

"First Violet, and now you? What's gotten into you both?"

"Many women cut their hair when they get married, Daddy."

"Not like that, they don't. Next, you'll be wearing pants like those schoolgirls we saw the other day. Maybe their fathers don't care, but I do."

"If I wanted to wear pants, they would already be in my wardrobe," she retorted. Her gray eyes had become angry slits.

"No, they wouldn't. I would rip them up and burn them. What about you, Downs? You're going to be her husband. Did you permit this atrocity?"

Downs hesitated, put in the bad position of displeasing either his bride-to-be or her father.

It must have been during the argument that Violet slipped out.

The moment he realized that his younger daughter was no longer in the suite, Stevens had gone to the window to check the yacht basin. He must have seen a vessel he recognized, because he became furious and insisted that they all go downstairs immediately.

A shriek brought Teddy out of her reverie. "Father, no!"

Ansel Stevens was there, grasping his daughter's arm. Arthur Downs took the other, albeit more gently. The girl wailed and twisted as they dragged her away from the water's edge and the young man from the Gangplank. He headed towards them, rage in his dark eyes, but the girl shook her head at him. "No, not now."

"Violet!"

"Stay there, Brockman," Ansel ordered the young swain. "I haven't finished with you."

Teddy watched Ansel drag the girl to her mother and another young woman. A friend, perhaps? Then she realized that the second woman with the short, slicked-down hair was Ansel's older daughter. How daring, to get an Eton Curl! Her father must have been apoplectic.

The women enfolded Violet in their arms and turned her towards the hotel. She stopped fighting and trudged between them. Poor child. Ansel still had the ugly, domineering side he'd had when they were young. He'd grabbed his daughter's arm the way he'd grabbed Teddy's arm that night, when—

The girl had slipped off to see her young man. He didn't seem to be a bad sort, but he was Jewish, and that wouldn't fly in the Stevens' social circles.

Arthur assisted his soon-to-be father-in-law in separating the pair, but that wasn't the end of it. Stevens indicated that Arthur should remain by his side. Once Violet had been taken away, the older man rounded on young Brockman.

"I told you to stay away from my daughter," he snapped, waving his finger. The sun glinted on his gold pinky ring.

"She's of age, sir. She has the right to see whomever she wants," Brockman replied. His accent wasn't local or even Southern; he was from New York, Arthur knew, or a kissing cousin of it.

"I'm surprised you had the nerve to sail over here, especially on a Friday."

The young man shrugged. "The sun hasn't set yet."

"Oh, yes it has," Stevens hissed. "You're going to leave my daughter alone from now on."

"That's for her to say, sir; not you."

"My daughter doesn't know what's best for her. What will it take for you to go away?" Stevens pulled his cigarette case out of his pocket and toyed with it. He took out a cigarette, then put it back. "You're doing brisk business right now, but you're dangling from a shoestring. I might be persuaded to grant you a loan."

The lad jerked his chin up. "This has nothing to do with money."

"Money will have very little to do with you if you don't take my advice. I'll ruin you. What do you have to say to that?"

"If you could have ruined me, you would have done it already," Brockman said. He took a step towards the men, and Arthur moved closer, ready to intercept. The young man's eyes flicked from one to the other of them. "Look here. You're her father; I'd rather have your blessing than fight. What can I do to get your permission to see Violet?"

Stevens put the case back in his pocket. "Nothing. You're the wrong sort for her. She's too young to realize how many bridges a relationship with you would burn."

Arthur became aware that people were gathering around them. A screaming young woman and her indignant

47

father were much more interesting than the gentle charms of an afternoon near the ocean.

"Sir, I think we might want to take this inside," he said, but Stevens waved him off.

"There's nothing more to say, nothing you can give her. You'd make a poor husband for any young woman."

Brockman's brows rose, but he mastered himself. He took off his fedora and ran his fingers through his dark hair before responding. "That's not true. I'm a hard worker, I come from a good family, I did well in school, and I've built a decent business from the ground up. Violet tells me your father did the same."

The older man was unmoved. "My father would have felt the same way about it. You're not our kind."

"Then ... I'll challenge you."

The old man sneered. "Challenge me to what?"

"I'll challenge you for the right to see Violet. I've seen you sailing your tub up and down this side of the harbor."

Stevens clutched a fist. "Tub? That's a fine vessel, and I paid a pretty penny for it."

"Too bad you didn't buy the oars to row it."

The retort brought laughter, and Stevens became aware that they had an audience. He raised his voice. "Yours is barely a sloop. It doesn't deserve to have a slip in this marina next to real yachts."

"If my boat is so lousy, what are you waiting for?" Brockman said. "Race me. Race me to Boca Ciega and back. If I win, I get to see Violet."

"Your boat isn't in the same class. It'd be like shooting fish in a barrel."

Brockman half-smiled. "And yet you hesitate. Perhaps the problem with isn't the yacht's class at all. Maybe it's the class of its captain."

This brought hoots and more laughter.

Ansel Stevens brought himself to his full height and glared down at Harry Brockman.

"You know what? I'm going to accept your challenge. But I'm going to up the ante. The loser of the race must also leave town. No, more than the town—they all run together here. Not only Saint Petersburg, then, but the entire state of Florida."

"Done," Brockman said, and the assembly cheered and clapped.

Dinner felt more public than usual. Arthur watched the furtive glances made to the Stevens' customary table in the dining room. He also caught a few people whispering to one another. News of the challenge had quickly made the rounds.

"I hope you're pleased with yourself," Mrs. Stevens said in low tones to her husband. "We're the main attraction tonight."

"Good," Stevens said, looking over the choices on the evening menu. "It will give that young upstart a larger audience to lose in front of."

"Harry is a good sailor," Violet said. "He's been to New York and back with his yacht to visit his family."

"Perhaps he needed another loan from his church, or whatever they call it," her father retorted. "Living on a boat may be fine for a single man playing at business, but it doesn't suit a man who is serious about things, including courtship. He probably has a girl in every port."

"Not with those ears," Evelyn said, bringing a chuckle from everyone but Violet.

Arthur's short-lived relief at the levity didn't last.

"You should have dinner with him," the young woman said. "Then you could get to know him and ask him what his plans are for the future. He's more practical than you think."

Ansel made a gesture for the waiter to come forward. "Where would we go? The galley of his boat? Certainly we couldn't sup in any respectable restaurant." The waiter arrived at his shoulder. "I'll take the ham."

"Oh, Father!" Violet sputtered. "You disgust me."

"She'll have the ham, too. We'll all have the ham," he told the waiter, waving him away.

Once the confused waiter had left, she leaned forward. "You may force us to eat ham, but you're the one acting like a pig."

Arthur's eyes shifted to Mac. The son and heir looked strangely untroubled by the rancor at the table. Was this normal talk for the family? His own family had always begun dinner with a prayer and finished with a glass of wine and discussions of what work needed to be done on the farm the next day. He hoped that Evelyn would not bring this tradition into their own family.

Stevens fixed his youngest child with the glare that meant he was not to be questioned.

"I am forbidding this for your own good," Ansel Stevens said. "You don't realize how many doors will be closed to you if you marry into that religion. In Miami, they have restrictive land covenants to keep Jews out of the good areas of town. They can't even rent hotel rooms at the beach there. This area isn't much better, and neither is New York, where they live cheek to jowl in ethnic neighborhoods. I don't want that for you, or for my grandchildren."

"You haven't beaten Harry yet," Violet said.

CHAPTER SIX

The morning was clear and, truth be told, a little on the chilly side. Cornelia slung the bag of rented clubs over her shoulder and followed her uncle out of the pro shop. She was glad she'd purchased a modest golfing outfit with a light sweater. The colors were a bit brighter than she would normally wear: light pink with a mint green diamond pattern. Teddy always said that pink was flattering. It was no more colorful than those worn by other golfers, even with the pink pom-pom topping her cap.

Uncle Percival was wearing two-tone shoes, knee-length acreage trousers, argyle socks, a bow tie, and suspenders. The short pants were a shock. When he'd taught her the game, his golfing trousers were the proper length. She was surprised no one was laughing at the old coot, even if the other men on the course were dressed in equally outlandish attire ... minus the suspenders.

They stepped onto the perfectly kept fairway and paused for a moment to admire the view. The lush green course, dotted with tropical plants, was a delight to behold.

Cornelia sighed. "I'm going to miss the gulf views and tropical greenery when I leave."

He patted her arm as they walked toward the tee. "From what you've told me, the Rockies have their own appeal. I'm looking forward to seeing them this spring. Do you know I have never been west of the Mississippi?"

"It is quite different. I look forward to showing you around. Maybe we can find time to drive into Denver and tour the mint. Have you ever watched new coins being minted?"

"No, but I'd be interested in seeing the machinery at work." The professor gestured. "There's the ladies' tee, my dear."

Cornelia snorted. "Only if you use it first."

"Ladies always go first. They say you are the weaker sex."

"No, we are the fairer sex. I'm thinking you should use this tee, too, at your age."

"Harumph. An active man of seventy-five shouldn't need to use the ladies' tee."

"If we were referring to an active man of seventy-five, I might agree. I've never understood your attraction to that number. You've been stuck there for years."

"I'm only a little older than seventy-five."

"At least a decade older."

Uncle Percival lifted a finger to his brow. "Really? I forget."

"That's poppycock. You never forget anything. I propose that we use the same tee for handicapping purposes."

"Are you making a wager?"

"Only if it will make this game begin faster."

Despite a pleasant sea breeze that played in the palm trees, the morning quickly became warm. By the ninth hole, Cornelia was ready for a break, not that she was willing to admit that to her uncle. He looked better than he had in some time. Maybe being drawn into the Greek chain dances and having more than one glass of ouzo at the festival was good for him. The irony of her uncle being in the pink while she wilted did not escape her. Thankfully, a foursome asked to play through.

Her uncle suggested they have a cool drink before playing the back nine.

"I've been thinking since Homosassa," the professor said as they walked toward the clubhouse. "The weather here is much more agreeable than Kentucky at this time of year."

"Yes. Snow and ice are more exciting for children than adults."

"I know that you need to go back to Colorado, but I would like to spend the rest of the winter here."

Cornelia was surprised, but pleased. The pneumonia he'd developed the previous November had given her a bad scare. The climate in Florida was damp, but at least it was warm. "The papers are full of real estate ads. I'm sure you could buy or design an excellent home."

He shook his head. "There are too many ads, not to mention some negative rumblings about prices. Besides, I would like to see more of the area before I purchased land for a winter residence. For the time being, I think I would be better off renting a place." He asked the waiter to bring them water before continuing. "I hadn't given thought to designing the house myself. The idea tickles my fancy."

"Just be sure it's not on swampland."

"Hammock land, Cornelia, hammock land. They never say swampland. But we digress. I need to ask your opinion on Teddy."

"Teddy?"

"If you return to Colorado, and I remain here, where will she go? I don't think she'd be happy in Kentucky by herself."

"No," Cornelia said. "She's not really farmer material, and the climate there isn't good for her lungs. The damp air at the festival had her coughing most of the night. It would have been worse in Kentucky. I could take her back with me until we can return together. I'll need to let Mr. Scroggins know that he should keep an eye on the farm for a while longer."

"I have a different idea," the professor said, "if you're both amenable to it. She doesn't know many people in Kentucky, and I know no one here. I propose that I rent a place large enough for the two of us. Outside of one disagreeable individual, she seems to be enjoying the climate."

"Speaking of disagreeable individuals ..." Cornelia said, nodding toward the front entrance.

The professor turned his head and saw a red-faced Ansel Stevens approaching the Moorish archway. His oldest son trudged along beside him, carrying both sets of clubs. Mac wasn't talking back, but the set of his jaw and the way his lips pressed together made Cornelia think that his silence was maintained with great effort.

"Does that man ever speak to his family without yelling?" Cornelia asked. "Whenever I see him, he is bullying one of his children."

"Young Mac isn't one to be bullied. He may not backtalk his father, but there's no surrender in his eyes. Mr. Stevens would be well advised to let him keep his aeroplane."

"Have you heard this argument before?"

Professor Pettijohn picked up the menu their waiter had left and glanced down the list. "No, but Mac there has bought himself one of the surplus jennies the military is selling. Apparently, his father doesn't approve. Wants him to get rid of it."

"How could you know that? Even I can't hear them at this distance, and my hearing is excellent."

Her uncle grinned. "And I have excellent eyesight. I don't need my hearing device to read lips. Mr. Stevens ordered him to sell the jenny and devote himself to the family business."

Cornelia took another sip of her water and sponged the sweat from her brow with her handkerchief. "Uncle, you're incorrigible."

"Isn't that what you love most about me, Corny?" His blue eyes crinkled at the corners as he chuckled. "Why don't we have a bite to eat before we go back to our game? The grouper sandwich sounds delicious."

She bit back the urge to remind him again that she hated that nickname. It was a beautiful day in one of the loveliest places she'd ever seen. The clubhouse was decorated in imported Moorish tiles, with graceful arching windows overlooking swaying palms and deep blue water. "I don't have the constitution for fried food on a day this warm, especially after indulging in all those exotic Greek dishes last night. The seasonal fruit plate with pineapple sherbet should be quite refreshing."

Teddy filled out a postcard for Kathleen, a young friend she'd made in Homosassa, and dropped it off at the front desk of the hotel before starting her hunt for suitable hats. The city trolleys made visiting the stores of Central Avenue convenient, and quite economical.

She strolled through the shops she'd visited before, but none of the hats struck her fancy. Perhaps it was because she'd seen them during her first shopping trip, or perhaps it was because too many of them looked like ones from the clothing catalogs delivered to the house in Kentucky. She left Central Avenue and explored the connecting streets.

She finally stopped in front of a window with a sign: LAST DAY TO BUY FROM BERBER'S. She didn't know who Berber was, or why someone would want to buy anything from him or her, but there was an adorable straw hat on display next to the placard. It sported a broad jacquard sash across the front and tropical blossoms on the side.

The bell tinkled when she entered the store, a lonely call to the sole person on duty, a tiny middle-aged woman. She smiled at Teddy, but her hands, small and neat, clutched the edge of the counter.

"May I help you, ma'am?"

"Yes, you may," Teddy said. "I would very much like to see the hat in the window. The one with the jacaranda blossoms."

"An excellent choice. Please, have a seat by the mirror while I fetch it."

The hat was, indeed, an excellent choice. It was stylish, broad-brimmed enough to keep the sun out of her face, and the tropical flowers added a splash of exotic to the jacquard elegance.

Teddy admired the way it framed her face. It would go well with the light jacket she'd purchased during Thursday's expedition.

"Do you have a hand mirror, Miss, er ...?"

"Rena. I'm sorry, it's at the counter. I'll get it."

"Thank you, Rena." The bald announcement in the window hadn't done justice to the charming little store or the elfish woman working there. Her small display window held about a dozen hats, but inside the store, shelves were stacked with every style hat imaginable. Teddy had intended to buy a single hat suitable for afternoon functions, but she'd spotted at least a dozen others that she was dying to try on. They were all so lovely, and on sale.

When the woman returned with the smaller mirror, Teddy used it to check the bow in back. "Very, very nice. So, tell me, why is Berber's closing when it has such wonderful hats?"

"It's not exactly closing. Mr. Berber sold the store for a handsome sum to a man from Michigan. So today is the last day this place is Berber's." Rena took the mirror back and sighed.

"Will you be staying on with the new owners?" Teddy knew the answer already, but the question needed to be asked.

"No. He's moving his family down here permanently, and he has daughters to work in the shop. I was informed that my services would not be needed."

"But you keep an excellent shop."

"Thank you."

"Surely another store would be happy to have you. Do you have a place to go?"

Rena shook her head. "Not yet. I'm going to try my luck in Sarasota; I have a friend I can stay with while I look."

"I'm sure you will land on your feet." Teddy glanced around the shop again. Admiration filled her eyes as she examined the way Rena's arrangements complemented all the rich colors and textures of the hats. "Tell me, do you receive a commission for hat sales?"

"Yes, I do, but today," Rena said, "Mr. Berber told me I could have all proceeds."

Only the certain knowledge that Cornelia would be apoplectic kept her from buying more than three. One for the sun, one because she had to have it, and a broad-brimmed telescope one that would make a perfect gift for Cornelia.

Rena was all too pleased to help her. The two women spent a pleasant hour chatting about hats, fashion, and St. Petersburg.

Teddy wore one of her new purchases when she left the shop. The clerk was kind enough to wrap the one she'd worn and tuck it into her shopping bag. She paused to admire a beaded purse in a window display. It was too bad that Shirley was at work. The trip would have been more fun shared with someone who had an eye for style. That always ruled out Cornelia. She would have begrudged any time spent looking in shop windows. Besides, even her civilian clothes were a uniform: utilitarian, comfortable, and drab.

Two stores down, a shoe shop with a large banner proclaiming "Under New Management" in bright red letters caught her attention. She was about to enter, when she saw Violet Stevens and her muscular young man with the large ears going into a small corner cafe. Teddy was immediately famished. She feigned interest in shoes until the couple was out of sight, then headed toward the tantalizing aroma of fried chicken.

A pimple-faced youngster who looked uncomfortable in his crisp white shirt and black bow tie greeted her. "Only one, ma'am?"

Teddy nodded.

She smiled as he led her to a high-backed oak booth directly behind the one occupied by the pair. The boy couldn't have chosen a better table if he'd known she was as interested in sating her curiosity about Ansel's daughter as she was in satisfying her appetite. She couldn't see the couple, but the location gave excellent concealment with the added benefit of being able to hear every word the lovebirds uttered.

Violet requested coffee; her suitor declined to order.

Later, Cornelia would scold her for eavesdropping—if she found out. Teddy was used to her growls. Unlike the nurses she ordered about, Teddy knew what an old softie was behind that bark. Besides, she reasoned, she hadn't set out to spy on Violet. She had finished her shopping, and merely stopped for lunch at the closest place. It wasn't her fault that the couple happened to have chosen a cafe close to the hat shop, or that her waiter decided to seat her directly behind Violet Stevens and her beau. After the rough way her father dragged Violet away from the waterfront, she was concerned for the girl's safety.

The young man's voice was a pleasant tenor. "Violet, sweetheart, your father doesn't have the right to bully you.

Look at the bruises his rough handling made on your arm. I should have told him yesterday that we were already married, instead of trying to find a way to pry his fist open. If he lays a hand on you again, I'll break his neck."

"Please, Harry, that would only make things worse."

The fear in Violet's plea reminded Teddy of her own experience with the brute. Her appetite vanished.

"Nonsense." His tone was hushed, but the force of Harry's words reverberated. "Tomorrow, this cat and mouse game ends. Come with me in the race. You can stay in the cabin until we're underway. No. Wait. I have a better idea. Be my mate. Come up on deck beside me and show him that we don't give a fig."

"What about Mother? He'll take it out on her."

"Your brother Mac won't allow that. He is going to be with your father until this race is over. Afterwards, I told him that we are willing to take your mother with us or help her get away. You know how unhappy she is with that monster."

"He's not a monster, Harry, just strict."

In the silence that followed, Teddy formed a mental picture of the look of incredulity on Harry's face.

"Do you believe Father will keep his word?" Violet asked.

"He won't have any other choice. Everyone at the Yacht Club already knows about our wager. Your father cannot afford to welsh in front of his business associates. Construction is a business that demands absolute faith in a man's word. He would never get another contract. Trust me. Before Monday morning, it isn't going to matter what your father thinks of me."

"Oh Harry, I wish I were as brave as you. I'm not."

"Then I will be brave enough for both of us."

There was a long silence, and then short breaths that made Teddy believe she was weeping.

"Sweetheart," he said softly. "You are safe with me. All the happiness you could want is waiting for you. You'll see. There is nothing like being aboard a finely crafted yacht, coursing through the water at speed—the *Silver Breeze* has a cruising speed of over ten knots. It is impossible not to smile and love life under her sails."

She sniffed. "You make it all sound so wonderful."

"It will be wonderful, win or lose. No more sneaking around, no more living in separate places. We'll have a real honeymoon in the Caribbean; we'll tour Cuba, Jamaica, Barbados, and dozens of other islands. Then we'll come back and find a place on land to call home. Either way, you never have to be bullied by your father again."

The back nine played faster than Cornelia had expected. She shot two birdies back to back and was feeling proud of herself for taking the lead. Then the professor got an eagle on the seventeenth hole and tied the score. She still might have won if it hadn't been for an unfortunate incident on what should have been her final putt. As she approached the green, a Boston Terrier grabbed the ball and disappeared into the lush greenery near the water. She was about to give chase, but the sight of a gator made her reconsider. The loss of her ball gave her uncle the advantage, and he didn't waste the opportunity.

On the bus back to the hotel, he regaled the other passengers with the story. To her chagrin, he referred to her as "Corny" at least a dozen times while spinning his yarn. She took the annoying nickname and the jibes of the golfers with as much grace as she could muster. Over the years she had witnessed several golfing incidents, including one in the Philippines where a monkey leapt onto the back of the hospital surgeon as he started his swing.

She would have shared the story with Teddy, had it not been for the look of bewilderment on her face when they walked into the suite.

"Miss Theodora, it's good to see you're up and about," the professor said. "How are you feeling today?"

Teddy opened her mouth, but no words came out. She looked from one to the other. The professor looked like a binder boy who had consumed a half dozen pints of Rip Van Winkle's ale, slept far more than twenty years, and awoke still dressed to hawk real estate from the street corner. She had seen him in outlandish costume before, but Cornelia ... Never in her wildest imaginings would she have pictured Cornelia dressed in pastel shades of pink and green. Someone had spirited the real Cornelia away and replaced her with an enormous Easter egg topped by a huge pom-pom.

"When did you get that?" Teddy asked, pointing to Cornelia's golfing cap.

Cornelia reached up and adjusted the brim. "This morning. It was a gift from Uncle Percival. He wanted to play a round of golf, and I didn't bring anything suitable for sport."

Teddy thought the sport in question was to embarrass Cornelia. The smile beaming through Professor Pettijohn's snowy whiskers told her otherwise. He was delighted with the purchase. She refrained from comment. At least he'd gotten Cornelia out of mourning colors for a while.

Teddy had wanted to visit the Vinoy ballroom from the moment she'd had her first peek inside. She was positively glowing in a peacock blue sequined gown that captured the shimmering lights. Tonight, she'd taken special care with her makeup. After all, seeing Paul Whiteman's Orchestra live was a rare treat. It was easy to see that some of the color in her cheeks was excitement instead of cosmetics.

Cornelia was dressed in the gown Teddy picked out for her. She felt self-conscious in the pale champagne color, but both her companions assured her the dress looked wonderful. Her complexion was another matter. She had cheeks as rosy as Teddy's. Unfortunately, her color was from a golf outing with too much sun and too little face cream. The years spent in Colorado had done away with her tan. A brown paper and vinegar plaster had pulled most of the heat away, but the color would remain until the skin peeled. She trusted it more than the Noxzema Teddy offered. Cornelia was glad Teddy had refrained from those evil words, "I told you so."

Uncle Percival was his usual dapper self in a black evening suit that cost more than she made in a month. White shirt with his silver Wildcat cufflinks, white silk tie and vest, and a silk handkerchief in his breast pocket that folded into points as sharp as those on the lapels of his suit. Cornelia couldn't help noticing he had his hearing device discreetly tucked behind the handkerchief. The idea of her uncle listening to modern music was a little surprising.

The Paul Whiteman Orchestra was taking the stage in the Palm Room when the three of them arrived. It was a full house. Luckily, the professor had reserved a table at the edge of the dance floor with a great view of the bandstand.

"I do hope they play 'The Japanese Sandman.' It always reminds me of that evening in the desert when our shoes were filled with sand from dancing under the stars," Teddy said.

"You are such a romantic," Cornelia said. "My feet were just fine in sensible footwear. As I recall, you paid five dollars for those fancy heels you ruined. The next day your feet were blistered, and you limped for a week."

Teddy stuck her tongue out at Cornelia as they took their seats. There was no malice in the exchange. Teddy was smiling across the table in a way that made Cornelia's face turn a darker shade of pink. Soon, the first strains of a Gershwin tune had Teddy tapping her toes.

The music was lively, as were the dancers. Professor Pettijohn seemed taken aback by the acrobatics. Cornelia didn't want to know what he would think if she attempted the gyrations herself. Teddy, on the other hand, looked ready to jump into the fray at any moment.

He smiled at her. "Perhaps, Theodora, you'll favor me with a waltz if it isn't too old-fashioned for this crowd. That is, if they ever play a ballad."

"I'd be delighted," she said. "And don't worry, every band has an arsenal of ballads. Couples of any age want to hear something romantic."

A short time later the band played "Make Believe" and both Teddy and the professor left their canes at the table for a spin around the dancefloor.

Cornelia was distracted from watching her uncle and Teddy by an angry voice behind her. She turned to see Ansel's daughters: the tall elegant blonde, and the sweet-faced one with the dark curls.

"Daddy is being ridiculous about this, and you know it," the younger daughter said. "He has no right to choose whom we marry."

Evelyn's voice was softer, but the background music forced all conversations to be loud. "You don't see it the way he does. He's trying to look out for your future." She toyed with the marquise diamond on her finger.

Violet noted the gesture. "Just like he was looking out for yours, choosing your husband for you?"

Evelyn released the ring and clasped her hands together. "Daddy suggested that he was a good match, but the choice was mine."

"He's a good match for the family business," Violet retorted. Cornelia thought the girl's expression was too cynical for someone so young. "A nursery owner goes swimmingly with new development."

"It may," the older sister said coolly, "but so would a builder. He's trying to save you a lot of grief. You'd see it too, if you weren't stuck on the guy. He can't even join a club or stay in a nice hotel."

"I'd rather sleep under the stars on Harry's boat than be imprisoned by a comfortable life."

"Watch out. You may get your wish."

The sisters fell into what must have been an uncomfortable silence then, and Cornelia was abashed to realize that she had been eavesdropping. How many times had she scolded Teddy for that?

CHAPTER SEVEN

Valentine's Day dawned bright and full of promise. The ladies exchanged gifts before dressing for breakfast. Cornelia, straightening her new hat in the mirror, watched Teddy slip into her new stockings.

Cornelia's uncle was waiting for them when the pair entered the sitting room. His smile beamed out from his snowy beard. On the table beside him were two large vases of flowers: one filled with pale pink camellias, the other with bright pink roses. Between them sat a lacy heart-shaped box of chocolates.

"How beautiful!" Teddy said, immediately going over to sniff the roses. "You remembered it was Valentine's Day."

"I rarely forget dates," the professor said. "I'm afraid chrysanthemums are out of season, even here, Corny. I know they're your favorites."

"These are marvelous. I don't remember the last time I got flowers and chocolates on Valentine's Day. Thank you," Cornelia replied. She hadn't expected such a lavish gesture on his part.

After appropriate oohs and aahs were made over the flowers, the three went downstairs for breakfast. The entire dining room was abuzz with excitement over an impromptu regatta planned for the afternoon. The hoopla centered on the public wager between Ansel Stevens and Harry Brockman. Their race would determine which man left St. Petersburg— and young love was in the balance.

Looking around the room, Cornelia could see the worried expressions on the faces of parents with daughters of marriageable age. One red-faced father slammed his paper on the table. "Alice, I won't listen to another word of your romantic nonsense. That girl is from a good Christian family. Heaven knows what she's in for if she marries that man."

Alice started to say something, but her father was in no mood to listen. "The presumption of that young man is appalling. If you ever acted like that, I would lock you in your room until you came to your senses."

The girl burst into tears and ran from the room.

Cornelia balanced a sharp retort on the tip of her tongue. She had no right to intrude, but it was difficult to remain silent. Anti-Semitic sentiment was entrenched in the world and this man was part of the reason. If confronted, he would insist that he had no ill will toward the Jews; the world simply wasn't ready for mixed-faith couples. On some level, he was right. If Violet wasn't aware of the depth of prejudice in America, she was in for a rude awakening. Still, she couldn't meet his eyes when they walked past the table.

For the first day since they'd come to the Vinoy, Teddy did not have a headache or diminished appetite. The professor could choose a table near the windows, which afforded lovely views. He was also able to have his favorite breakfast, Eggs Benedict, which was a specialty of the hotel. Cornelia chose steak and eggs with a side of hash browned potatoes.

While Teddy pondered her choices, the professor brought out the real estate ads. "I looked at the paper while I was waiting for you to wake up," he began. "There are a couple of rental options that piqued my interest. What do you think, Cornelia?"

He handed her the *Times*. One of the properties was nearby. The other was near the golf course. She didn't know that much about that part of town, but the houses were all new and looked expensive.

"Which one do you want to see first?" Cornelia asked as she passed the paper to Teddy.

The professor beamed. "I would have bought flowers before if I'd known they would make you so agreeable."

Cornelia turned the corner onto Mirror Lake Drive and was pleased to see the small lake lived up to its name. Sunlight reflected on glassy water, and the right side of the street had an unobstructed view of the waterfront. She was apprehensive of the small walkways that ran along the steep banks of the lake, though; neither Teddy nor her uncle would have an easy time on that path. One slip of the foot, and her elderly uncle could slide into the lake.

Uncle Percy hadn't said a word since leaving the dining room. He obviously didn't want to talk. The earpiece to his hearing device still dangled from his suit pocket.

Cornelia stopped in front of the house and looked at her uncle. She made sure he had a full view of her face, since he was still being childish about the hearing device.

"This is it," she said. "I don't see any sign of the rental agent."

Professor Pettijohn put the earpiece back in place and turned the tiny knob on top of the device. "Neither do I."

He pulled his watch from its pocket and checked it against the one he wore on his wrist. "We're six minutes early. He should already be here."

Cornelia hoped so; she didn't need to be lectured again on the importance of punctuality.

"We could look at the outside," Teddy suggested.

The professor contented himself with examining the roof tiles, shaded porches, and exterior conditions for the first quarter of an hour. His frown deepened each time he stopped to check either the watch in his pocket or the one on his wrist. For the next quarter, he paced the walk, looked down the street, and grumbled each time he looked at his watches.

Teddy and Cornelia retreated to the back of the house on the pretext of viewing the condition of the garden.

Five minutes later, the garden gate banged closed. Professor Pettijohn tromped through the grass to where the two ladies stood admiring a gardenia bush. "It's time to go," he announced. "I have no interest in renting a property from a man who can't be bothered to show up for an appointment."

Teddy sighed. "They've painted the stucco such a pretty shade of blue. I would have liked to see the inside."

Uncle Percival turned and marched away without another word.

He was a stubborn old mule whose pace belied his years. Cornelia was obliged to trot, as she had as a youngster following him down the streets of Lexington. She caught him by the arm as they neared her automobile. "Where are we going next?"

"To do a little investigating. Please take us on a tour of the neighborhood, Corny."

She complied, turning at the next street and making a large loop around the house they'd been looking at.

"Stop," Professor Pettijohn shouted.

Cornelia slammed on the brakes.

"What's wrong?" Teddy asked as she looked for some cause of alarm.

The professor pointed to a large black car with "Hale Developing Co." painted on the door. "That's the fellow who was supposed to meet us at the house."

"Really, Uncle," Cornelia groused. "You nearly gave me a heart attack. There could be a dozen cars painted with that sign."

He opened the door. "There's one way to find out."

She caught his sleeve. "You are not going over there and make a fool of yourself."

"Certainly not." Indignation dripped from his voice. "I am going to find out if our rental agent ignored our appointment for a more lucrative one."

"In that case, I'll go."

"I don't need to be protected," he snapped.

"Of course not," she replied, in a more conciliatory tone. "I was trying to keep us on time for your next appointment. Surely I can climb those steps much faster than either of you."

The mention of his next appointment sent him scurrying for his pocket watch.

Cornelia was out of the car before he could recover from his distraction.

Within minutes of entering the house, Cornelia reappeared. Her rigid spine and the set of her square jaw confirmed his suspicions. The bounder had stood him up. These land agents had the character of lemmings, blindly following each other off a cliff in pursuit of another sale.

"I was right," the professor said, when Cornelia opened the door.

She nodded.

He checked his watch. "Much as I would enjoy instructing Mr. Hale in proper business manners, we no longer have the time. We need to set up the camera so I can film the yacht race, and we'd better be early if we want a good view."

St. Petersburg had transformed Cornelia's ancient uncle into an excited five-year-old with free reign in an ice-cream parlor. Mechanical novelties were spread out before him and he wanted to taste them all. The park would have been excellent for birding, but she hadn't been able to pry her field glasses away from him once since they'd arrived in town.

Today, he'd found a new reason for "borrowing" them. Delight danced in Professor Pettijohn's eyes. "The mezzanine is a great place to set up the camera. We'll get the start and finish of the race on film. If you angle the camera correctly, we can also have some excellent footage of the pier construction."

By the time they reached their suite, it was obvious that Cornelia was the "we" who would be behind the camera. On the first part of the trip, he handled his precious camera while she lugged his tripod from place to place. Somewhere between Citrus and Pinellas County, he became the director as she filmed his masterpiece. She didn't mind cranking the moving picture camera, but it was irksome to be taken for granted.

The professor sat at the edge of his chair watching hired boats set up the racecourse. "I've never watched a regatta with sailing vessels before. The ones held on the Ohio River were between magnificent paddle-wheeled steamboats. I'll be interested to see how this race is conducted."

Cornelia relented and smiled at her uncle. Despite his antics, she was glad they had this time together. Even though it had started as a ruse, wintering in Florida was a good idea. The sunlight and sea air were putting some color back in his face. She would have told him so, but the black earpiece of his hearing device dangled from his breast pocket. He'd had it in his ear when they left the room. The race chatter around them must have made it difficult for him to distinguish what was being said.

She settled into the tall-backed rocking chair beside him. His excitement was contagious. She leaned back in her seat, enjoying the clear blue skies and soaking in the warmth. It was a perfect day for watching boats speed across the bay, their motors leaving a trail of white-capped waves in the deep blue water. There was irony in using motorboats to set up the racecourse for sailing.

In the yacht basin, young Harry was ready to cast off. His mate didn't look like much of a sailor. He was a wisp of a boy. Something in the lad's stance pricked a memory. "Uncle, may I have my field glasses for a moment?"

"You will give them back before the race starts." It was a statement, not a question.

Cornelia pretended not to notice. She looked into his deep blue eyes and enunciated each word to make it easier for him to read her lips. "Of course, Uncle. I want a better look at the yachts." What she really wanted was a better look at the first mate.

One glance confirmed her suspicions. Violet had joined Harry against her father and Mac. Her face softened as she watched the young couple get underway. The determination in Violet's face reminded her of Teddy as a young woman. Her father might not know it yet, but he had lost something far more precious than a race today.

Cornelia handed the glasses back to her uncle and took her place behind the camera. The yachtsmen had a calm day for racing sailing vessels. No speed records were in danger of falling. The wind was light and fluky over dead calm water. At least Harry had the good sense to take advantage of the tidal flow. When the yacht club horn blasted a signal for the race to start, he tacked starboard and gracefully brought the bow of the *Silver Breeze* leeward of the tidal stream. Wind filled white sails as the youngsters sailed past the new pier, gaining an early advantage over Ansel. The older man pulled his hat low over his brow and copied the move.

Professor Pettijohn cheered as the distance between the boats widened. "That was superb. You did capture that on film, didn't you, Corny?"

Cornelia bristled at the nickname. He looked so excited that she resisted her usual retort. "You should have some good footage of the construction crew applauding the maneuver."

He winked at her. "That's my girl."

In that moment he so reminded Cornelia of her father that she had to look away to get her emotions under control. A wink was such a silly thing to get all teary-eyed about.

She glanced over to where Teddy stood clinging to the railing, giggling with young Shirley. Teddy was such a romantic. Cornelia wasn't sure if her hatred of Ansel or her sympathy for Violet was at the forefront of her mind. Either way, she would be inconsolable if the pompous bully managed to win.

Ansel was closing the gap, but Harry was still in the lead when they rounded the point. Once they reached the gulf side, their speed would pick up. Still, it was going to take the boats a while to get to Saint Petersburg Beach and make the turn. She filmed a moment longer before returning to her seat and picking up the copy of Willa Cather's My Mortal Enemy that she'd discovered in the hotel library.

She was still absorbed in her book when her uncle nudged her. "Here they come."

The boats were barely visible on the horizon. It was pointless to try filming them at this distance. There was no arguing with her uncle, though. She stood up and took her place behind his camera. As they came into range, Harry appeared to be in the lead, but neither boat moved at more than three knots. The distance tightened, then Ansel made an egregious error. His boat turned sharply into the path of the *Silver Breeze*. Harry barely managed to avoid crashing into the broadside of the *Nittany Nob*. Ansel neither acknowledged the penalty flag, nor righted his boat. His sailing became more and more erratic as they approached the finish line.

There were no cheers when Harry glided across to the finish. Hotel guest were on their feet craning to get a better look at the *Nittany Nob*. The boat was in trouble. Neither Ansel nor his son had the wheel. Cornelia watched in horror as Ansel's boat drifted out of the channel.

The vessel edged closer to the pier with each slight gust of wind.

Workmen scurried to get out of the way.

Judges' motorboats sprang to life.

Harry turned the *Silver Breeze* and followed in their wake.

The workmen realized that the sailboat was going to crash. One of the laborers grabbed a piece of lumber and tried to push Ansel's craft away from the construction.

He was too late.

The *Nittany Nob* collided with one of the floating construction cranes.

A steel beam broke free of its chains and hit the water, creating a wave that swamped the boat as it pushed hard against the crane. Both vessels began to list.

More and more people from the hotel crowded the veranda. Filming was impossible.

Cornelia removed the camera from its tripod seconds before a clumsy guest stumbled into her while vying for a spot near the front of the mob.

She managed to right herself and hold onto her uncle's camera. Then she noticed that his chair was empty. Professor Pettijohn was leaning over the railing, transfixed by the scene on the pier. Goliath couldn't have pried her field glasses from his hands.

The crowd on the veranda didn't disperse until the ambulance screamed its way out of the one clustered at the pier. Whatever had happened aboard the *Nittany Nob*, there was at least one survivor.

CHAPTER EIGHT

Shirley went home. The trio returned to their hotel suite. They sat in silence for a long while, each struggled to digest what they'd watched. Cornelia waited for a cue from Teddy, who had known and detested the man. There was none forthcoming. Her companion stared out the window, pale and quiet, legs tucked underneath her on the sofa.

Uncle Percival, never one to sit idle for long, pulled his watch from his vest and checked it against the clock on the side table, one of three he'd brought with him on the trip. He picked the clock up and adjusted it. After several more uncomfortable moments, the professor produced a small tool kit from a pocket and began removing the back of the timepiece.

A knock at the door interrupted the unpleasant silence. Cornelia didn't know whether to be annoyed or grateful, but she rose from her seat to see who it was.

She was surprised to see someone she knew—a man with curly dark hair and the beginnings of a five-o'-clock shadow on his face. Mitchell Grant, the reporter from the *St. Petersburg Times*.

"Mitch?"

"Hello, Miss Cornelia. May I come in?"

"Why, certainly." She let him inside and closed the door. Mitch was a welcome sight, but why had he come?

Teddy was on her feet, even smiling. "It's good to see you. How have you been?"

"Oh, I've been fine," the young man replied. His eyes scanned the room. "Never been in one of the rooms here. It's the Ritz. I'd be afraid to touch anything in a room like this; I might leave fingerprints."

"It's very nice to see you, Mitch, but it's been a ..." Cornelia searched for a good word, but could only find bad ones. "... a difficult day. What brings you here?"

"Business, I'm sorry to say. Did you ladies watch the race today?"

"Race? I presume you mean the disaster at the Pier," the professor said. "Bad business, that. Yes, we watched it from the veranda."

"You saw the sockdollager at the end, then."

"We could hardly have missed it."

"I guess not." Mitch rubbed his brow before continuing. "Look, what I'm getting at is that I've heard Miss Teddy knew Mr. Stevens, the guy who cracked his boat up."

"You heard it?" Teddy exclaimed. "From whom?"

"From Mrs. Stevens. More like overheard it. She was talking to the police."

Cornelia frowned. "The police? What did she say, and where did you overhear this?"

Mitch winked. "The walls at Mound Park Hospital have a good echo. Besides, the lady wasn't quiet about it."

"Well," Teddy said, "I knew him when I was young, but that was some years ago. Is it relevant for some reason?"

"It became relevant when Mr. Stevens died," Mitch blurted.

Teddy gasped—a real gasp, not one of her affectations—and sat down in the nearest chair. "Ansel's dead?"

Cornelia went to Teddy's side and took her hand. She didn't know whether to offer condolences or say good riddance. When in doubt, keep your mouth shut.

"I'm sorry, Miss Teddy, I didn't realize you hadn't heard." Mitch said. "I hoped you would be able to tell me more about him for my article. I can hardly ask his wife."

"Oh—of course you can't," Teddy sighed. "Let's see, what do I know? Ansel was originally from Erie, Pennsylvania. His family has been in construction for a long time—oh, and he was named for his grandfather Ansel. Ansel Senior was in partnership with his brother Conrad, but bought him out, I believe."

Mitch took notes, although Cornelia thought he didn't seem particularly interested. Writing an obituary was probably not the sort of work a newspaper's crime writer would enjoy.

"Young Ansel was studying business at Behrend College when I knew him, but I—I left for nursing school in New York before he finished his education. I don't know if he pursued a graduate degree or not."

"I appreciate the information," the young man said. "Perhaps you have a personal story about him you'd like to share? Bring the article to life."

Cornelia knew that Teddy's personal story about Ansel was one she would not want to share. Mitch waited patiently while his interviewee gathered her words.

Another knock from outside interrupted the conversation. Cornelia was relieved, but the feeling was short-lived.

A young woman in a crisp navy suit stood at the door. Her cloche hat and curls did little to soften the sharp hazel eyes under them. "I'm Roberta Hornbuckle, society writer for the *Evening Independent*. Is a Miss Theodora Lawless here?"

Mitch turned and scowled. "Bobby! Get out of here. This isn't one of your galas or fetes."

'Bobby' strode into the room. "The Stevens are a prominent family in St. Petersburg, which makes it my business."

"And what led you here?"

"You did, Mitch. When the widow began squawking about Miss Lawless, you lit out like a dog with cans tied to his tail. I just followed the racket."

Teddy stood again. "Squawking about me? Exactly what did you overhear, Mitch?"

The professor, who had continued to quietly work on his clock, set it down. "Is there a reason to believe that Mr. Stevens' death was not the result of his crash?"

"It might not be," Mitch said. "The docs at the hospital said there was something odd about it. Like maybe something else caused the accident in the first place."

A bad feeling crept into Cornelia's belly. "That has nothing to do with us," she snapped. "I think both of you should leave."

"But it does involve her," Bobby said, pointing at a pale-faced Teddy. "This woman, Theodora Lawless, has publicly assaulted Ansel Stevens on at least two different occasions—and now he's suffered a violent death."

"Which we watched from the veranda," Cornelia said. "There are at least two dozen witnesses. Before that, we were having breakfast downstairs in a room full of people." She seized the woman's arm, turned her around, and frog-marched her towards the door.

"Miss Lawless, call me!" Bobby shouted as she was shoved into the hallway. "The *Evening Independent* wants your side of the story."

"You don't want to talk to her," Mitch said to Teddy. "She's little more than a gossip columnist."

"And you're a crime writer," Teddy said. "Maybe you should tell us why you are here, Mitch."

"The guy is dead, and it doesn't look natural," the reporter replied. "When the police asked Mrs. Stevens about enemies, your name was the first thing out of her mouth."

"And you thought you'd talk to the murderess first?" Teddy retorted. "You lied when you said you needed more background information. You were hoping for a hot story."

"Oh, Miss Teddy, don't you know me better than that?"

"No," Teddy said, crossing her arms. "I don't."

"Out you go," Cornelia said, reaching for his arm.

Mitch ducked her grasp and headed for the exit on his own. "I'm on your side, ladies. Let me know when you're ready to talk."

"There's nothing to talk about," Cornelia said, locking the door behind him. She leaned against it for a moment.

"The police will be next," Uncle Percival said.

Cornelia sighed. "I know."

Teddy rifled through the wardrobe. "What does one wear when being questioned by the police?"

"You've been questioned by the police before." Cornelia snatched the half-empty Ball jar from the woman's free hand.

"That was in France; I wore my uniform. This is a civilian interview." She stretched out her hand. "Give it back."

"No. Drunkenness is its own offense."

"At least it would be true," Teddy said. "When that cad was alive, I was blamed for things I didn't do, and now that he's gone, I'm still being blamed for things I didn't do. It isn't fair."

"There's not a lot of fairness in this world, but you should keep it on your side," Cornelia said, stowing the resealed jar away in its suitcase. "What about wearing your pink frock?"

"That's a good idea," Teddy replied. "Pink is sweet and harmless. Let's do that."

"Yes, let's."

When they returned to the sitting room, the professor was examining the newspaper. He straightened and removed his bifocals.

"Ah, there you two are. I've been looking for legal representation in the area."

"Surely we won't need it," Cornelia said. "Teddy was in public view the entire time."

"Mmm, perhaps," her uncle said. "It's still best to be prepared."

The knock, when it came, was heavy and seemed to echo in the room. Cornelia steeled herself and approached the door.

"If you're from the press, we're not giving interviews," she said, fingers resting on the handle.

"We're not the press. This is the police."

Teddy and the professor both stood and smoothed their clothing at the same time.

When Cornelia opened the door, two officers entered. The one in plain clothes was short and wiry; the uniformed officer was stocky. The pair removed their caps.

"We're sorry to bother you sir, ladies. I'm Detective Joe Knaggs, and this is Sergeant Duncan. We've come to speak to a Miss Theodora Lawless," the wiry one said.

"That would be me." Teddy sounded surprised, little actress that she was.

The professor moved in front of Cornelia and extended his hand. "Professor Pettijohn, resident of Midway, Kentucky. These are my nieces, who are also my nurses. How may we help you gentlemen?"

"We're investigating the accident that happened earlier today at the Pier," the stocky one said.

Cornelia forced her face into a grimace that resembled a smile. "Come in, please. I'm Cornelia Pettijohn."

"Thank you, ma'am," Knaggs said. His hair was cut military-style, with a little Brilliantine to keep it under control. "Sorry to interrupt your afternoon, but with the calamity earlier today—"

"With the yacht. Yes, it was horrible," Teddy said.

"We've been informed, Miss Lawless, that you knew Ansel Stevens, the man involved."

"Yes, I knew him long ago. We grew up in the same area."

Knaggs took out a notebook. "So, you knew him well?"

"He managed to surprise me a few times," Teddy replied.

The men waited. Teddy did not elaborate.

"We understand," Duncan said, "that you weren't on good terms with Mr. Stevens."

Teddy leaned forward, peering at the uniformed sergeant's badge. "Pelican."

The stocky man was startled. "What?"

"On your badge. A pelican." She gave him an innocent smile. "How delightful."

Duncan shifted from one foot to the other. "Er, yes."

"A nice touch," the professor added.

"Thank you," Knaggs answered in Duncan's stead. "Now, Miss Lawless, could you tell us about your relationship with Mr. Stevens?"

Teddy's smile never wavered. "We were engaged to be married when we were young. Our parents considered it an advantageous match. I did not."

The officers were quiet.

Teddy, Cornelia, and Uncle Percival were quiet.

Knaggs stared at Teddy.

Cornelia stared at Teddy.

The professor stared at Teddy.

Teddy stared at the badge and kept smiling.

Finally, Sergeant Duncan harrumphed. Without his cap, he looked like his mother had spit-shined his bald head. "Could you tell us more, ma'am?"

Teddy raised her gaze leisurely. "I decided I wasn't ready for marriage. The reason was rather our business, not anyone else's. I considered it a private matter when I was seventeen, and still do."

"We have also been informed," Duncan replied, "that you assaulted the deceased in public recently."

She sighed. "I slapped him. If there is a fine to pay, I will pay it. He was brutish over the breakup. Encountering him again was a surprise, and I was unprepared to be polite."

Duncan muttered something under his breath, and Knaggs took over. "Where were you when the accident happened?"

"She was on the veranda downstairs," Cornelia said. "In public sight."

Knaggs continued to watch Teddy. "Were you on the veranda?"

"Yes," Teddy replied.

"And before that?"

"Here, dressing for the yacht race. A light jacket over a tea dress. Oh, and the professor gave us those lovely flowers." She gestured to the nearby table.

"I see," he said, not bothering to look. "What did you do yesterday?"

"I shopped for a hat suitable for afternoon events. I chose a lovely one with silk jacaranda flowers."

Knaggs wrote something down. "Well, you could hardly be expected to attend a yacht race without a new hat."

Teddy brightened. "Exactly! I'm glad you agree."

"Where did you do your shopping?"

"Downtown. I purchased the hat at Berber's, plus two other hats. Do you need to see them?"

The officers looked at one another.

"No, ma'am, we'll take your word for it," Detective Knaggs said. "And before you shopped?"

"Before that, I ate breakfast in the restaurant downstairs. And before that, I took a soak in the tub. I was asleep before the bath, so I can't make an account for myself during that time."

Knaggs half-laughed, half-snorted. "Quite a thorough description. Miss Pettijohn, did you shop yesterday with your sister?"

It wasn't the first time they'd been mistaken for sisters, which Cornelia had never understood. Teddy was thin as a whippet, while she'd often thought one of her ancestors was a fireplug.

"No, I went golfing with Uncle Percival. Before that, we had breakfast downstairs. After the game, we had a snack."

Knaggs made more notes before shifting his attention to the professor. "And you, sir?"

"The account for my day is largely a duplicate of Corny's. Except no one bought a new hat for me."

"Don't call me Corny," Cornelia muttered, and the officers smiled.

"I'm so sorry, Professor," Teddy said. "I'll get you a new hat, too."

"You should, after stealing my fedora in Homosassa."

"I gave it back."

"It is unwearable. I've been letting it air out, but the scent of your perfume lingers."

Detective Knaggs closed his notebook. "I think this is all we need for the moment. How long will you three be staying in Saint Petersburg?"

"I plan to stay here for the next month or two, though I may make some excursions elsewhere. Cornelia must return to Fitzsimons General Hospital in a couple of weeks, but Teddy will be staying in Florida with me."

Knaggs tilted his head. "Fitzsimons, ma'am? Are you Army?"

"Yes, I am," Cornelia said. "I'm the chief surgical nurse at Army Hospital Number 21. Teddy and I both served through the Great War."

"Where were you stationed?"

"Verdun," Cornelia said.

Knaggs half-smiled. "Lorraine. Me and Morty both. We were lucky; a lot of guys didn't come back."

Teddy was almost amongst them. "I wish both of you a pleasant evening," Cornelia said.

The officers made their farewells and departed.

Teddy hugged the professor. "You poor man. I'll get you a new hat, I promise. I'm so glad that's over."

Cornelia wasn't as sure.

CHAPTER NINE

Cornelia closed the door behind the officers. Her hand toyed with the chain latch for a moment, but she didn't use it. "Between the police and the press, we aren't going to have any peace here. We should get away from the hotel for a while."

"Wouldn't it be better to stay in?" Teddy asked. "Out there we'll have to deal with the entire mob. I would rather deal with them individually."

Cornelia came over, put her arms around Teddy, and enveloped her in a protective hug. "You shouldn't have to deal with this at all."

Teddy wept on her shoulder for several minutes.

"I need a drink," she muttered, between sniffles.

"No," Professor Pettijohn said. "Cornelia's right. You need to get away from the hotel and not to the sort of places you've been visiting. You'd run into the same crowd there that you would in the hotel."

"Do you have something in mind?" Cornelia asked.

The glint in her uncle's eyes and the sly half smile that peeked through his snowy whiskers told her he had a ready answer.

He picked up the newspaper from the side table. "I think this might fit the bill." He pointed to a small advertisement near the bottom of the page.

Cornelia's eyes widened. "*No, No Nanette*? What is that?"

"A live performance, by a local theatre troupe that performs in the high school's gymnasium." The professor's smile broadened as he spoke. "The crowd here is more accustomed to Broadway. It is doubtful that a cast without a professional venue would attract the hotel guests."

"It is reported to be an engaging production, delightfully funny, with dancing and a number of popular songs." Cornelia said. "What do you think Teddy? Are you up to seeing a sentimental comedy?"

"It's better than a sentimental tragedy," Teddy sighed. "Yes, I would love to escape for the evening."

They entered a raucously loud and crowded hotel lobby. A knot of people blocked the entrance to the dining room. Cornelia looked closer and saw that the steps were blocked by a hungry pack of reporters. Those loathsome creatures surrounded the Stevens family, jockeying for the spot closest to the widow. The ones who couldn't get close enough to be heard above the noise fired loud, injurious questions at Mrs. Stevens.

She caught a glimpse of the new widow when Mac shoved a burly reporter hard enough to topple him and several cohorts to the floor. Mrs. Stevens wore unrelieved black. Her hat was draped in layers of black mesh heavy enough to block her own vision. Still, it gave her a buffer from the vultures. Her son edged her down the stairs, and the girls were flanking her on each side. The older one, Evelyn, spotted Cornelia and gave her a poisonous look. Then she pointed at the three of them and said something to the closest member of the Fourth Estate. The reporter turned in their direction.

Cornelia extended her arm to stop her companions. "Get back in the lift now," she said in an urgent tone. "Go up a floor. Get off and walk to the other lift. I'll get the car and wait for you at the far door."

Teddy and the professor immediately retreated to the elevator doors.

Cornelia charged across the lobby, intent on beating the pack to the exit. The reporter from the *Evening Independent*, the only female in the bunch, broke from the group and made a beeline for Teddy. As she did so, a man followed and grabbed her by the waist. It was Mitch.

"Grant!" the woman hissed. "Let go of me." She kicked backwards with her sharp heels and freed herself—but the brass elevator doors had already closed. The reporter had to content herself with unleashing her anger on Mitch.

"Serves him right," Cornelia muttered. She wasn't ready to forgive him for leading that woman to Teddy's door. Mitch was smart enough to know better.

Cornelia awoke later than usual. The image of the yacht crashing into the pier kept invading her dreams. Ansel wasn't at the helm, though; Teddy was. She turned over to look for her companion. After they'd returned from the play, Teddy had downed half the contents of a Ball jar by herself. Judging from the wadded pile of blankets, it hadn't been enough to keep her from an equally restless night.

She sat up and patted the pile in the area where Teddy's shoulder was most likely to be. "Time to get up."

A moan was the answer, followed by, "Why?"

Cornelia sighed as she opened the curtains to let in the morning sun. "Because Uncle is probably already dressed and waiting to have breakfast with us." She could picture her uncle moving from one of his clocks to the next as if that would make Teddy get dressed any sooner. Between his obsession with punctuality and hers with alcohol, Cornelia couldn't win. She was always defending one of them to the other.

"You go. I'm certain he doesn't want to be seen with me today."

"Well, I want to see you, so get up."

"It's so awful," Teddy whined.

"It *is* awful," Cornelia agreed, "but the gossip will be worse if we go downstairs without you."

"You know how to hurt a girl!" The pile of blankets sat up and parted, revealing Teddy. Her close-cropped curls had gone awry during the night and resembled a herd of silver buffalo preparing to jump off the left side of her head.

Cornelia didn't hide her smile. "You should go get freshened up. I would suggest starting with your new hairdo."

"I dread going down there," Teddy said. She reached for her robe.

"We can't eat every meal out," Cornelia said. "Our hotel suite is on the American plan. All our meals are included in the price of the room. Each time we eat elsewhere, we are wasting Uncle Percival's money."

Teddy approached the mirror and stopped. "'Freshen up' was rather an understatement, don't you think? My appearance needs major renovations."

They were later than usual to the dining room, but they were still serving breakfast. Percival pointed to a table near the French doors, but Teddy pleaded that they sit elsewhere.

"My eyes are still strained from the theater; they're not ready for full sunlight. Perhaps a nice dark corner ..."

The professor indicated the newspaper he'd picked up from the front desk. "I planned to look at the real estate ads this morning. There might be some prospects we could visit later when your eyes have, er, recovered."

Cornelia suggested a nearby table. "Perhaps that would be a good spot. It has decent light, and Teddy could sit facing away from the windows."

They accepted the compromise and persuaded the maître d' to seat them at their compromise table. The attendant came for their breakfast order and offered them coffee. Teddy asked for tea and toast, her usual breakfast the morning after the night before. She normally liked an ice pack as well, but the room was a little formal for that.

"What about the Eggs Benedict?" Percival asked.

"The theater also affects her stomach," Cornelia said. "I'll take the eggs and bacon."

"But the dish was invented as a remedy for 'theater stomach,'" the professor protested. "What could be milder than ham and eggs on toast?"

"I don't think I could look at that without getting sick," Teddy said.

The professor had no argument for that. "The same as my niece," he told the waiter. Once the young man was gone, he added, "Let's not do the theater tonight, ladies. I would like to be able to order what I please without fear of creating another spectacle in the dining room."

He placed the *Saint Petersburg Times* face down on the table and sorted through the sections. When he found the real estate section, he folded the sheets until only the ads were exposed.

Cornelia was puzzled. The elderly professor believed in precision, punctuality, and a proper sequence in everything. In all the years she'd known him, her uncle had read the newspaper in precise order, from the front page to the classifieds. *The front page.* Of course, the old dear was protecting Teddy. Ansel's death would be the lead story.

The same thing must have occurred to Teddy at the same time; she eyed the newspaper. "Why did you start from the back, professor?"

"I decided I should go directly to the real estate section to save time," Percival said. "We'll also want to cross-reference the locations with a map of the county."

Her brows wrinkled. "It's upside down. What are you not showing me?"

"We don't need to trouble ourselves with the news right away," he dissembled. "This is supposed to be a vacation."

She reached for the stack of newsprint; he laid a hand atop it.

"Let me see," Teddy demanded. "It's about his death, isn't it? Did you read about it already?"

"Not the entire article. It was continued on page three." He met her eyes. "Do you really want to see?"

She sighed. "Yes. Otherwise, I'll be thinking about it all day."

The professor relinquished the *Times*. She drew the front section out and flipped it over. The server returned with Teddy's tea. He placed it beside her plate, where it was ignored.

"'Tragic end to yacht race; prominent developer dead. Murder?' Hmm, why murder?"

Yes, why? Cornelia waited for more. She noticed that her uncle was no longer reading the classifieds. With her uncle's gift for quick memorization, he had to know at least some of the article's contents.

Teddy studied the article further, then read aloud: "'Stevens' son, Nimrod'—oh, dear, Mac hates people using his first name—'states that during the race, his father fell ill and collapsed at the helm. He attempted to render aid, but to no avail. The Stevens vessel, the *Nittany Nob*, crashed into the new city pier, which is still under construction. Mr. Stevens was rescued by workers and rushed to the Mound Park Hospital, where he subsequently died. The Saint Petersburg police are investigating the death as suspicious for reasons that they are not making public at this time.' Well, that's not fair."

"I'm sure Mitch felt the same way. Or did someone else write the article after all?"

"Oh, he wrote it. He even used some of the information I gave him. Maybe he was simply interested in getting details about Ansel."

"That female reporter disagreed, and so do I," Cornelia replied. "He smelled a scoop and followed it to you."

Their food arrived, and she tucked into it, as did the professor. The eggs were done to perfection, and the bacon was crispy. These disappeared rapidly, while Teddy's toast grew cold.

"Oh, dear, the police have been questioning Mac," Teddy said, turning to page three. "As the only son, he stands to inherit the business. If they knew him like we do, they wouldn't bother. The boy was always a straight arrow."

"An arrow is dangerous under the proper circumstances," Cornelia replied, but she, too, had trouble picturing Mac as a murderer. "What about Violet's young man?"

"He's mentioned," Teddy said. "He lives on his boat and might have gained access to Ansel's vessel when they were both in the same marina. The police didn't question him at the time because no one realized it was murder yet."

"He works in construction, but lives on his boat?" Uncle Percival commented. "That's an interesting way to travel from job site to job site."

"Look!" Teddy's voice went up an octave. She covered her mouth and flushed. "I'm in here," she whispered.

Cornelia took the article away and read:

The police have also questioned Miss Theodora Lawless, who is visiting Saint Petersburg with her family. Miss Lawless is alleged to have publicly assaulted Mr. Stevens because of a personal dispute.

"That's not too bad," she reassured her companion.

"Assaulted," Teddy said. "It sounds so harsh. It was just a slap."

"Well, there was the kicking incident as well."

"My foot slipped."

"It must have been the wax on the floor."

"Ladies," Uncle Percival said, "engaging as the article is, I think it is best put into the past, now that it's been read. There are several prospective homes we should visit this morning. Once we are further from the Stevens family, matters will have a chance to calm down."

The professor reached for his paper. "As for the article, we can't hold that against Mr. Grant. Reporting crime news is his job."

Both women glared at him.

His ears turned red, but he didn't retract his comment. He took the wire of his hearing device out of his ear, cleared his throat, and turned back to the classified section. "There is a house in Roser Park that's available for the remainder of the season. That might be a good place to start our search. I'll contact the agent and arrange a time to view the property."

Cornelia wasn't going to let him weasel out of it that easily, but further discussion was going to wait until he could hear every word.

CHAPTER TEN

Behind the wheel of her Dodge Brothers sedan, Cornelia's clenched jaw began to relax. In the back seat, a subdued Teddy gazed out the window. She doubted that the stately old live oaks dripping with Spanish moss were giving her comfort. At least they were away from reporters, whispers, and accusations on the drive through suburban streets.

She wasn't sure why her uncle wanted to go house-hunting today. Perhaps the expense of staying in a lavish hotel was behind his desire to rent a house. She doubted that, though. He was so happy with his excellent view of pier construction.

It was hard to stay mad at her uncle; the old dear was right. Mitch was a crime reporter. The Stevens murder had enough sensational features to make headlines for weeks. He would be a fool to ignore Teddy's involvement. The idea of Teddy being a suspect tightened the muscles in her neck again to painful levels. Perhaps she shouldn't have slapped him in public or kicked him in the ankle. But after what he did, that Stevens creature deserved much worse treatment.

"Where are we headed?" Cornelia asked her uncle.

The old man handed her a sketched map with the route from the hotel to their destination marked.

Cornelia's brow furrowed. "Isn't this a little too far out of the city, Uncle?"

"I think you'll approve when you see the neighborhood. Brick streets, trolley service, and electric street lights. It's also within blocks of Mound Park Hospital."

She glanced at Teddy again. "You make it sound like a modern utopia."

"I think that's what Mr. Roser had in mind. Locating enough paving brick for eighty blocks of his development is quite an accomplishment, not to mention a considerable expense."

She chuckled. "What makes you think he didn't do that to sell more houses?"

Professor Pettijohn shook his head. "When did you become such a cynic? You had such high-minded ideals when you were young."

"When I was a girl, we didn't have men on every street corner hawking property day and night."

"I see your point, Corny. These Florida land deals never stop. Not that I have room to complain." His blue eyes crinkled at the corners as he laughed at himself. "I was never much inclined to take time off when I could be productive."

Cornelia wasn't laughing. "I don't feel comfortable about these Florida land deals. The prices are insane. People buy and sell land in the same day. Eventually, there will be nobody left to buy."

"I agree; that's why I decided to rent instead of buy a home this winter. The rent may cost as much as buying a house in Kentucky, but it isn't as crazy as the home prices."

She smiled at him.

"If it makes you feel any better, Corny, the Rosers moved here from Ohio long before the land boom. All of the houses in that neighborhood are over a decade old."

"Have you been reading up on all the local developers? You seem to know a lot about this one."

"How could I not know about Charles Roser? He invented my favorite treat, Fig Newtons. Made his fortune from the recipe."

Cornelia stopped to let a gaggle of children cross the street. "Really, Uncle?"

"Yes, really. He and his wife sold their factory and the recipe. They moved from their small town in Ohio to Saint Petersburg."

Once the road cleared, Cornelia handed the map back to her uncle. "What made him decide to become a developer? That seems like a big leap from running a bakery."

"He made a couple of hotel investments, but didn't go beyond that for a while. His wife liked the warm climate, but she missed the kind of community they left behind. He set out to create one."

"You can't create a small town by building houses at the edge of a city."

"Maybe not, but I think the Rosers came close. They bought a few small parcels of land and built houses and small shops. Then he donated land for neighborhood parks and a public school. He also built a home for nurses near the hospital and contributed funds to build a hospital for coloreds. I'm looking forward to seeing how his vision turned out."

"I guess you'll get your chance soon enough. Right, Teddy?"

At the sound of her name Teddy turned to look up front. "What?"

"We were talking about Roser Park."

"I'm sorry, dear. I wasn't paying attention."

The professor turned in his seat. "Never mind. It wasn't important. If you'd like, we can forgo looking at houses until another time."

Teddy forced a smile. "You're so sweet. Thank you for the offer, but I wouldn't dream of having you miss an appointment on my account."

His face reddened to the point that his snowy beard glowed pale pink.

Cornelia turned onto Roser Park Drive and motored through a canopy of green above dark red streets and walkways. The neighborhood was indeed as beautiful as her uncle made it seem. Houses varied in style from Mediterranean to Bungalow. Cornelia had to admit the Rosers had come close to creating a small town feel in their neighborhood. The area was also more hilly than she expected. Many of the homes had retaining walls next to the walkways and were perched atop landscaped slopes with flights of stone steps leading to their doors. She couldn't picture her uncle making that climb.

Arthur spent the night at the Vinoy, sleeping on the couch. He called the assistant manager of his nursery the following morning to let him know that he would not be coming in. He could still remember how difficult it was when his parents passed away. It was more important that he be with Evelyn and the family than to go to work. She was going to be his wife, and by extension the Stevens were his family now.

Once or twice, he regretted his decision to stay. He didn't know what to say to Evelyn. She had to be so hurt. Then the police showed up. Detective Knaggs was civil, but the morning was spent in further interviews—a waste of time, in his opinion. Nobody had anything useful to say. Afterwards, Evelyn volunteered to contact the staff of both Stevens offices about the death: the office here, and the one in Erie. Arthur offered to escort her downstairs to make those calls.

"Bring your jacket," she said, draping her own over her arm.

After several calls, during which his fiancée assured more than one employee that they still had jobs, Evelyn gave the phone back to the concierge. She exited the double doors and descended the marble stairs, Arthur at her well-shaped heels. He glanced idly at the palm trees planted in front of the hotel. They looked good now, but in a few decades they would be tall enough to obscure part of the view. Perhaps seeing palms and water together was part of the intent.

At first, he believed that Evelyn was seeking sunshine and fresh air to clear her head. She'd been devoted to her father, and his death must have been a terrible blow. He remembered how shocked he'd been when his father dropped stone dead between two rows of dwarf lemon trees. Mother was already gone, and there were no other relatives to help him with arrangements. He hadn't known what to do.

Arthur had never been a churchgoer, but the local parson had come immediately to assist, and his neighbors had been invaluable. He thought about what needed to be done as he kept pace with Evelyn, who strode with purpose down Bayshore Drive. Let's see—would they bury him here, or send the body back to some family tomb? How did you even ship a body? How long would the police keep it?

She halted abruptly at a trolley stop. He was puzzled, since there was a stop directly in front of the hotel.

"Where are we going, dear?" Arthur asked.

Evelyn turned, and stared at him intently. He saw tears in her eyes for the first time. She'd borne the trauma of last night with seemingly no emotion at all, but he saw emotion now, and it was fury.

"Arthur, do you still want to marry me?" she snapped.

"Of course I do!" He tried to take her hand, but she wasn't cooperating.

"Nothing has changed how I feel," he added.

She moved closer and hissed: "Then help me send that woman to the chair."

"Woman? Which woman?"

"The one who killed Daddy."

They rode the trolley without talking. The other passengers didn't notice; the locals were chattering about work, and the visitors were busy consulting their maps. Evelyn pulled the cord to stop, and they disembarked. She headed towards a brown building with purpose. To his surprise, it was the headquarters of the *Evening Independent*.

Introducing herself as the daughter of Ansel Stevens, the man who had been murdered the day before, got the secretary's attention quickly.

"I want to speak to Miss Roberta Hornbuckle," Evelyn demanded.

"The—but miss, she's just the society reporter. Wouldn't you prefer to speak to—"

"*Miss Hornbuckle*. She's the reporter I'm most familiar with, and the one in the best position to help me."

93

"Let's see if Mr. Webber has more integrity than Mr. Hale did," Professor Pettijohn said. "The house should be about two blocks down on the right."

"I hope the street is more level there," Teddy said.

"If not, we'll keep looking," the professor promised.

The agent was waiting for them when Cornelia stopped in front a two-story prairie style house with a pair of oak rocking chairs on the front porch. He got out of one of the rockers when he saw them stop, and hurried down the walk to greet them. The man reminded her a little of the young land agent who had come to their rescue in Ocala when her car's water pump sprang a leak. Mr. Webber was tall and lean with sandy hair curling out from under the ubiquitous straw boater every man in Florida seemed to own.

"You must be Mr. Pettijohn," he said, holding out his hand to the professor. "It is good to meet you in person."

"Professor Pettijohn. Retired."

"My apologies. Professor Pettijohn." Webber led them into the house and pointed out the large living room with red oak floors and a substantial fireplace. "All the floors are oak," he said, "except for the solarium. Those are slate to help regulate the temperatures."

Cornelia glanced through the door to the solarium and noted the ivory rattan furnishings with jungle print pillows. She could picture her uncle soaking up the sun while reading the morning paper.

Their agent pointed to a door at the back of the foyer. "The ladies will be interested in this. There's a large kitchen through there with all the modern conveniences, including an electric refrigerator."

"Excellent," the professor said, heading for the door.

Teddy joined him but went to the sink to test the taps. "City water?"

Webber nodded. "The best part is, you never have to worry about the pipes freezing here."

Uncle Percival examined the refrigerator, peering into it more than once. "I've been considering purchasing one for my home kitchen. A man must keep up with the times. Don't you agree, Corny?"

Cornelia was surveying at the steep stairway. "Are there any bedrooms on this floor?"

"Not on this floor, but there are four ample-sized bedrooms and a full bath upstairs."

The professor looked from his agent to the shiny white refrigerator and back again. "I'm sorry, Mr. Webber, that won't do. It is a fine house, but we must have at least one bedroom on the ground floor."

"I'll see if I can find you something more suitable, then. Do you like this neighborhood?"

"Yes, I do. I also like the house design, outside of needing a downstairs bedroom. If you do locate such a house, we can be reached at the Vinoy under the name of Percival Pettijohn."

CHAPTER ELEVEN

When Detective Knaggs arrived at the station, there were already several messages connected to the Stevens case. Two were interview requests from the local newspapers, but the others called for an arrest. Three messages were from prominent clients of the business, demanding that Harrell Brockman be clapped in irons, two were from the Stevens family, demanding the arrest of Theodora Lawless, and one was from the mayor's office, demanding that *someone* be arrested because the tourists wouldn't feel safe.

He closed the door to his office and reached for the phone. He paused, withdrew his hand, and frowned. What was the point of calling his chief? This was the guy's first week on the job. By the time his superior figured out what was what, somebody else could be resting his butt in the Chief of Detectives chair. The division had been through three chiefs in as many months. Who knew how long this one would last?

Instead of sitting, Knaggs put his hat back on and headed for the door. Sooner or later he would have to talk to the chief, but he would like to be positive of someone's guilt first. He needed to interview *everyone* involved, not just the son and Miss Lawless.

Brockman was at the top of his list. He had not provided the police with an alibi yet. Ansel Stevens' spat with Brockman had been near the hotel, but not in it. The young man couldn't have easily tampered with Stevens' clothing because the Vinoy was restricted. Miss Violet was there, though, being kept away from her suitor after the girl's recent arrest. The way the two of them were sneaking around, who knew what she would do for Brockman? It wouldn't be the first time a young girl had been tempted into wrongdoing by an older man. Some of the most heinous crimes he'd seen were twisted acts of love.

As he drove across town, he thought about his own daughter. How would he feel if she brought a Jewish man home to dinner? Knaggs wanted to believe he would be more understanding than Stevens, but the sign posted at this end of the Gandy Bridge sprang to mind. "No Jews wanted here," was a powerful message.

As a father, would he be any less resistant than Stevens? He wasn't the kind to burn a cross in a man's front yard; what would he do to protect his little girl from the hateful side of such a match? He pushed those thoughts out of his head as he neared the construction site.

Arthur wasn't convinced that barging into the offices of the *Evening Independent* was going to help them prove Miss Lawless was a murderess. He wasn't even sure the woman had anything to do with his future father-in-law's death, but his fiancée was adamant that the silver-haired nurse had killed her father. He took the seat furthest from Roberta Hornbuckle's desk and tried not to look as uncomfortable as he felt.

Evelyn's voice dropped an octave as she leaned closer to the society columnist. "The old man claimed they were both his nieces, but the Lawless woman isn't related to the Pettijohns at all."

The reporter, Miss Hornbuckle, took notes.

Arthur hadn't remembered her name, but she'd attended their engagement party and had written a flattering portrait of him. She'd called him a successful businessman and lamented the fact that one of the area's most eligible bachelors was taken. He couldn't help wondering why they were here.

"Are you certain they're *not* related?"

Evelyn nodded. "Yes, her family comes from Pennsylvania like ours. There are some relatives on her mother's side from New York and New England, but no one from Kentucky."

"That sounds like information the police should have," the reporter said. "Why would she be traveling with them to Florida? Why would any of them feel the need to lie to the police?"

"I was hoping you could find out," Evelyn said. "I don't know much about Theodora Lawless in the present ... but I can share some juicy tidbits about her past. I was there when Mother told the whole sordid story to the police."

Harry Brockman didn't look up when Detective Knaggs pulled his Ford into the gravel drive. He was on the roof hammering a layer of tar paper over the plywood. The young man's white shirt was transparent with sweat and clung to his arms like a second layer of skin. The dark hair that showed under his Greek fishing cap was as wet as his shirt, but not a button was undone. His tie hadn't even been loosened. He had removed his suit jacket, but not his vest. His hammer tapped out a steady rhythm; each arc of Brockman's arm drove another roofing tack into place.

He was doing the same hard labor as his crew, but nobody would mistake young Brockman for a common laborer. Knaggs had a certain grudging admiration of the young man. He could see how Mr. Stevens' youngest child would be smitten with Brockman, ears notwithstanding.

Knaggs unfolded himself from the Ford and closed the door. The sound of the door closing caught Brockman's attention. Knaggs waved him down from the roof and waited for him at the base of the ladder.

"I've got a few questions," Knaggs said, when Brockman reached the ground.

Harry took a handkerchief from his pocket and wiped the sweat from his face and neck. "What can I do for you, detective?"

"You can start with what you were doing the night before the race."

"Of course." He motioned to a group of folding chairs under a cluster of live oaks so old that ferns grew from the tops of the branches. Harry took a blanket off the top of a washtub and pulled a Coke from the ice water. "Can I offer you a cold drink?"

Knaggs eyed the bottle.

"There's jars of water too, if you don't care for sugar."

The detective wondered if there were bottles of beer tucked deeper in the layers of ice.

"Coke's fine," Knaggs said.

Harry pulled a bottle opener from his pocket and popped the cap off the Coke before handing it to the detective. He pulled another from the tub and took a long swig before settling into one of the chairs.

"The day before the race was the Shabbat," Harry said. "I spent the night at the Jacobs'."

"The Jacobs?"

Harry smiled. "I have a small kitchen on my boat, but I'm not a particularly good cook. Even if I were, I don't have the time to prepare Shabbat meals or a place to store them. So, I made a bargain with Hyman Jacobs, the president of our congregation. I supply him with labor and materials to fix up the storefront we use as a temple, and he invites me to his house for the Shabbat. Once a week, I spend the night in a real bed."

"What time did you arrive at Mr. Jacobs' home?"

"The first time was around eight in the morning."

"The first time?"

"Yes. I had breakfast with them and visited for a few hours. After lunch I had an appointment, so I went out for a while."

Knaggs took out his notebook. "Where was this appointment?"

Harry's face colored. "I met Violet."

"I see."

"I just met her downtown. She had some coffee and we talked."

"Where did you have coffee?"

"I didn't. Ordering anything would be a violation of the Shabbat."

Knaggs groaned. This was almost as bad as talking to Miss Lawless. "Where did you *not* have coffee, then?"

"That cafeteria downtown, I can't remember the name. I'm sure you know the place. The whole block smells like fried chicken."

Knaggs made a noncommittal noise. "And next?"

"We took a walk. I escorted her back to her hotel. Then, I went back to the Jacobs' home for dinner."

"The family could verify that you were not at the marina the night before the race?"

"Of course. Hyman took me back to my boat the next morning. He and the family all stayed to watch the race." He paused. "They were very kind when it ended."

"What about Miss Violet? Her father was adamant that she end your relationship. Instead, she was seeing you behind her father's back."

Harry's smile vanished. "Are you asking me if she killed her father? That's outrageous. Violet wouldn't hurt a fly."

"She did want you to win the race. Maybe she didn't mean to kill her father. Are you sure she didn't want to put Daddy out of commission and out of your lives?"

Harry was on his feet. "Violet wouldn't think of harming her father! She is the sweetest, kindest soul alive. I won't have you impugning her character."

"Mr. Brockman, it is my job to question everyone's character. I would be a sorry policeman if I didn't."

"You have a sorry job."

Knaggs sighed. "That may be, but someone put poison on Mr. Stevens' cap."

The sun was still high in the sky when the three snowbirds returned to the Vinoy, and Teddy announced that she was going to swim.

"In February?"

"Yes, in February. The water couldn't be any colder than Steamboat Lake in Colorado, and the air is probably the same temperature."

Cornelia remembered the scandalous swimsuit Teddy had purchased. "Perhaps we should swim tomorrow. Aren't you tired?"

"I'm tired of waiting for agents who don't come, tromping up and down stairs, and turning faucets on at strange houses to see if the plumbing works. A nice splash in the ocean and some sun would be quite restorative."

"I agree," the professor said. "We've been in Florida for two weeks, and we have yet to visit the beach."

What could she do? The lunatics outnumbered the sane. They went to their respective rooms, and she donned her sensible swimdress and new beach shoes while Teddy pulled the straps of her suit—more like a corset trimmed with ruffles—over her bare shoulders.

"You said you would wear a robe with that," Cornelia reminded her.

"Yes, I did." The younger woman examined her hats, which were beginning to pile up around the room, and chose the new straw one she'd brought home from her shopping trip on Saturday. There was always a selection process Teddy adhered to while dressing, even though the outcome was almost invariably her most recent purchase.

They returned to the shared sitting room, and Cornelia was confronted with her uncle's beachwear. His striped silk beach robe hung loose over a bathing suit cropped a good two inches above his knees. He'd always been a peacock, but this... Her gaze raked over the brilliant blue bathing suit that exposed pale skin and masses of leg hair as snowy white as the piping on his suit. She could barely fathom a man of his years appearing in public in a suit that exposed his knees. He was as bad as Teddy.

"Uncle Percival! You will catch your death of cold."

The professor puffed up in response to being scolded like a child. "I don't intend to swim, Corny, even though it's warmer today. I might wade if it's not too windy at the shore.

"When we get to the front desk," he added, "we can make the arrangements for chairs and an umbrella."

"And I can call Shirley to see if she can join us," Teddy said. "If you don't mind."

"Not at all," the professor said. "We can request more chairs. Corny, would you mind carrying my tripod again?" The question was rhetorical. He wasn't wearing his hearing device and turned away before she could answer. The professor tied his farmer's hat under his chin and fastened his robe. "Are we ready, ladies?"

Shirley was pleased to be invited to an afternoon at the beach. She arrived with an armful of towels and her own umbrella, and had brought her mother with her, a pleasant surprise. Anna Wheeler had a stylish bob, but it was nearly as gray as Cornelia's.

Uncle Percival immediately rose and offered her his seat. "Please take my chair, madam. Perhaps we can procure an extra one from the hotel."

"Oh, don't worry about that," Shirley said, "I brought a towel to sit on. You get comfortable again, sir."

"I'm pleased to meet you all," Shirley's mother said. Her voice, like her daughter's, bore the lilt of a southern accent.

"I'm glad you could join us, Mrs. Wheeler," Teddy said. "It's a lovely day, especially for February."

"Call me Anna, dear. February is my favorite month here. Much better than back home; it's supposed to be rainy and cold in Knoxville today."

"I suspect Kentucky would be the same," the professor said.

"Kentucky! Well, I'll be. Whereabouts?"

Percival smiled. "Midway, madam, although I lived and taught in Lexington for many years."

The social niceties went on for a bit, then Teddy stood and removed her terrycloth robe. Her limbs were exposed to the sun, bare and alabaster. "I'm ready to get in."

"Me too!" Shirley said, taking off her own robe. The swimdress—nay, the slip—she wore was pink and even shorter than Teddy's. "How cold do you reckon the water is today?" she asked, putting on her beach slippers.

"I'm sure it's freezing. Are you coming with us?" Teddy asked Cornelia.

Cornelia rose to her feet, feeling dowdy and prudent at the same time. She did not remove her robe or sun hat. "Of course. Someone has to play fire extinguisher."

The water was as cold as she supposed it would be, but it didn't stop Teddy from splashing and squealing in the surf beside Shirley, who was decades younger than her. Almost everyone in the ocean was young; their elders had the sense to stay on shore and enjoy the sun. All the elders but Teddy and her, of course. Short swimdresses and exposed skin, male and female, surrounded them. Even the girls in the Philippines had worn longer shifts to swim in during the hot summers.

Shirley must have recognized some of the other youths, because she was sloshing over to a group of them with Teddy in tow. Introductions were made, and the chattering began. Cornelia thought that her teeth would join in.

She was surprised when Teddy made an early farewell and withdrew from the group. She waded back to Cornelia.

"Let's go check on Uncle Percival," she said.

"Did the water finally get too much for you?"

"No," she said, "but I think Shirley might be acquiring an admirer her own age."

Cornelia glanced back, and saw a young man speaking to their friend. "That was an excellent decision, Teddy. She deserves someone better."

They headed back to their encampment, where Percival and Anna hadn't moved from their seats.

"The Gainesville place was the best," Anna said. "We all gathered around the fire to heat up our food. Afterwards, we sang songs. Shirley was scarce sixteen and they all doted on her. It was a one-way trip for us, so we used a car tent, but the regulars had housecars in all shapes and sizes."

They must be talking about the Tin Can Tourist Camp, Cornelia realized. She remembered the housecars, most of which were either cars with trailers permanently attached or trucks that had been modified in outrageous ways. Uncle Percival had been driving, and he'd followed the line of homemade rolling shelters into the campsite. She and Teddy feared that they would never get him back on the road. The professor wanted to know all the details of the modifications, and the owners were, of course, so proud to share them.

"I'm glad you've come back," her uncle said. "I want to test the water myself, and a short scene of us enjoying the ocean would be a good addition to the film."

Cornelia obliged her uncle by once again setting up his camera and filming the group. This time, she was happy to be behind the camera. The last thing she would want was to be captured on film in her bathing costume. She pulled her beach robe tighter around her waist just thinking about it.

Teddy procured a copy of the *Evening Independent* before they went down to dinner.

"Miss Hornbuckle's version of the story," she said. "'Ansel Stevens thought he was racing against his daughter's suitor, but little did he know that he was racing against Death as well,'" she read aloud.

"A florid beginning," Cornelia commented.

"Builder Harry Brockman issued his challenge in seamanship on Friday, after Stevens caught his daughter Violet strolling in the park with the younger man. The loser would have to leave town—Brockman without his prize, or Stevens, with his daughter. It seemed that Stevens would win either way. Instead, he collapsed near the end of the race, ramming his yacht, the *Nittany Nob*, into the pier currently under construction near the Vinoy Hotel. The conclusion of the police: poison."

"Do they say why, or which poison this time?" the professor inquired.

"We'll see," Teddy said. "'When Stevens was examined by the doctors, they discovered a rash across his forehead that conformed to the band of his cap. At first, they assumed that the rash was caused by his sweat, since the cap was damp. Once they suspected poison, however, they alerted the police, who are having the item analyzed.'"

"Ah, we are still left in suspense," Cornelia said. "Now, about dinner—"

"There's more!" Teddy cried. "We have since learned that the cap was already on the yacht Sunday morning, having been delivered to the *Nittany Nob* sometime since their last sailing. There was a card from the Saint Petersburg Yacht Club with the cap, and it bore the burgee of the Club, but the Club's officers say that they sent no such gift. There are no named suspects, but of course there is the vexed Mr. Brockman, Miss Theodora Lawless, an aggrieved former fiancée'—how in the world did she learn that? '—of Ansel Stevens, only son N. McKinley Stevens, who stands to inherit the business, and, of course, any number of rival builders who would benefit from Mr. Stevens' unfinished contracts."

"She took a swipe at everybody," the professor said. "Now, is that the end?"

"It is."

"Then let's have dinner. Swimming makes me hungry, even when I'm merely watching it."

When the trio returned to their room, they discovered Detective Knaggs and Sergeant Duncan leaning against the wall outside their hotel room, waiting for them.

Knaggs straightened and stuck his notebook back into his jacket. "We need to have a word with you three again. Something needs clearing up."

"Of course," Uncle Percival said, unlocking the door.

Cornelia had another bad feeling in the stomach. The pair of officers didn't sit down, and the one had his notebook out again.

Her uncle didn't sit, either. His hearing device was in his ear and his face had the calm expression he wore when he was in the middle of tricky negotiations. "You said you needed clarification, gentlemen. How may I assist you?"

"Professor Pettijohn, we have made inquiries since our last visit," Knaggs said.

Duncan broke in. "And you want to know what we found out? She ain't your niece." He jerked a thumb towards Teddy. "You're not related to her at all."

Knaggs made a quieting gesture at Duncan. "Why would you say she was your niece, when she's not? She came from Colorado with your real niece, so why didn't you just say she was a friend of your niece? More importantly, why are you paying for her to stay in this hotel?"

Cornelia held her breath. Teddy had no good reason for being with them outside of friendship. What Knaggs was implying was scandalous, but the truth was illegal.

The professor didn't blink. "Really gentlemen, you look like men of the world."

He walked over to Teddy and put a protective arm around her shoulders. "I'm sure I can rely on your discretion. I claimed she was my niece to avoid gossip. You see, gentlemen, Miss Lawless and I are engaged to be married."

Shock forced Cornelia into a seat. She listened, speechless, as her uncle continued.

"I realize that Theodora is perhaps twenty years younger than me, which would make us subject to talk. We wanted to avoid that while we shopped for a honeymoon cottage and made all the necessary arrangements."

Twenty? More like thirty or thirty-five, Cornelia thought.

"If you have done a thorough checking, you will discover that she and I have been looking at rentals to live in whilst we search for our cottage in Paradise. I assure you that she has been staying with my niece, her maid of honor, in the other side of the suite to avoid the appearance of impropriety before the ceremony."

Teddy, teary-eyed, took the professor's arm. "Oh, sweet Percival, I'm so sorry. I told you we should have eloped."

He patted her hand fondly. "Nonsense, my dear. You deserve a proper wedding with all the trimmings. Before you came along, I took for granted I would die a bachelor. You have made an old man very happy."

All the color had drained from Cornelia's face. She clung to the arms of the chair and did her best not to gape. *Insane, both of them.*

Knaggs harrumphed. "Well, that does explain a few things, sir. Were you aware that Miss Lawless' former fiancé was in Saint Petersburg before you traveled here?"

"Absolutely not," Professor Pettijohn said. "If I had known, we would have chosen Naples or perhaps Marco Island for our nuptials. I want no distraction from our future happiness."

"A pity that you didn't elope," Knaggs said. "It would have saved us some time."

"My apologies," Cornelia's uncle said. "Can you forgive a romantic old fool for making your job harder?"

Once the officers were gone, Cornelia's shock turned to anger. She bounded out of the chair and rounded on her uncle. "Now look what you've gotten us into. Engaged? That preposterous lie is going to come back on us. Then what?"

"It seemed to be the best explanation," her uncle said. "It stopped them from asking more personal questions. An engagement rather neatly explains why we're traveling together. I can't believe I didn't think of it before."

"I can't believe you thought of it at all," Cornelia snapped. "You realize that now people will expect the two of you to marry, and sooner rather than later."

"Hmm." The professor rubbed his white-haired chin. "We can always break the engagement if we need to."

"Now, wait a minute," Teddy said. "One broken engagement is bad enough. Another one will make people think I'm a shrew."

"They already think you're a murderess," Cornelia said. "How much worse could the gossip get?"

"A woman can have any number of good reasons to kill a man, but getting jilted twice makes her sound like an ugly spinster."

Cornelia smacked herself in the forehead as she sank back down in the armchair. They were both hopeless. "You *are* a spinster. Just not an ugly one."

"That's hardly the point. I'm already suffering from public humiliation."

"I can't fake my death again; you can only get away with that once. I could simply marry her," Uncle Percival said. "Then we could argue that she wanted Stevens alive, so he could see that she'd found a better prospect."

"They'll think she's a gold digger."

"Nonsense, they'll think I'm an old fool."

"They'll think both," Cornelia snapped, "and they'll be right about you."

CHAPTER TWELVE

The trio had breakfast at a table that provided a splendid view of the water and the distant beach. Despite the hour—and, more importantly, the cool morning air—there were young men and women splashing in the surf.

"That water must be freezing. They'll catch their death," Cornelia said.

"But they'll look good for one another while they're doing it," Teddy replied. "The mating dance pays no heed to weather."

This morning, Uncle Percival was able to have the Eggs Benedict, a new favorite of his. Teddy had been too amused by the engagement story to take more than her standard medicinal dose of alcohol.

"So, what do you think of the concoction?" Cornelia asked after the professor tried it.

"I've always loved the dish, but their version is very good," he said. "A little rich to eat regularly, but pleasant as an indulgence."

He extended a hand and casually rested it on the morning newspaper, which he'd placed next to Cornelia. His fingers wiggled, and she glanced down. The police department had a new chief of detectives. Is that why Knaggs and Duncan were being so aggressive? Then, she saw the article beneath it. Mitch had provided an update on Ansel Stevens' death.

"Mystery Woman Delivers Death Cap to Stevens," bold lettering said. Below it, in smaller lettering: "Police Confirm Nicotine Poisoning."

Cornelia moved her tea cup onto the newspaper, blocking Teddy's view. The poor thing was just coming out of her state of melancholy. There was no need to put her back in it. She took another bite of her eggs, and followed this with a sip of tea.

On Saturday, marina employees saw a woman climb onto the Nittany Nob, *carrying something wrapped in tissue. Suspicions of imminent theft were alleviated a few moments later when she descended sans the item. This item is now believed to be the captain's cap.*

After cautious examination of this cap, police determined that a liberal dose of nicotine, possibly from an undiluted insecticide, had been applied to the interior band. Also, the burgee of the Yacht Club had been sewn onto the cap by hand. Nicotine deaths are rare, but they can happen.

"This was no act of impulse," Detective Joseph Knaggs said. "This was ruthless murder."

The woman was described as white, slender, and approximately five feet and a half tall. wearing a stylish dress of either blue or green. Her hair was concealed by a dark hat, but is believed to be light, perhaps blonde or bleached.

Anyone who knows or suspects the identity of this woman should contact the police.

Well, with that description, it could be half of the women in Saint Petersburg. Maybe not half; the mystery woman was closer to her height than Teddy's, and Cornelia had been the tallest nurse in her class.

The professor, who had been studying the Real Estate pages, turned to Teddy. "Since we are now publicly engaged, my dear fiancée, I have a suggestion for the day. They're promoting some waterfront property in Tampa Shores today, and I think we should go see what's available."

"Tampa Shores?" Cornelia took up the cue. "Where is that in relation to the Vinoy?"

"It's not as far as Tampa. The town is better known as Oldsmar, named after the car manufacturer. He invested in some of the land there."

"I see," Cornelia said. "Do they sell the cars there, or actually make them?"

"The local product appears to be tractors. It's a farming community." He shrugged. "Where would an old mechanical engineer feel more at home?"

A farming community appealed to Cornelia, but Teddy looked a little disappointed. "Waterfront. Does it have a beach?"

"It is advertised as having one," Uncle Percival said, "but we've all seen how land agents exaggerate. Why don't you two go upstairs and freshen up, while I make a few phone calls?"

Teddy headed for the elevator, but Cornelia lagged behind and turned so Teddy couldn't read her lips. "Wouldn't Mac and his father have smelled nicotine?"

"They would have. Unfortunately, it smells like fish," the retired professor from the Agricultural and Mechanical College of Kentucky informed her. "Not an unusual smell in a marina."

Arthur had finished his own breakfast and was preparing to leave for work when the phone rang. It was Evelyn.

"They're headed for Oldsmar today," she whispered. "Can you believe our luck?"

"What? Why are you whispering?"

"Because the old man hasn't gotten on the elevator yet. He and the concierge are busy with something. Are you coming to get me, or should I take a taxi there?"

When they arrived in Oldsmar, Cornelia was impressed with the thoughtfully laid out streets that led from the downtown area to the bay. The beach itself was small and unimpressive, but the enclosed bay was a turquoise jewel flanked on the far side by the trees of Safety Harbor. Gentle waves lapped at the sand, and Cornelia felt that if the vacant

111

lot they were standing on were empty of people, it would be a lovely place to sit and enjoy the view.

Unfortunately, the beach was full of would-be homeowners who had been invited to a "Gold Rush" by Mr. Prettyman, a local land agent. He wore the straw boater and jacket that seemed to be the dress code for selling real estate in Florida. His assistants welcomed the would-be homeowners to the lots being sold, spreading them out, and handed each a trowel or child-sized shovel. Their host extolled the virtues of the area, wheedling the women with the nearby farms, restaurants, and library, and the men with the excellent crabbing and fishing to be had in the rippling bay.

"Home construction will be handled by the Oldsmar Land Development Company, which will be more than happy to tailor your future home to your needs."

"I thought this was Tampa Shores," one of the other customers asked in the Maine accent they'd become familiar with at the hotel.

"This area is still in the process of being developed," Prettyman assured him, "and is currently referred to as Tampa Shores."

Because the name is more attractive to tourists, Cornelia surmised.

The land agent answered a few more questions as the remainder of the lots filled, then announced that the Gold Rush was ready to begin. "On my signal ..."

He blew a whistle. "Dig!" his assistants shouted.

Sand flew as the buyers, none of whom had likely seen the business end of a real shovel in their lives, scraped the ground and flung their burdens in all directions. There were many loud complaints.

"Keep digging!" Prettyman urged them. "There's treasure everywhere in Tampa Shores."

Teddy stabbed her patch with her shovel a few times, then knelt in the sand and began sifting it like a prospector. Cornelia bent and used the inexpensive trowel she'd been provided, not particularly surprised to find more sand underneath the surface sand. The professor simply rested on his cane and watched the people dig. He looked from the crowd to the plat displaying the lots, smiling slightly. *He's probably entertained by the fools here*, Cornelia, who had no faith in real gold lying under the ground, thought.

"Look!" Teddy cried, holding up two golden coins. "I found some! Do I get to keep them?"

The agent grinned. "They're yours, young lady. Now picture a fine new home here, with the lovely vista you see around it. Add a chaise-lounge for the inside, a sturdy Olds Chair for the outside—product of the local mill—and you'll have many pleasant evenings to watch the water."

Teddy closed her eyes briefly. "It sounds relaxing, but I bore quickly. What sort of social life flourishes here?"

"All your lovely heart desires," Prettyman assured her. Cornelia found his flattery stomach-turning. "There's a Woman's Club that's responsible for the local library. If you're seeking entertainment, a casino is going up not far from here, and Tampa Downs will be opening later this year."

The tourists would follow. Why, Cornelia wondered, were people so hell-bent on improving places that needed no improvement? The ocean and lush vegetation of Oldsmar were beautiful, so of course the land had to be paved over and the water crisscrossed by bridges. The live oaks of Safety Harbor, which stretched gracefully over a bay almost shallow enough to wade across at low tide, would fall to the axes of developers too blind to see that they were destroying what made this place valuable.

"Murderess!" a voice screamed, jolting Cornelia out of her grumblings. She turned quickly to see who had shouted.

It couldn't be ... but there they were: Arthur Downs, with a somber expression on his face, and Evelyn Stevens, who was the accuser. She was clad in black from head to toe, including a velvet cloche trimmed with black felt flowers and a net veil. It was stylish, but hardly suitable for digging on a beach.

"That woman killed my father!" Evelyn pointed at Teddy.

Teddy, arms and knees covered with sand, sat up on her heels. Her face was flushed from a combination of physical exertion and the start of a sunburn. "I did not," she snapped.

Evelyn turned and buried her face in Arthur's shoulder. He took up the refrain. "You were a nurse. I'm certain you knew the perfect poison to use on Mr. Stevens."

Behind Arthur, a young woman scribbled furiously in a small notebook. She was partially hidden by the Prettyman truck, but Cornelia recognized the reporter who'd followed Mitch to their hotel.

Many of the would-be homeowners had stopped digging and were watching the show. The land agent approached the two families, an appalled expression on his face. "Ladies! Please, no more—"

The professor's voice boomed, drowning him out. "That's slander, young man. Watch what you say about my fiancée."

Sweet Jesus, Cornelia thought. Her uncle was digging this hole of lies deeper and deeper under them. Didn't he care that the woman with Evelyn was a reporter? Clearly, the Stevens family had chummed up with the sneaky little troublemaker. She would love to smack that smug expression off Arthur's face, but that would only add to the trouble.

"Why are you hounding us?" Evelyn asked. She took a handkerchief out of her purse and pressed it to damp eyes. "Can't you leave us alone?"

"My dear girl," Percival said gently, "we aren't hounding you. Rather the opposite; we believed getting away from the hotel would spare your family some rancor. I brought my bride-to-be here to find a future home."

"Bride-to-be?" Arthur sneered. "You must be older than Moses. She's taking advantage of you, you old coot."

Cornelia started to speak, but her uncle spoke up.

"I'd part the Red Sea for her," the professor said. "But I'll settle for parting your hair with my cane if you insult her again."

Prettyman stepped between the two families. "Gentlemen, ladies, this is not the place to settle your differences. I'm going to have to ask you to leave."

"I fully agree, and shall bid you adieu," the professor said, taking Teddy by the arm. "Come, dear."

"They started it," Teddy muttered as she was led to the car.

Cornelia handed the land agent's shovel back to him and followed. "Well, that was a bust," she said, sliding into the driver's seat. "I'm sorry, Uncle Percival."

"I wouldn't have purchased land from that man anyway," the old man replied. "Based on his plats, some of those lots were underwater. I believe that 'land agent' in Florida may just be another term for 'crook.'"

After their return to the hotel, the trio took dinner in their room. No one felt sociable or had a desire to run into the Stevens family again. The professor turned in right after dinner. He claimed that he planned to get up early. Cornelia could see the dark circles under his eyes.

Teddy went downstairs to hear the Paul Whiteman orchestra, over Cornelia's protests. She insisted that either she was going to dance her troubles away or drink them away. Given the options, Cornelia relented, but not before warning her of the risk of running into one of the Stevens family members.

"Mrs. Stevens is in mourning. She's not going to be out dancing."

"Young Violet or Evelyn might," Cornelia countered. "Evelyn would probably bring Arthur with her."

Teddy pondered for a moment. "If you're so worried about me running into one of the children, you should come along. You could dance your distress away, too."

Cornelia simply wasn't up to it. The afternoon's confrontation had renewed her disgust with humanity in general, and the Stevens family in particular. Teddy had promised Uncle Percival that she wouldn't resort to liquor again, but Cornelia began seriously thinking about raiding her companion's stash.

When Teddy had gone, she decided that she must put worry aside. She picked up the Willa Cather book she was reading and forced herself to concentrate on it. Cornelia

115

normally derived great pleasure from reading, but the memory of what happened in Oldsmar kept nipping at her nerves. Why in the world would Evelyn Stevens show up there? Arthur had a business in Oldsmar, but would he really bring his grieving fiancée to a land sale? She was sure Evelyn was trying to pin her father's murder on Teddy. Would Arthur be party to an orchestrated scene like that? Perhaps he hoped it would distract Evelyn from her grief. Men were sometimes uncomfortable with women's tears.

The outside door of the suite slammed shut. The door to their room flew open. Teddy stomped in, clutching a newspaper in her hand. She was flushed and gasping for air.

"What's wrong?" Cornelia jumped to her feet, alarmed.

"That Hornbuckle woman!" Teddy flung the newspaper down on a bed. "She worked fast. I wish Mitch had throttled her; I'd like to."

Cornelia picked up the offending object, the newest edition of the *Evening Independent*. Behind her, Teddy yanked off her shoes and flung them into the wardrobe.

"'Disgraced Socialite Prime Suspect in Murder,'" she read aloud. "What in the world?"

"That's only the headline," her companion snapped. She ripped off her bandeau and slammed it on the dresser. She almost followed suit with her pearls, but thought better of it. "That insufferable witch! Everyone was pointing at me and whispering!"

The article was on the front page, unusual for a society column. Cornelia read further:

City police have been looking for the mystery woman who was seen climbing into the Stevens' family yacht last Saturday. She was described as being of tall stature, slender, and wearing a drop waist turquoise dress embroidered with butterflies. Her cloche hat was dark blue or navy, and witnesses believe her hair was light blonde or silver. The woman may have used a cane for assistance while climbing onto the Nittany Nob.

Bobby's characterization of the 'mystery woman' was certainly more detailed than Mitch's. Probably because she was a society columnist. The part about the cane was interesting; that bit hadn't been included in the *Times* article. Had she put that in to further incriminate Teddy, or had Mitch omitted the detail to protect her?

The subject of her train of thought interrupted her. "Did you see the part about my past in Pennsylvania yet?"

"I hadn't gotten that far." She looked at the article again:

According to sources in Erie, Miss Lawless was engaged to marry Ansel Stevens in 1883. Announcements were made and gifts sent, but shortly before the wedding Miss Lawless left him for the lights of New York—and the charms of another young man. Stevens broke the engagement with cause, one that would have embarrassed the Lawless family if he had sued for breach of promise.

It would take the warm breezes and palm trees of Florida to bring the two together again in explosive fashion. Since her arrival in Saint Petersburg, Miss Lawless has publicly assaulted Stevens twice and has hounded his family. Local police have taken a strong interest in her whereabouts the day before the ill-fated yacht race, given the witness accounts from the marina.

Anger—and fear for Teddy—swelled inside her. "This woman should be sued for libel. And her newspaper, too!"

Today, Theodora Lawless and her new fiancé, Percival Pettijohn, were digging for gold in Tampa Shores, or at least Miss Lawless was. An unpleasant confrontation ensued when Oldsmar nursery owner Arthur Downs showed up with his fiancée, the stylish Evelyn Stevens. They confronted the gold-digger, and Professor Pettijohn gallantly rose to her defense, creating a scene. The northerners were asked to leave the premises.

"I knew this was going to happen," Cornelia said. "Uncle Percival didn't think of the consequences when he said you were engaged. He's doubled the scandal." She considered sharing her belief that Bobby Hornbuckle was being used by the family, but that would only fuel Teddy's anger.

"That's not making me feel better." Teddy grabbed one of the bottles of Coca-Cola she'd purchased, then opened the case with the Ball jars.

"Remember what you promised Uncle Percival," Cornelia reminded her.

"I remember, but I need something." She filled a glass halfway with the soda, then topped it off with the pale liquid from the jar. "This day has been awful."

"Well, if you're going to do it anyway," Cornelia said, "give me some. I've had a bad day, too."

Teddy mixed a second drink, more soda than booze, and handed it to Cornelia, who took a deep draught.

She coughed and almost spit it back into the glass. "You said you had leftover rum from our visit to Homosassa."

"Never waste good rum on a bad night."

"You're right; Mr. Scroggins' product is probably a better pairing with this miserable day."

CHAPTER THIRTEEN

The drive to the airfield was made in uncomfortable silence. Cornelia feared it was a mistake to intrude upon Mac after yesterday's heated exchange with his sister. Telling Uncle Percival that they should stay in their suite, though, was worse than trying to keep Teddy from excessive drinking. She was almost looking forward to returning to Colorado. Twelve to eighteen-hour shifts in a hospital operating room were less exhausting than spending her leave with the two of them.

She shifted down to make the turn onto Tyrone Boulevard. The Dodge Brothers sedan glided onto the long open stretch of road, and she pressed the accelerator. Unlike the tourists' areas of Saint Petersburg, Tyrone Boulevard was a mix of residential and business areas, dotted with clusters of old live oaks and the occasional bay or banyan tree.

The tranquility of driving along in early morning quiet allowed her mind to relax. She forgot about everything except the rumble of the engine and the pleasure of being behind the wheel of her sedan. *It's too bad that I have to stop*, she thought with a mental sigh, as she turned left onto the access road to the airfield.

A young man in greasy overalls greeted her at the gate. She rolled down the window. Smoke from the engine of a nearby jenny and stench of burning castor oil made her stomach churn. Cornelia fought back the bile. She'd never understood how the airmen got used to the scent.

"Can I help you?" the young man asked. "You folks lost?"

"Not lost. I'm looking for Mac Stevens. He is supposed to have a warehouse or workshop around here."

"Gosh. Not on the field." He waved at the acres of fresh mown grass. "We ain't even got a hanger built yet. She's coming along fine, though. The best airfield this side of the bay."

The pride in his voice made Cornelia smile. She wasn't sure what he did at the airfield, but he had the flying bug as much as any of the young airmen she'd known. He would find a way to soar above the clouds. "There must be someplace near the field that men work on their planes."

He looked her over as he considered the matter.

Cornelia tried to look less intimidating. It was too bad Teddy was sleeping it off this morning. Her natural charm would have had the information by now.

Professor Pettijohn pointed to the camera and tripod in the back seat. "Mr. Stevens invited us to film his aeroplane. We're already late. Are you sure you can't help us?"

"Shucks, mister, I'm sure he won't mind. Go back that way until you see an open field to your right. There's a couple of old warehouses hidden behind a stand of trees. You can't miss his. 'Stevens and Wells' is painted across the front in letters about two yards tall."

"Much obliged," the professor said, as Cornelia turned around and headed back the way they'd come.

Mac was surprised when he opened the door to his office and saw Cornelia standing there with the motion picture equipment. The shock disappeared, replaced by confusion.

"Nurse Pettijohn? After what happened yesterday, I didn't expect you would want to have anything to do with me or my family."

Cornelia looked him in the eye. "Do *you* think Theodora murdered your father?"

He was taken aback by the question. "No, of course not."

Professor Pettijohn smiled. "Good. Then we'll consider that a closed subject and move on to what we came to see."

"Uncle Percival, please. Show a little restraint." Cornelia placed a hand on Mac's arm. "Allow me to at least offer our condolences. Whatever else he was, Ansel was your father. I am sorry for your loss."

"Thank you, ma'am," Mac replied. "I didn't like Father very much, but I did love him. Do you know what I mean?"

"Yes," she said. "I know exactly what you mean. Our loved ones are not always easy to like. Differences build up into walls that keep us apart."

"It is ironic. Father always wanted me to be like him. I didn't realize until he was gone that we were too much alike in all the wrong ways."

"I would say you took after him in the right ways," Professor Pettijohn said. "You grew up to be a strong, independent, and hard-working young man. Those are not flaws; they are the building blocks of success."

Mac's voice cracked. "Not in his eyes. We were always at odds. I think that's why the police have me pegged as his killer. They've questioned me three times now."

Cornelia had her doubts about the police having him pegged as the killer, given the newspaper reports, but she nodded. She wasn't sure who was responsible for Ansel's death. Her instincts told her that Mac was a good man, but in the right circumstances good people were as capable of murder as bad ones.

"Young man, your father was blinded by his own desire to live on through you," her uncle said. "That isn't something a father has the right to ask of his son. Believe me, I know what it is to break with tradition. My father was a farmer, and his father before him was a farmer. I was an engineer."

He paced the floor as he spoke. "Father never understood that. The family farm was passed on to me because I was the eldest son. It made no practical sense. My younger brother was a born farmer; he managed his farm, and the one that I inherited, until the day he died. Now I lease the land out until I pass it on to the next generation. I hope that among my sister's progeny I can find a farmer."

"I wish I believed that I could be a builder," Mac said. "Or that one of my sisters had been born male. It would make my life easier. But enough about that. Let me show you around the shop."

Cornelia picked up the camera and followed the them into the warehouse. Along one wall was a long row of identical wooden crates, each stamped "CurtissOX5." She set up the camera and panned down the row.

"Those are the backbone of our business," Mac said. "Kicker, or rather my partner, Yancy Wells, was an aircraft mechanic during the War. Before that, he worked for Curtiss building airplane engines. There were thousands of surplus engines made before the war ended. The government unloaded them cheap."

Cornelia smiled at the memory of the lanky mechanic nicknamed for his propensity to kick troublesome engines with the heel of his boot. Nobody ever figured out how his system worked, but engines no one else could start hummed after a good kick from Yancy.

"So, you went into the aeroplane business," the professor said.

"That's how it started. We had the idea of building our own planes, using the surplus engines, but a lot of other guys had the same idea. Some of them still go into planes, but here in Florida, boats are way more popular. We started modifying the engines for use in racing boats. Now we have customers willing to wait months to get one of our custom-designed boats. We've reached the point where Kicker spends all his time helping racers maintain the engines, while I produce new boats."

He uncovered the vessel he was working on, and the professor grinned. "I believe I had the pleasure of riding in one of your boats. A young man in Homosassa has one similar to this."

"I wouldn't be surprised. Kicker and I have been producing them for about eight years."

The professor peppered him with technical questions.

Cornelia filmed for a little while longer, then left the camera on its tripod and had a seat on one of the crates while the two men climbed into the boat and examined the engine. She wished she had brought her book along. There was no telling how long her uncle would keep pestering Mac with his questions. Instead, she tried to piece together what she knew about the murder. Ansel had been poisoned by the sweatband in his cap, which sounded far-fetched, but had worked. Teddy's motives had been made public by Miss Hornbuckle, but there were plenty of other motives to go around.

It was no secret that Mac didn't get along with his father. As the eldest, he stood to inherit the bulk of the business. Mac claimed he didn't want the business, but that didn't mean he wouldn't want the money. His share of the family fortune would build a lot of boats and airplanes. There was also plenty of opportunity: being on the boat with his father during the race gave him easy access. It was no wonder the police were hounding him. When they'd seen him striding towards the hotel the other day, was he coming from the marina?

Then there were Violet and Harry; she couldn't see one of them acting without the other. The picture of Ansel dragging his daughter away from Harry was indelible. Harry's anger, the fear in Violet's eyes, the way she mouthed the word "no" when Harry took a step toward her. If Ansel had found out about their secret meetings, they might have motive.

Ansel's objection to Harry's courtship had led to that ill-fated race. Violet's young man clearly found the way he treated his wife and family contemptable, based on what Teddy had told her. With Harry sleeping on his boat near the *Nittany Nob*, he had plenty of chances to poison anything in Ansel's possession. But why would he, since he was already married to Violet?

Arthur and Evelyn were another pair she couldn't separate mentally. They hadn't stirred up her suspicions until they showed up at Oldsmar, pointing their fingers at Teddy. Their collusion with that reporter was as underhanded as the Harding administration. Was Arthur conniving enough to hatch a plot to get rid of his father-in-law and have Teddy take the blame? Plotting to get control of a family business through marriage wasn't anything new. It was a big step from fiancé to murderer, but he wouldn't be the first ambitious man to make the leap—especially if Evelyn were equally ambitious.

Ansel's wife, Florence, and his girlfriend couldn't be eliminated either. She wasn't sure 'girlfriend' was the right word for Shirley's relationship with Ansel. But Teddy had spilled the beans that he had a wife and children. She didn't like thinking of Shirley as a murderer. For that matter, she didn't want to think of her as seeking a 'sugar daddy', as Teddy would say. But either or both could be true. Discovering that you were the 'other woman' in a love triangle could lead to murder. The fact that Ansel was a man of means made it more probable. A suite at the Vinoy was a long way from a car tent in a Tin Can Tourist camp.

As for Florence, the knowledge that her spouse was a philanderer wasn't nearly as powerful a motive as the possibility that one of her children might have killed their father. Whatever her relationship with her husband, Florence was devoted to her children. She and Mac supported Violet's choice of Harry as a husband. Florence was afraid of Ansel, but even the most timid mother could become fierce in the protection of her offspring.

"Cornelia!"

Her uncle's voice startled her. A trace of red crept into her cheeks. "Sorry, I was lost in thought."

He patted her on the shoulder. "Theodora is going to be fine. She might even be awake by now. Why don't you go check on her?"

A rueful smile spread across her face. She could remember a time when neither of them would have been asleep at this hour. Cornelia considered sleeping past six to be a luxury. Even on leave, she was too wide awake to lay in bed longer.

"Are you ready to leave?" she asked.

"Mac will give me a ride back to the hotel later. We're going up in his plane to get a better look at the new developments around the bay." His blue eyes twinkled. "He's also invited us to go out, to test out the new boat ... when things settle down, of course. That should be a great help in my house hunt."

Trekking through the lobby amid stares and awkward silence was not going to be easy, but it was that or slinking in the back door of the hotel. She'd lived too long to let a few gossips make her cower. Cornelia put on a brave, albeit sweaty face, and handed her automobile over to the valet. Chin high, she strolled past the doorman and headed toward the lift. She gritted her teeth at the whispers intended to be overheard. There was a temptation to gaze back and match a face with the words. She focused on the brass doors instead, and kept putting one foot in front of the other.

Despite the gossip, Cornelia was relieved to be back at the hotel. After years in Colorado, she had become unaccustomed to Florida's humidity. It seemed odd to be sweating in the middle of winter, but it had been a while since she was in a climate where February temperatures could reach eighty degrees. Carrying her uncle's camera around didn't help. Next time he wanted to film Florida, she was going to let him tote his own equipment.

She let herself believe that lie for the few seconds it took to lug the tripod to her uncle's room. As she stowed the camera in the wardrobe, she was greeted by the faint aroma of bay rum mingled with leather polish and machine oil. The scent took her back to her childhood. She turned to leave, but lingered in the doorway to glance around the room at his clocks, his leather luggage arranged by size, and engineering journals stacked on the bedside table with their spines in perfect alignment. During the week they had spent in Saint Petersburg, he had managed to make the room his own. The old dear with his gadgets, obsessions, and sheer brilliance was going to have her wrapped around his finger as long as he lived.

Her own room lacked any sort of order. She didn't see Teddy anywhere, although there were plenty of signs of the condition she was in the previous evening. The wardrobe door hung open. One of Teddy's shoes and several articles of clothing lay crumpled in the floor. Her covers were in a twisted lump in the middle of the bed. She frowned at the sight of the Ball jar Teddy had opened. It sat empty on her nightstand.

Last night, Cornelia had taken a single drink, and the jar had been almost half full when she dozed off on one of the Vinoy's comfortable beds.

Cornelia sighed. She hoped that Teddy hadn't had more after they left the hotel. There was already too much gossip. Then, she regretted her assumption. Teddy and Shirley were probably out shopping, or perhaps only Teddy. Shirley had a job, after all. Cornelia unpinned her hat, placed it on a shelf, and set about putting the room to rights. At least the maids wouldn't have reason to join the rumor mill.

In half an hour she was freshly bathed, dressed in one of the cotton frocks Teddy had bought for her, and headed to the veranda with her book. She found a rocker with a nice view of the yacht basin, ordered a glass of sweet tea, and settled in for a much-deserved respite from the chaos.

Three chapters later, she was pulled out of the story by a commotion. She tried to ignore the disagreement until she heard a voice that made her plant her face in her hands. "Not again," she groaned.

CHAPTER FOURTEEN

Teddy didn't leave the room until noon. The first time she woke up, it was Cornelia telling her it was time for breakfast. Teddy's response had been a rush to the bathroom. No, there was no way she would make it downstairs, much less sit through a meal in the dining room. Her head rang like an out-of-tune xylophone, and her stomach felt like the percussion section had shifted to the bass drum. After her first bout of illness, she begged Cornelia to give her regrets to Uncle Percival.

"Oh, Teddy, you know he asked you not to drink," Cornelia said.

"I know; I'm sorry. Let him go eat whatever he—" The picture of the Eggs Benedict swam behind her eyelids, and she was ill again.

Then, she was alone in the bathroom with the cool, cool porcelain. After the worst of the nausea had passed, Teddy crept back to bed. She was wracked with guilt over breaking her promise, but she hadn't realized how awful the day would be when she'd made it. She pulled the bedclothes over her head to block the light and succumbed to the soothing darkness.

The second time she woke up, she returned to the bathroom and mixed a dose of BC Powder. There wasn't much of it left; a visit to the pharmacist was in order ... once the sun wasn't as bright. Back under the covers, although she didn't sleep this time.

Once she felt well enough, she rose, bathed, and dressed. Instead of face powder, Teddy applied Magnolia Balm to her sunburned cheeks. No rouge was needed today. Cornelia and her uncle still weren't back, so they had probably gone off to explore after breakfast. She could either be sad that she wasn't with them, or find something else to do.

Teddy settled on working with her needlepoint. It was quiet, didn't require going outside to do, and was something she'd planned to work on anyway. She remembered how beautiful the ocean had been on the afternoon in the park. How much blue floss did she have, and in how many hues?

Eventually, she decided that she did need to have more light to create the small stitches that would lend a proper subtlety to the hues. It would also be nice to see the ocean while she worked on her creation—and get some fresh air. She'd been stuck inside long enough.

Evelyn had convinced her mother to leave her room. They stared out at the water, saying nothing. Sunshine and fresh air were supposed to help with grief, but pain and anger still throbbed deep inside the younger woman. Father had been murdered, taken from her. He had given her everything: her first pony, her education, and more control of the business than anyone else, even Mac. She had been his favorite, immune from his darker moods, his lashings out. Although there had been a spat about her hair, it would have blown over quickly.

A movement in the corner of her eye drew her attention. It was *her.* Theodora Lawless had crawled out from under her rock to warm herself like the reptile she was. She glanced at her mother, who was still gazing at the ocean, then inched herself closer to the Lawless woman. Closer ... closer ...

As usual, the veranda was crowded, but she discovered an empty seat at the far end and pounced on it. Out came the floss, and the project began anew. She interwove blue with aqua, ultramarine with navy. The light playing on the water should be gold—no, white. Maybe silver. Did she have silver in her basket? Teddy opened it to search inside, and jabbed someone with her elbow.

"Excuse me," she said, and discovered Evelyn Stevens standing over her. "You again?" Teddy snapped. "I wish you would leave me alone. Why are you following me?"

"Following you?" Evelyn turned to her mother, who wore a dismayed expression. "I would say rather that you were putting yourself in my way. Oldsmar yesterday, and now here."

"I'm staying at this hotel, just like you," Teddy said. "Of course you're going to run into me at the hotel."

Florence, who had come over, was staring at Evelyn. "You went to Oldsmar yesterday? I thought you were out making arrangements."

The young woman waved a dismissive hand. "I did, but Arthur needed to do some things at home, and I had to get away for a while."

"We went to Oldsmar to get away from *you*," Teddy said. "And to look at properties. Why did you show up at the Gold Rush?"

"It looked like fun, and I wanted to think of something else besides—" she covered her face with her handkerchief.

Florence put an arm around her offspring. "Must you be so churlish to my daughter? She's done you no harm."

"No harm?" Teddy exclaimed, loud enough to draw looks. "You mean, besides following me—with a reporter—and publicly accusing me ..." Other hotel guests were staring now, and she shut her mouth.

"You did, though, didn't you?" Evelyn cried. "Daddy was rich, and he caught on to your ways in time. Now you're leading that little old man down the garden path."

"I generally follow *him* down garden paths," Teddy retorted. "No one leads him anywhere."

"Men aren't as bright as they think," Evelyn sneered. "You knew my father was going to blow the whistle on you, let him know that you were a fallen woman."

Teddy jumped up, dumping her basket in the process. "That isn't true! Your father lied about me to protect his own reputation, and he didn't care how badly he hurt my family in the process."

Florence released Evelyn and rounded on Teddy. "My family has nothing to hide! Ansel was a man of sterling reputation," she proclaimed.

Teddy was sheet white, rouged cheeks making her face a clownish comedy again. "He was charming as long as he got his own way. When he didn't, he had a cruel temper."

The other woman winced briefly, then spat: "I'm sure you brought it out of him, you hag!"

This brought jeers from the gathered spectators. Teddy took a step towards Florence, but Cornelia had her arm. "Come with me."

"My needlepoint," she protested, and Cornelia let her go long enough for her to snatch it up.

"Killjoy!" a member of the assemblage hurled at Cornelia's back as they left the veranda.

Teddy clutched her basket to her chest once they were in the elevator. "Oh, that was horrid."

"We need to talk." Cornelia prayed that her uncle wasn't back from the airfield yet.

For once, her prayers were answered. There was no sign of the professor. She steered Teddy into their section of the suite and closed the door. She dropped her book on the bed and removed her hat. "Set your basket down over there. Come sit with me."

Teddy did as she was told. Cornelia put her arms around her, and Teddy sobbed. "I'm such a fool, I really am."

"You're not a fool. This has been a trying time."

"I am a fool," Teddy said. "It was crowded, and I bumped Evelyn by accident, and then I accused her of following me around."

Cornelia fetched the box of Kleenex Teddy kept with her makeup. "Well, they have been following us around. I'm fairly certain that little stunt she pulled with the reporter was planned."

Teddy dabbed a tear away with a tissue. "Why would she do that?"

"It's possible that she really thinks you killed her father. You did assault him twice."

Her companion took exception. "Only once she knows about."

"She can read. The papers have reported the second time, too," Cornelia countered. "I'm more concerned about the effect this has had on you. You've been moody—"

"—and churlish," Teddy said. "Let's not forget churlish."

"You've had some provocation with the Stevens family. What I'm worried about is the amount of alcohol you're consuming."

"I have a lot of sorrows to drown."

"I think you're trying to pickle them, and you're preserving them instead. You've been sick almost every morning since we came to the hotel. You drank nearly an entire jar of moonshine by yourself last night. That's a pint of whiskey. I'm just grateful you chose the smaller jar size for the trip."

"I was afraid if one broke, I would lose more hooch."

Cornelia placed her hands on the sides of Teddy's face and looked into her eyes. "Your liver is what you'll lose if you keep this up." Her voice was fierce. "It's making you sick, it's making you sadder, and it's making you churlish. You promised Uncle Percival that you wouldn't overdo it. Now, I'm asking you. You have the therapeutic dose you're supposed to take. Limit yourself to that. Will you promise?"

Teddy's eyes shimmered with tears. "I promise."

"Good. After dinner, I'll talk to Uncle Percival about changing hotels. He's had his fun, but we need to get away from here."

Uncle Percival returned from the airfield shortly thereafter. By then, the ladies had freshened up. He regaled them with the story of his exciting flight around the bay, then excused himself to bathe and change for dinner.

"He should have done that first," Teddy said. "He stinks of castor oil."

"They use it to lubricate the engines," Cornelia replied. "Flying aces need to have strong stomachs."

Once the professor was clean and smelling better, the trio left their suite for the dining room. As they entered the lobby, though, two young men sprang up from a pair of overstuffed chairs and intercepted them.

"I beg your pardon," the professor said, "do we know you?"

No. A bad, bad feeling seized Cornelia by the stomach. She instinctively reached out to clutch Teddy's hand. The fingers were cold.

One of the men addressed her companion. "Are you Miss Theodora Lawless, latest of Fisher's Mill, Kentucky?"

Teddy, already straightened up to her full height, lifted her chin higher. "I am."

"Come with us," the officer said, showing her his badge. "I think you would rather do this outside than here." He indicated the now-silent lobby, filled with hotel patrons.

"How considerate of you," Teddy said, sweeping past him.

Explosions of magnesium and the click of cameras began as the officers pushed open the double doors. Bobby Hornbuckle was there with a camera crew. Mitch was nearby with his own crew, but had the grace to look sheepish.

Cornelia shoved a businessman aside at the valet station and demanded that they bring her car immediately. "This is an emergency." The hapless young man who delivered her car gaped when she asked for directions to the jail, but made no comment. She rewarded him with a five-dollar bill.

She barreled up Fifth Avenue, hands in a death grip on the steering wheel. "This should not be happening."

The professor kept an equally firm grip on his seat and the roof of the car. "Slow down, Corny. We know where she's going to be."

"Don't call me Corny!" she roared. "This is monstrous! We need to stop this."

"My apologies," her uncle replied, continuing to clutch his handholds as they made a sharp turn. "We're going to get her out, Cornelia."

"How? We're miles from home and she doesn't have a lawyer."

"Actually, I began researching attorneys again after the police visited the second time. Watch out for that cart! I contacted two promising candidates while you were dressing for Oldsmar."

"You were already convinced this was going to happen, and didn't warn me?"

He shot her a glance. "Did you really have no notion that the family would push for her arrest?"

She glared at him and nearly passed the entrance to the jail. She corrected at the last moment, and the Dodge's wheels squealed in response. "They have no reason to arrest her."

"They have a reason," Uncle Percival said. "The question is, what evidence do they have?"

"None," she retorted, "because she had nothing to do with it."

"Then they have something they think is evidence."

Knaggs awaited his chief suspect in a side room within the women's section of the jail. The room usually served as a waiting area for disappointed parents and the husbands of errant women but was usually empty on weeknights. He wondered what a woman of her social set thought of the institutional grey paint over concrete block. Then Knaggs remembered that she'd spent years in the army. The jail was pure luxury compared to the camps he remembered.

He'd set up a table and two chairs for the interview. The interview room was short of comforts but afforded a little privacy for questioning. When the patrolmen brought the spinster in, he stood and indicated the empty chair. "Please sit here, Miss Lawless."

"Thank you," she said, and did so, arranging her limbs with regal grace.

He plopped down in his own seat and took out his notepad. "Now—"

"Where is my attorney?" she asked.

I should have known she would be difficult. "This isn't a formal interrogation. We're just talking."

"It certainly seems like an interrogation. I've been charged with murder, so I'm not a witness. We're in a private room now, and you have a pen and paper ready to go."

Knaggs slapped the pad down. "Okay, then, let me advise you of a few things, Miss Lawless. Does that suit you?"

She leaned forward and clasped her hands together. "Please proceed, Officer."

"You were engaged to Ansel Stevens. He broke it off, and since then, you've had a personal vendetta against him."

"Wrong! He didn't break it off, I did. As for a having a vendetta, I didn't even know he was here till I arrived at the hotel."

"You behaved like you did. You assaulted him in public at least twice."

"That wasn't a vendetta, that was simple enmity. We did not part as friends."

He made a note. "Simple enmity; I like that."

"I'm glad I amuse you."

"It's no pleasure to me. Where were—" he said, then stopped himself. "No questions; this isn't an interrogation. So, here's another item: you can't account for your whereabouts for approximately two hours the day before the race. That would have been Saturday."

"Yes, I can," she retorted. "I was searching for a hat."

"No one saw you searching for one." The woman opened her mouth, and he raised his hand to stop her. "You say you purchased the hat at Berber's, but there are no witnesses to be found. Not even the woman who sold it to you."

"My dear fellow, I have a receipt."

"That only proves you were there at some point during the day. You had plenty of time to get to the marina and back."

"I spoke to the clerk there at length. She was a pleasant woman."

"That's what you tell me, but if I took people at their word, I'd be a poor policeman."

Theodora Lawless huffed and raised her chin. "A good policeman would check my alibi. You should be searching for that woman. Her name is Rena, and she was going to find a new job in Sarasota."

"Do you have a last name for this woman?"

"No, but her former employer should."

"Do you know the name of the friend she was staying with?"

"We didn't become that familiar," Miss Lawless admitted. "But dislike and a lack of witnesses are hardly enough to muster a charge of murder. After my attorney makes inquiries in Sarasota and finds that woman, you'll have egg on your face."

The moment had arrived. Knaggs reached into his pocket and pulled out the envelope with the hair comb. He shook it out onto the table, a smidgen beyond the woman's reach. It shimmered in the morning light. "Is this yours, ma'am?"

He was surprised by her smile. "Why, yes! I wore it to dinner the first night we were here, but I lost it somehow. Maybe it came off when I walloped Ansel. Where did you find it?"

He grinned despite himself. "We found it in the *Nittany Nob*, Mr. Stevens' yacht."

Finally, he had the pleasure of seeing Miss Lawless shut up.

CHAPTER FIFTEEN

The Pettijohns were not permitted to see Teddy that evening; she was being interviewed by the police. There was also no bail to be paid, since she wouldn't be arraigned until the morning. The matron advised them to return then with some personal items for their friend; she would probably want to dress differently for court.

"Will you at least be providing dinner?" Cornelia asked, almost babbling. "She—she didn't have a chance to eat."

"We'll give her something," the matron said. "It won't be Vinoy-level cuisine, though."

Cornelia spent a sleepless night turning from one side to the other, lying on her back, and even her stomach. She'd slept through wailing sirens and dropped bombs, but the empty bed next to hers spoke loudest of all. Finally, she climbed into Teddy's spot, which smelled of her perfume and, faintly, of moonshine. Only then could she drift off.

In the morning, Teddy was escorted to a private room and introduced to her attorney, Morgan Cosgrove. Cosgrove was a slender man who appeared to be in his forties. His suit was well-tailored, and his reddish-brown curls had been tamed with Brilliantine.

"Miss Lawless," he said, "A shame we must meet under these circumstances."

"Yes, a shame." Teddy was dressed in the simple blue suit Cornelia had selected—dark, conservative in cut, with a skirt that covered the knees.

They both sat. The attorney produced a pencil and paper. "Before we head to court, I'd like to be prepared. Could you give me a short description of what happened between the deceased and yourself?"

"We were engaged when I was young and foolish. I broke off the engagement, and he spread lies about me that hurt my family. Last week was the first time I'd seen him in ... well, many years."

"So, you didn't know he was staying at the same hotel before you arrived?"

"No, the professor chose the hotel. He wanted to watch the construction of the pier."

Cosgrove nodded. "The professor. That would be your fiancé?"

Teddy fluttered her eyelashes. "Yes."

The attorney raised a brow. "He just wanted to see the construction?"

"He's a retired professor of engineering. Percival is an inventor and has many patents. I am a lucky woman to have found someone so intelligent," she gushed.

"I'm happy for you both. You struck the deceased in the dining room of the Vinoy last Wednesday."

"No, I struck him in the face. I was overcome with rage; I've often pictured what I would do if I saw the rotter, not what I *wouldn't* do. So I did it."

"Er, yes. You assaulted him again later that evening. You were still unprepared?"

"He was dancing with a young innocent girl at the Coliseum, and I knew he was married. I got angry again and kicked him in the Achilles' heel. I'd say that was spite. I probably should have stopped at alerting the girl."

"Well, you're not up on charges for spite. So, tell me, did you poison Ansel Stevens?"

"Of course not. If I had, I wouldn't have chosen nicotine. Strychnine is much more painful."

Cosgrove pressed his fingers to his temple. "Please don't say that in court."

"What if they ask me?"

"They won't ask which poison you preferred, Miss Lawless. Just whether you poisoned him or not. Don't volunteer information, especially not that sort."

"Well, I didn't poison him at all."

"You did not purchase a captain's cap and coat the interior with nicotine?"

"No, that would hardly be practical. If I were going to use nicotine, I would have added it to his abominable little cigarettes. The poison in the hat might not have absorbed into the skin in sufficient quantity to kill him, especially if it didn't get damp enough. Inhaling it would be much more effective."

Now Cosgrove winced. "Please don't say that in court, either."

"Am I volunteering information again?"

"In the worst way. Stick to yes and no answers whenever possible."

Teddy cocked her head, puzzled. "If you say so, but how will I get them to like me?"

Cornelia and the professor watched the arraignment from one of the rear benches. Closer to the front, a smug Evelyn Stevens sat with her mother. Several reporters lingered at the corners of the room. Bobby Hornbuckle and Mitch Grant were among the pack. Each pointedly ignored the other.

Teddy was, again, advised of the charges against her. She pled not guilty and her attorney, Mr. Cosgrove, requested that she be released until trial or be offered bail. Both were denied. The attorney seemed relieved when Teddy was quietly taken away, which Cornelia considered odd.

The pair were permitted to see her briefly before she returned to her cell. Much as she hated her uncle's pretense of engagement to Teddy, it did open doors for them. Cornelia had packed Teddy's tin of Oreos in her purse and slipped her a few when the matron wasn't looking. "Did they ever give you dinner?" she asked.

"They did. It was a simple sandwich, but there were times in the field I would have been happy to have such fare. I didn't know nursing would prepare me for prison."

Cornelia shuddered. "Don't say that. I still can't believe they charged you over gossip."

"They had more than that." Teddy leaned closer. "Remember that first night in the dining room, when my hair comb disappeared? It reappeared in Ansel's yacht. Someone is framing me."

The Pettijohns met briefly with Morgan Cosgrove after Teddy was taken away.

"Miss Lawless seems to know a good deal about poisons," the attorney said. "How did she come to have this knowledge?"

"She was a nurse during the Great War," Cornelia said, "and spent a good amount of time in the dispensary. Chemistry was one of the subjects she excelled in at Bellevue."

"That is not favorable for our side," Cosgrove said, "especially if she tries explaining to the judge which poison is the most painful or how she would have administered it."

Pure Teddy. "Oh dear."

"Exactly. I have tried to dissuade her from saying such things on the stand, but it would help if every moment of her time could be accounted for from your arrival in Saint Petersburg to the time of the victim's death."

The ride back to the hotel was not a silent one. "People are so willing to think the worst of unmarried women. Why must they always think the worst?"

Her uncle sighed. "It's their job to think the worst, Corny. A murder has happened, and of course people are feigning innocence and grief."

"Don't call me Corny. His family certainly isn't doing a good job of feigning grief. Outside of making funeral arrangements, I haven't seen tears from anyone but Evelyn, and those were for dramatic effect. I daresay none of them liked him, except maybe her, and some had more reason to hate him than others." *Especially his wife, if he'd pushed her around like he did Teddy.*

"Teddy also had good reason to hate him. He ruined not only her reputation with his words, but her father's. Your dear

140

one has been estranged from her kinfolk for decades, and no one would blame her for being bitter and vengeful. She also has a superior knowledge of drugs and poisons, even for a nurse."

He really *had* been eavesdropping that first night. In a way, it was a relief. She didn't have to explain things to him now. "They don't know Teddy like we do. She's the most caring—"

"We all think we know people, dear, but anyone can be pushed to murder given the right reason ... or deep, festering emotions."

"Are you saying that you think she really killed him?"

Her uncle patted one of her hands, currently engaged in a death grip on the steering wheel. "You and I know better than that. But the police regularly deal with people who have been pushed beyond their limits in some form. They have to look for the worst."

"It doesn't help that she assaulted him publicly," Cornelia mused.

"That's why I'm certain she didn't poison him," the professor said. "People who use poison usually do so to conceal their actions. Our Teddy has been out in the open and ready to slug the man."

Cornelia drew a ragged breath. "Oh, Uncle, what are we going to do to get her out of this?"

He drew himself up in the seat. "We're going to find the killer."

They took a late lunch in their suite and shared the information they already had. Did Teddy really lose the hair comb in the dining room? Yes, Cornelia had seen it bounce on the floor and then slide under the Stevens' table. She'd tried to retrieve it, but the head waiter appeared with his protests at that moment. Anyone in the family could have recovered and kept it. Why would perfect strangers do that?

"Perhaps she was already planning murder," the professor said, "and she saw it as an opportunity to point police attention elsewhere. Since we know at least one of the killers was female."

"So, it was Florence, Violet, or Evelyn. We need to learn more about the family, and where they were on the day—or perhaps days—before the race."

A plan was made. Cornelia would try to learn more about the family members, including where they were during the time between Brockman's challenge and the race, while Uncle Percival would visit the Yacht Club and marina to learn more about where the *Nittany Nob* was kept and who might have visited it. They would compare notes during dinner.

Cornelia found that she was genuinely hungry, despite a stomach that had clenched like a fist all morning. Now that they were taking action, she felt a world better.

Evelyn sat in the lobby, waiting for the Pettijohns to finish lunch. The old coot had hired an expensive attorney for the Lawless woman; she wanted to see what he would do next. In his shoes, she would be looking for someone, anyone, else to pin the crime on. It was troubling that he'd visited Mac yesterday, even before the arrest.

When the pair left the dining room, she trailed behind and watched from the door. They stopped at the valet station, and Evelyn scanned the nearby street for a taxi. There was usually one loitering out there for businessmen and tourists who wanted to travel beyond downtown.

The old man and his niece talked while their car was retrieved—then, to Evelyn's surprise, they split up. The niece got into the car, while the old man headed for the trolley stop. Evelyn waited until the car left, then exited the hotel herself. She got the taxi driver's attention, and he pulled into the Vinoy drive to pick her up.

Nearby, the trolley was gliding to a stop for its prospective passenger.

"Do a short loop," she instructed the driver, handing him a couple of bills, "and then come back around to follow that trolley."

Learning about the Stevens family was going to be a challenge. Teddy made friends easily and loved going to places with other people; Cornelia preferred quieter, more solitary pastimes. They hadn't tried to get to know the other patrons of the hotel after the first disastrous evening, since it increased the risk of running into Ansel and his family.

Still, there were things she could learn, if she had the proper help. Shirley and her mother seemed to be the best prospects. The young hairdresser certainly had not known enough about Ansel, but his daughters were both well-kept and fashionable. Women often shared their personal lives with their stylists, which would be useful. There was a chance the Wheelers would know who did their hair.

The concierge helped her find the location of Anna Wheeler's salon, staring at her doubtfully the entire time. He was probably trying to picture her with a bob, or worse, that Eton crop. Teddy would probably look delightful with slicked-down hair and kiss curls, but with her square jaw and build, Cornelia was more likely to be arrested as a man wearing women's clothing.

She had the valet fetch her car, and she took off for Third Street North. Uncle Percival had been interested in using the car himself, but the places he needed to go were within walking or trolley distance. Who knew where she would wind up?

Anna Wheeler's salon was located next to a barber shop. There were as many young women occupying chairs in the barber shop as men, and as she approached, Cornelia saw freshly-bobbed girls leave both establishments.

Inside the salon, the walls were plastered with pictures of different hairstyles and advertisements for beauty products. She saw an ad for Lifebuoy Health Soap, the best soap to shampoo bobs, Colgate's Brilliantine "For giving gloss and softness to the hair," and a poster of Claudette Colbert advertising Player's Cigarettes.

Both Wheelers and a third stylist were busy with clients, while a young woman at the front counter spoke to the newest arrival. There was a separate area with a table containing nail buffers, sticks, and polish. Army regulations would probably forbid most of the styling offered here, but a manicure would be more subtle and likely to fade before her return to Colorado.

Shirley spotted her. "Miss Cornelia! How are you doing today?"

"Badly. Have you heard the news?"

"Oh, yes!" Anna Wheeler said. She was busy taming a customer's wild curls. "It's horrible. Are you looking to drown your sorrows in a new coif?"

"No, I think the Army would disapprove of anything adventuresome," Cornelia said, "but Teddy always said—says that a manicure is therapeutic. Do either of you have time?"

"I'm nearly finished here, if you don't mind waiting a few minutes," Shirley said. "Mrs. Babcock's hair is always a treat to work with. So well-behaved."

Mrs. Babcock appeared surprised. "It never behaves well for me."

"You need to let it do what it wants to do," Shirley cooed. "We're never satisfied with our own hair. I would love to have your natural waves."

Cornelia sat and let Shirley finish her blandishments of Mrs. Babcock. She studied the array of Cutex products as she waited. Powders, nail pastes, and polishes. Teddy would be familiar with all of these. To her, they were a mystery.

The young redhead plopped into the chair opposite her. "You must tell me what's happened. Why on earth would they arrest poor Teddy?"

"The family appears bent on it—at least the female portion." She mustn't lump poor Mac in with the rest of his family. He'd said he didn't believe Teddy was a murderess, and the lad had been truthful in other areas.

"I assume one of them is his wife." Shirley wrinkled her nose. "I asked around about her after I learned the truth from your friend. She's a bit of a Mrs. Grundy."

"I've had that term applied to me a few times, too," Cornelia said.

"You're not all that bad. You're serious, but you mind your own potatoes." She finished cleaning Cornelia's nails and began to apply solution to the cuticles.

"Well, I'm afraid I need to look into Ansel Stevens' garden. Somebody wanted him dead, and Teddy's freedom depends on my finding that person. Can you tell me what else you've learned about him and his family?"

"Not that much. He and his family are from Pennsylvania. I reckon they came down here to make money—it's the local hobby. He has a wife, two daughters, and a son, according to the papers."

"Teddy and I knew the son from the Great War. He was wounded, and we were among his nurses."

Shirley's eyes widened. "Teddy didn't tell me she'd been in the War. I assumed when she referred to visiting France, it was because she could afford to."

"No, we were there to help the young men who were wounded. Would you be kind enough to let me know to whom you spoke about the family? I don't really know anyone here, so I don't have much of a starting place."

"I asked someone I knew, Lucy Rivers. I saw the Clara Bow-style curls on the dark daughter and guessed—correctly—that it was her work. Clara Bow's an actress," Shirley added.

"Yes, I saw her in a film with William Powell last year. Where would I find Lucy?"

"And give her the rest of our trade?" the girl teased, stopping when she saw Cornelia's scowl. "She owns the Movie Star Gallery. The bad news is that her salon is in the Stevens building—as in *Ansel* Stevens. You might run into the family there."

"I will deal with that if I have to. Just tell me where it is."

"You're really brave," Shirley said. "Let me apply some Nail White, and I'll write out directions while you're drying."

The Gallery was also busy; it was Thursday afternoon, and many of the young clients were preparing for social events over the weekend. The business was at least triple the size of the Wheelers'. Cornelia counted six stylists, one manicurist, plus two sales girls at a counter stocked with products and cosmetics.

She approached the counter. "Would it be possible for me to speak to Lucy Rivers?"

"Lucy's with a client at the moment," one of the women said, not lifting her eyes from a schedule book. "Do you have an appointment?"

"No."

"Do you want to set an appointment for a cut?" The attendant then raised her head and saw, really saw, the middle-aged, square-jawed woman standing in front of her. "Oh, I'm sorry, ma'am ... are you the mother of one of her clients?"

"No," Cornelia said, "but if I could buy a bit of her time today, I would appreciate it."

The attendant excused herself to go check, and after the exchange of a sum that would have paid for a styling and a tank of gasoline, Cornelia was led to a cushioned seat near a stylist's station that was larger than the others.

Lucy Rivers was directing the air of a metal hairdryer onto the mud-encrusted tresses of a client when Cornelia sat down. Cornelia knew the substance was likely henna, which was much in vogue these days due to the influence of Miss Bow, but it looked like mud to her.

After applying the mud, the stylist wrapped the hair with a towel "to keep in the heat." She left the client reading a magazine and approached Cornelia, who stood.

"Hello, I'm Lucy Rivers. You're the second person to buy my time this week," she said, looking down into Cornelia's eyes. "I must be famous."

The second person? Cornelia was trailing in someone's wake. How would Teddy handle this? She managed a smile. "Your work is distinctive. You do remarkable work with curls."

"Thank you," Lucy said. Unlike Violet or her previous client, Lucy had no curls. Her hair was peroxide blonde, as short as a man's, and brushed back from a perfectly oval face. Powder covered but could not entirely conceal freckles. Her bare arms were tanned and muscular. Cornelia didn't know much about hair dryers, but the device Lucy had wielded looked as heavy as a machine gun. It was mounted on a metal rod attached to a wheeled base instead of the tripod the heavy guns used, but the shape was similar. "So, how can I help you?"

"I'm looking for information. On the Stevens family."

"Again? You know the family works upstairs; you could go up there if you have questions. Are you a reporter, too?"

Cornelia had a question ready, but the words took her aback. *Reporter?* "No, but I'm familiar with a few of them. Male or female?"

Lucy grinned, revealing a small gap in her teeth. "Male. I didn't think men kept track of women's fashion."

"He must be dedicated," Cornelia said, nodding. She would bet it had been Mitch Grant. "I understand that most of the family only comes down during the winter. The son lives here year-round and works for the business. What about the wife and the daughters?"

"You get right to the point, don't you? I don't know what the wife does, but Violet lives here in Saint Petersburg with her brother. She works for the business, too. Probably more than the brother. He has a new thing going with some speedboats."

"Indeed. What about the other sister?"

"She and the dapper have been working in the office for a couple of months, I think."

Confused, Cornelia asked, "Dapper?"

The question earned another grin. "Dad of a flapper; that's Violet's term for him. I got the impression that she's feeling crowded these days. I read in the paper how her father didn't like her fella, and he was racing Mr. Stevens for the right to see her. Romantic. That could be right out of a movie."

"Does she talk a lot about him? The young man."

"Oh yes. He sounds like the eel's hips, coming from New York to live on a yacht down here."

Cornelia was unaware that eels had hips. "Did the mother also work in the office?"

"Not that I know of. She has Violet running from work to this and that cultural event, so she's probably not the type. Is that all you need to know?"

Since Cornelia still didn't have an idea who the real killer was, she needed to know a lot more. If only she knew which questions to ask ... "Do you do the mother or the sister's hair, perhaps?"

"Her sister became my client last week. I finally got to snip off that horrible Charleston cut. The mother probably goes to her hotel's salon. Matronly but nice, ya know."

Now we're getting somewhere, Cornelia thought. In order to resemble Teddy, Evelyn's heavy blonde hair needed to go. "That was a daring style, but becoming to her. How did you talk her into it?"

"I didn't have to; it was her idea. She said she wanted to do something a little wild before she got married. Men can get all possessive once they've put a ring on a girl. You can't blame her for wanting to make a decision or two on her own. Her instincts were right; it was the berries on her."

So, it was Evelyn's idea. *I knew it!* Cornelia's mind raced, looking for something, anything else to ask. "Do you know anything about her father or brother?"

Lucy hesitated, then said, "I'm sorry for staring. I'm thinking about that bun. You could do with a new cut yourself. That bun is too severe." She extended her hands, creating a frame. "You have good thick hair; a darkening rinse and a trim around the face would take twenty years off of your age."

Cornelia felt her cheeks pinken. "Thank you for the suggestion, but I'm still in service to the Army. They frown on such things. What you see is regulation."

"I bet the men would be happier if they didn't. If you can't have anything modern, have you considered trying a French Twist when you're off duty? Not one of those elaborate Victorian dos, just pull all of it back into one twist. It would have a softening effect and be more attractive."

"Thank you for the advice. Could you tell me more about Evelyn's father?"

Lucy frowned. "He was my landlord; I said hello to him in passing, but he was gone most of the year. I'm more familiar with the son, but not much."

CHAPTER SIXTEEN

The professor took the trolley to the Yacht Club, which was only a short hop away. The basins of colorful yachts made for a pleasant view. When he arrived, he introduced himself to one of the secretaries as a prospective resident of Saint Petersburg, and he was invited to speak to a representative of the Club.

Soon, he was ensconced in a comfortable chair that overlooked the yacht basin and the bay. In the distance, the pier was once again taking shape. Percival could have enjoyed the view for an hour, but he was here on a mission. He focused on the young man who occupied the office.

"Thank you for seeing me. I've been on many riverboats and steam vessels in my time, but I would like to learn more about yachting, perhaps try my hand at it. I've been watching them elegantly glide across the waters from the Vinoy, and I think sailing would be a perfect way to enjoy life in retirement."

"Oh, I quite agree," the young man, name of Lafferty, said. "And this area is perfect for it. You can explore the Bay and the Gulf of Mexico easily from here, and Sarasota isn't that far away, especially when you can get there by water."

"That does sound convenient. I understand Sarasota is rather a lengthy drive by car."

"You could cut down on the distance by taking the new ferry to Bradenton, but why bother when you can sail from our port to theirs?"

Both men laughed.

Lafferty gave him a tour of the headquarters, detailing the advantages of membership. "We have regular smokers, usually on Monday or Tuesday nights, card nights, plus various dinners, dances, and balls. Our Ladies' Auxiliary is also quite active. Are you married, sir?"

The old man puffed out his chest. "I'm engaged to a lovely woman. She loves parties and dancing."

"Congratulations, and it sounds like she would enjoy a membership as well."

The next part of the tour was outside, where Lafferty took him on a walk to the marina basin. It was the central basin, not the northern one where the *Nittany Nob* had been docked. The professor let Lafferty blather about slips and rentals for a short time, then stopped him.

"These vessels are very fine, but I think the yachts in the basin closer to the Vinoy are closer to the sort I would want to purchase. I've been eyeing them from the veranda each day. Could we go up there? I would appreciate your guidance."

Lafferty succumbed to the flattery, and they took the young man's car up the street. A short time later, they were ambling alongside the expensive vessels in the north basin. The walking surface was irregular, so the professor used his cane for additional stability. The sun glinted off the decorative ball, shaped like the head of a wildcat. This was no accident; Percival wanted the workers to notice and remember him.

"Visitors from all points of the compass come to enjoy the warm waters of the bay," his host said. "You'll find vessels from many ports here."

"I would enjoy broadening my own horizons," Pettijohn admitted. "I come from a landlocked state. The yachts themselves seem to come in a broad variety. Do you give lessons in sailing?"

"At your service," Lafferty said with a slight bow, "and we even have yachts you can rent. No point in making a purchase if you don't know what you're comfortable with yet."

"Oh, that's quite marvelous," the professor replied. "May I see them?"

Viewing the rental vessels took a good bit of time, especially with the number of questions the professor asked.

He led his guide around the basin, feigning interest in specific vessels, so the workers would get a good look at him. When Lafferty gave signs of winding up the conversation, Pettijohn threw out an offhanded query.

"I'm wondering; these vessels are all roped in their slips, but it's hardly like they're padlocked. What's to stop a stranger from boarding a nice one and sailing away with it?"

"Ah," Lafferty said, and pointed. "The marina has men to watch over the yachts day and night. Plus, there are the regular workers. If someone they don't recognize approaches a boat, they inquire what business that person has on the dock."

"There must be many people who come to explore, though, sight-seers and the like. And perhaps there are deliveries. Or are deliveries made to yachts?"

"Delivery men have to check in with the patrol first. Between the police, the marina employees, and the marina guards, your vessel would be secure, sir."

"That's good to hear," Professor Pettijohn said. "I am reassured."

The men bid their adieus. Lafferty returned to the Club, and the professor purportedly returned to the Vinoy to consult with his fiancée.

From a distance, Evelyn sat on one of the green benches the city provided for its white citizens and watched the entrance of the Yacht Club. She'd thought Pettijohn would confer with the attorney, or perhaps engage a private detective. Instead, he was investigating things himself. He had to be; why else would he visit the Club after his fiancée had been arraigned for murder?

She moved to a closer bench, marveling at the level of self-deception love could create. The mystery woman had clearly been Miss Lawless: a stylishly dressed woman with a cane and light hair? It *had* to be her.

Mr. Lafferty, a gentleman she recognized from previous visits to the Club, left the building with Professor Pettijohn in tow. They crossed to the marina and began touring it, Lafferty pointing out features while Pettijohn nodded. The old man must have evinced an interest in yachting as a ruse.

When they got into Lafferty's car, a wave of disappointment rushed through her. Was she going to lose him now? Oh, why hadn't she requested her father's car be brought around instead of hiring that cab? The vehicle went north, so Evelyn briskly walked that way. Perhaps the man from the Club was merely driving him back to the hotel.

She continued her walk, heading north, and stopped at the sight of Lafferty's car parked near the yachts next to the hotel. Evelyn scanned the vessels and caught sight of the old man's cane. The sly old coot had maneuvered his way into the scene of the crime. She slowed her walk and entered the park in search of another seat.

Twenty minutes later, Lafferty got into his car alone and left. The old man returned to the Vinoy. Evelyn was torn between following him or speaking to Lafferty herself. She decided it was best to stay on her original trail.

Once Lafferty was gone, the professor strolled to the Vinoy and enjoyed a cup of coffee, resting his legs. Thus restored, he returned to the northern yacht basin. After studying the men working there, he approached the one that appeared most likely to be the watchman.

"Good afternoon," he said, and introduced himself. "I'm the insurance appraiser for West Coast Casualty, Incorporated. We are the insurers for the pier they're building here."

The man looked puzzled. "I didn't know you could insure a pier."

"You can insure anything of value," the professor said. "You may have seen me at the pier late last week, inspecting the property."

"I did." The younger man gazed at the pier, brushing a fly away from his collar. "You were there with a camera and a woman. I didn't know women could use movie cameras."

Pettijohn leaned closer. "She's my niece. I try to throw a little work her way. Spinster."

"Ah." The nodded wisely, "I have a maiden aunt. The old dear spends the season working as a nanny to the spoiled offspring of one of those Yankee couples."

The professor's southern accent became slightly more pronounced. "I'm glad I have it on film now, considering what happened last weekend."

"I bet! Damaged, and it's not even finished yet."

"It's better off than the poor vessel that rammed it." The professor pulled out a notebook. He didn't really need one, but it made him look more official. "The pylon is still sound, but they'll have to replace some of the supportive beams and repour a section of concrete. So, tell me, are you one of the men who patrol here? May I have your name?"

"What for?"

Pettijohn made a dismissive shrug. "The company wants more information on the circumstances of the incident, so they requested that I learn more about what happened with the yacht, the *Nittany Nob*. You probably saw me speaking to Mr. Lafferty about it a little while ago. He was kind enough to take me on a short tour."

"Oh yes! I did see you with him. Striking cane you have."

"Thank you. The wildcat is the mascot of the University of Kentucky, or at least that's what it's called now. I taught engineering there when it was still the Agricultural and Mechanical College. You said you were one of the watchmen?"

"Um, yes I am. Sorry. Irvin Murray." He stuck out his hand, and the professor shook it.

"Pettijohn. Pleased to meet you. Most of the details I need are routine. The *Nittany Nob* was moored here before the race last Sunday, I believe. Did you see the person who delivered the captain's cap?"

"I wasn't here. The guy on duty was Gene Cross, the weekend man."

The professor wrote the name down. "Gene Cross. Does he only work weekends? I can get his information from Mr. Lafferty, but I'd rather speak to him in situ, where I can see what we're talking about."

"He works tonight, should be here around seven." Murray grinned. "Of course, it'll be dark then."

"I'll bring my niece to protect me." They both laughed, and then Pettijohn looked at his notebook. "So, the cap was delivered here. Do people bring gifts to the marina frequently?"

"It's not unusual for yachtsmen to send items they want on board for a planned cruise, especially if they're taking guests out or they want to fly a special flag."

"I see. Where do the owners pick those items up?"

"Sometimes we store the items at the office, sometimes we put them on the yacht, especially if it's something the owner will be using shortly."

"Which category did this item fit into?"

"Gene said the lady put it on the boat herself. But you should double-check with him."

Evelyn took a seat on one of the benches again. Pettijohn had returned to the yacht basin and was speaking to the staff. He was in better physical condition than his cane implied. Hours had passed, and the afternoon sun was sinking low. She wished she'd brought a book with her, although it would have defeated the purpose of observing the enemy. Maybe she should have called Arthur for company, but no ... he'd missed enough days of work. Her father had been the one to press for their match—she hadn't been as interested—but Arthur was proving himself such a dear during this horrible time. He must really love her.

Finally, the professor ascended the sidewalk from the marina and turned in the direction of the Vinoy. Evelyn watched as he re-entered the hotel, and she made haste to the curb. She caught a trolley south; she didn't have much time left.

The secretary was busy putting things into desk drawers when she entered the Yacht Club office. Her shift must be almost over. The woman straightened, though, and smiled in greeting.

"May I help you?"

"I'm sorry to disturb you so late in the day, but it's urgent that I speak to Mr. Lafferty before he leaves."

The Room Service staff were becoming increasingly familiar with the Pettijohn family. The gentleman who brought

154

dinner inquired after the wellbeing of their absent companion. Cornelia crossed her arms while Uncle Percival assured him that Teddy was doing fine and tipped him for his trouble.

Once the attendant had left, she said, "They're all talking about her. She would be mortified."

"I think she wouldn't mind someone asking how she is. Let's pool our information and see what we have."

Cornelia described her encounter with Lucy. "I'm not that encouraged by the information I got. I learned that all the children work in the Stevens office, and Florence has an active social life."

"Actually, that is something of value," Uncle Percival said. "It means that they all had time to themselves, during which they would have the opportunity to arrange the poisoning."

"Including Florence, if they were all out of the room. Any of them could have done it, which brings us no closer to discovering which one of them is responsible."

"We need to combine your information with hard data. I hope to acquire some this evening," he replied, and told her what he had learned at the marina. His description of himself as an insurance appraiser brought a smile to her face, as he'd hoped it would.

"The evening man comes on duty at seven. We'll give him a little while to settle in, then see if we can acquire a first-hand description of our gift giver. In the meantime, would you pass me the coffee?"

They donned jackets before they left the hotel, since they would be walking near the water. The dark waters lapped gently at the seawall. On a different occasion, she would have enjoyed listening to it. Uncle Percival was making that difficult.

"Remember that you're my niece, but also my assistant. So, look officious. I'm sure the Army trained you to do that."

"Among other things. I'm still surprised that the watchman bought that line about your being in insurance. If he talks to the people in the Club, he's going to know he's been bamboozled."

"I said officious, not pessimistic."

They climbed onto the walkway of the basin. Cornelia took her torch out of her purse in case it was needed. She'd brought her service revolver for the same reason. The professor had his cane and, one assumed, his rapier wit.

A few electric lights illuminated the slips where the yachts were moored, but once they left the orb of the street lamps, the torch proved useful. Wearing jackets had also been a wise move. The breeze coming off the water was much cooler than the night air.

Most of the yachts had been abandoned for the evening, but a few still had people aboard them. Cornelia wondered if some owners lived on their boats like Harry, or if the marina permitted that.

Uncle Percival patted her arm and pointed to a lone figure walking along the dock area that jutted into the water. "I believe that may be the man we need to interview." He trod across the boards at a healthy clip, and Cornelia feared that he would stumble over one and fall into the water. "Slow down. He's not trying to get away."

"No, but briskness keeps the blood moving when your limbs are cold."

"You have a point." She increased her pace.

The man stopped walking and waited for them to approach.

"Good evening," the professor said, not—quite—puffing. "Gene Cross?"

"That's me," the young man replied. "Were you looking for me?"

"Yes," Pettijohn said. "Your daytime counterpart, Mr. Murray, referred me to you."

From behind them, a voice spoke. "We meet again, sir. Is this your niece?"

They turned to see two men in raincoats.

"Mr. Latterly," the professor said. "How pleasant to see you again."

Latterly didn't look like he felt the same way. "You lied to me, Mr. Pettijohn. Or should I say, Professor Percival Pettijohn?"

Uncle Percival tugged at his collar. "I wouldn't say it was a lie. More an omission."

"There was definitely an omission," Lafferty said. "The gentleman with me is Tate Fowler, one of the managers of the marina."

Fowler tipped his trilby in greeting; the professor nodded in return.

"You omitted the part about being the fiancé of a murderess," Lafferty said. "Dragging me all over the grounds, sneaking in questions about marina security, hoping to find a loophole—"

"Come, come," Pettijohn said. "I was not looking for a loophole. I wanted to get more information than the newspapers provided, which, to be frank, made it sound like anyone could stroll in here and leave tainted garments for unsuspecting yachtsmen."

Cornelia bit her lip to keep from laughing; the watchman suppressed a chuckle.

"That's not so," Fowler said. "And, as you've learned, you can't lie your way into privileged information."

"I beg your pardon; the woman in question was in public view and this is a municipal waterfront. All I want is a firsthand eyewitness account. If you maintain that this is information the defense is not entitled to, I shall have Morgan Cosgrove request a deposition from the witness through the court system."

Gene Cross didn't look particularly happy about this notion. Neither did the other two men.

"Very well," Fowler said. "Although I think the *Evening Independent* was prepared to describe the woman down to her"—he glanced at Cornelia—"perfume. Our staff noticed the woman climbing onto the vessel. They approached to ensure that she was not a thief or some form of adventuress. When she descended promptly from the vessel *sans* her package, Cross investigated. He went on board to check the item and saw that it was a captain's cap, an item quite common around here. We saw no reason to investigate further."

"Since the item was left with a card from the Yacht Club?

That struck a sore spot with Lafferty. "No!" he snapped, Adam's apple bobbing. "Any nincompoop could have written our name on a card! Honestly, if we had sent him a gift, I would have simply walked to the dock and delivered it by hand to save time and money."

"Of course you would have," the professor said soothingly. "Perhaps, then, Mr. Cross could tell us more about the woman who delivered the cap."

"Everything I know, I told the police," the watchman said.

"Mr. Cosgrove will collect those reports, but perhaps I have different questions," Pettijohn said. "What time did she arrive?"

"Around two-thirty or so."

"Around two-thirty. Could you be more exact?"

Cross sighed. "No sir, I was working at the time, not checking my watch."

"She was described as having pale hair. Was it blonde, white, or silver?"

"I told the police I couldn't see her hair at all," Cross said, "just the cap. The reporters kept pushing me to guess, and a female one asked if she had light or dark eyebrows. I said they weren't dark. That's all I said, sir."

"In other words, they made a deduction."

"More like a guess, in my opinion," the watchman said.

"Now, if that's all ..." Fowler said.

Cornelia edged closer. "Was she carrying a cane?"

The local men looked at her as if she'd sprouted another head.

"Oh yes," her uncle said. "The descriptions from the press disagree. Did she carry a cane?"

"She was twirling it," Cross replied. "Like it was a toy."

"So, it was decorative."

"Not like yours, sir. It had the usual hook handle."

"There you go, questions answered," Fowler said. "Cross, please ensure that Mr. Pettijohn and his niece get off the property safely. He has no vessel moored here."

"And I will thank you not to return to the Yacht Club, sir," Lafferty added.

"Come along, Cornelia," the professor said. "Clearly, we will be joining the Power Boat Association instead."

Once they were back in their suite, Cornelia grumbled, "Well, that was embarrassing."

Pettijohn was also unamused. "At least we confirmed that she had a cane," he said, rubbing one of his knees.

"It won't free Teddy." Cornelia debated parking the car on the street again, then decided on the valet service to spare her uncle's legs. They were both exhausted. She nosed the Dodge into the entrance of the Vinoy.

"It makes it more evident that Theodora is being framed," the professor said. "The woman went to the trouble of being noticed with a cane. She's made a few errors, though; Theodora doesn't have a cane with a hook handle, and she always draws her eyebrows on before going out into public."

That doesn't help much, Cornelia thought. *We need to prove she was somewhere else entirely.*

CHAPTER SEVENTEEN

Teddy paced along the side of the cell facing the corridor. Her second night in captivity, with more to come. Tomorrow was Friday, and unless something miraculous happened, she would be stuck here over the weekend. Lord, she could use a drink. Her head was killing her. Worse, her cough had returned. The sea air was delightful when the sun shone, but at night it was cold and clammy.

"Hey, Curly, how about you sit down?" one of her cellmates said. "You remind me of a baboon at the zoo."

Teddy stopped and hugged herself, rubbing her arms. They felt shaky. *She* felt shaky. She also wished she were still alone, but the accommodations for female prisoners were limited. An hour earlier, the police had deposited two suspected prostitutes in the cell with her. Just like men, to take the lion's share of the cells and expect the murderesses and pro skirts to share quarters.

"If you think it's cold here," the woman said, "be glad ya weren't out with us. That wind gets cold at dusk."

"I'm not cold," Teddy said, "Merely a little nervous."

"Sit down, you're giving me the heebie-jeebies," the woman said again. "What's your name?"

"Teddy."

"I'm Minnie." Minnie was a skinny woman with a frizzy bob in the no-man's-land between brown and blonde.

Teddy plopped down beside her and sighed. Her stomach hurt.

"So," the woman said, "Haven't seen you before. You're pretty dolled up. Where are you working?"

"Oh, I don't work any longer," Teddy said. "I'm a pensioner."

"You have a pension? Who did you work for?" Minnie asked.

"The Army," Teddy replied, then realized what Minnie was talking about and burst into laughter. "Oh, how dreadful that sounds."

"So do we," the second woman, shorter and rounder, said. "The Army, the Navy, the Pipefitter's Union..."

"I was a nurse," Teddy said. "But I'm sure your service is appreciated."

The women guffawed, but it wasn't ill-natured. Not entirely, at least.

"So, whatcha doing in here? A raid at the tea room?"

"No. I'm afraid I'm in for murder."

The women's eyes widened.

"Murder? Who'd ya kill?"

Teddy shook her head. "I didn't. All I did was slap him. And kick him once."

"Who was he?"

"I used to be engaged to him."

"Oh." Minnie jabbed Teddy with her elbow. "Served him right, I bet."

The night wore on, and Teddy felt like she was getting worn down with it. Her stomach was in knots, and she was unable to eat what the matron called 'dinner'. Her cellmates, who had grown to three, were snoozing in their seats, which allowed Teddy to pace to her heart's discontent.

The cough was worsening. She was surprised that the other women could sleep through the noise. Teddy remembered lying in a hospital bed after the gas attack, the nurse gasping for air alongside her patients. The gasping and choking echoed in the ward, which only ended when death brought peace.

Down the corridor, a door opened and closed. Men's voices murmured, and she was jolted out of the gruesome reverie. She *knew* one of those voices.

"Chago!" she whispered, rushing to the bars. "Chago!"

Santiago Aldama, as dapper as she remembered, turned at the hiss. His smile was brilliant, then confused. "Miss Teddy?"

He turned back to the matron. "The ladies over there. May I speak to them?"

She nodded, and the gangster approached the cell. He clasped Teddy's hand in his. "Miss Teddy, how did you get here? Did they catch you in a raid?"

"No," she said, "I've stayed sharp. There's been a horrible misunderstanding, though. And I feel so awful."

He looked at her intently, then released her hand. He moved to block the view of the matron and produced a flask from his vest.

"Oh, Chago, you're so sweet," Teddy murmured before taking a long swig. Rum, bracing and fiery, rushed down her throat and into her body, filling it with heat that went down to the toes. Her stomach clenched one more time, then released, sending her blood back to her brain.

"Where is your friend?" he asked, taking the flask back. He shook it briefly; it was empty. He put it away. "And her uncle?"

"They're off trying to help me," she said, standing a little taller. "They know I'm innocent. All I did was slap him. Well, I kicked him too, but that was later."

Chago briefly glanced back at the matron. "Is she the one who checked you in?"

"No, that one went home before they served the gruel and water."

He turned to the uniformed woman, who was watching them with a mildly interested expression. "Ma'am," Chago said. "All the ladies in this cell, they are employees of Mr. Wall."

"You mean those are his professional skirts."

"No, ma'am, these are the showgirls from his casino. Minnie, Juanita, wake up," he said. "I'm paying bail for all of them."

The woman pointed at Teddy. "Isn't she a little long in the tooth for a showgirl?"

"Oh no, ma'am, she's their dance instructor."

"I could show you my can-can," Teddy offered.

"I'd rather not see," the woman grumbled.

Teddy looked hurt. "I do a charming can-can."

The matron rolled her eyes and walked away.

Chago escorted the women to a black Oldsmobile Six. He offered the front passenger seat to Teddy. "Which hotel am I taking you to, *senorita*?"

Teddy ached to be back with Cornelia, snug in the bed, but that wouldn't do. If Knaggs had any brains—and she was sure he did—he would head for the Vinoy as soon as the matron discovered her mistake and alerted the authorities. With a thrill, she realized that she was on the lam. "No hotel. I don't think that would be a good idea."

"Can she make up her mind in the car?" Minnie said. "I'm freezing on the hoof."

Teddy, abashed, quickly got in. She'd forgotten how much less her cellmates were wearing. "I'm so sorry, ladies. Let's get warm."

The women got themselves situated, while Chago started the car and turned on the floor heater. "Okay, no more complaining. Where am I taking you, Miss Teddy?"

"Well, is there a club near here?"

The Cuban laughed. "You don't know where they all are by now?"

"We've only been here a short time," Teddy said. "The only club I've seen was the Gangplank."

"Ah," He put the car in gear, no longer smiling.

Clearly, this wasn't one of his boss' clubs. She had made a *faux pas*. They drove silently out of the lights and turned down a darker street. Teddy decided that she needed to get back into Chago's good graces. He had, after all, ransomed her out of prison and provided her with the elixir of life.

"You know," she said in an offhanded tone, "the clubs here are set up *so* cleverly. They've planned in advance for police raids."

"You don't say." Chago's eyes were still on the road. He turned from Fourth Street North and headed into an unfamiliar neighborhood, giving a wide berth to a pair of zozzled young men.

"I love the secret exit at the Gangplank," she added. "It reminds me of a pirate story."

Chago finally looked her way. "How did you find this secret exit?" he asked in an equally casual tone.

"Oh, there was a raid. They had the flashing lights, of course, but then I saw the barkeep running towards the chimney with a ledger. I figured he knew what he was doing, so I followed him. When we got there, he ducked into a tunnel, and I kept on his heels."

The Cuban finally laughed again. "Miss Teddy, you really are an adventuress. You could have gotten stuck, or worse, he could have become angry with you."

"He wasn't pleased, that was for sure. But there was no time for him to chastise me, what with the police nearby. So, he ran for his boat instead."

"You were near the water, then?"

She had him hooked. "Yes, it was in the trees near the dock. It was a clever escape route, and I daresay it would be a useful way to bring goods into the club, too."

"That's a real smart setup, then," Chago said. "Maybe I should check it out for myself sometime."

"Not tonight, please," Minnie said from the back. "I need to go home and put my feet in Epsom salts."

The poor woman; jail was hardly a place where she could put her feet up. "Is there a club close to here, Chago?" Teddy asked. "I need more sustenance."

"The Candlelight Club is a fine place, and not far from here," Chago said. "Or I could take you back to Tampa with me."

She was genuinely touched. "I am flattered you would ask," she said. "But I'm so hot you could get in trouble for helping me as much as you have."

"Since I found you in jail, you're probably right," he replied. "What did they get you on, anyway?"

She opened her mouth, but Minnie replied for her. "Murder."

"Murder?" Her rescuer turned to her, and Teddy nodded. "I can't imagine you hurting someone on purpose."

"Oh, I could murder someone if I had to. But I didn't do it, even though I had good reason to strangle the rat."

They were traveling through the jungle north of the urban center now, where they could only see as far as the car's headlights, which lit up the fronds of cabbage palms and the ghostly drapes of Spanish beards from the trees.

The Candlelight Club was located near the shore. Across the bay, Teddy could see the lights of Tampa.

"Are you sure this is where you want me to leave you?" Chago inquired. "Not back at your hotel with your friends?"

"Yes," Teddy said. "I'm so grateful to you, Chago. I'll repay you for the bail when I can walk into a Western Union again."

"*De nada*," he replied. "Here's a couple more bucks for the cover charge. You watch after yourself."

The bouncer at the door looked a little surprised to see a silver-haired woman among the shebas clutching their pearls, but her money was equally green.

Teddy headed directly for the bar. The cocktail special for the night was the Bees' Knees. It was sweet, cool, and brought peace in its wake, even if it bore the tang of bathtub gin mixed with the real thing. It was also gone too quickly.

She stood at the counter, shuffling through the change that Chago had left her. "Could I get one leg of a Bee's Knees?" she asked.

The barkeep snickered. "Sorry, lady, it's either a regular cocktail or no cocktail. Maybe someone will spot you a couple of nickels."

Teddy looked at the piano, currently empty. Behind it and several instruments, she saw that the musicians were smoking. "What if I played some songs?"

"We already have musicians," he sneered.

166

"They're on break. Could I play a little, and see if I get some tips?"

"You're going to have to ask them, not me."

She approached the three men, who stood and straightened their jackets. "Excuse me, but could I play a song on the piano? I could really use some change for giggle water."

They looked at one another. "Yeah," one said. "We got another fifteen before we go on again. This bunch don't like choir music, though."

"Drat, and I meant to lead them in a singalong of "Ave Maria.""

This left them laughing. She climbed the steps of the stage, wiped the moisture out of her glass with a napkin, and set it on the piano.

Teddy looked around at the crowd, then struck up "Everybody Stomp". The young people immediately started to dance, while the older ones tapped their toes. She put real flair into her playing, doing flourishes and glissandos.

When she finished, there was clapping. She raised her glass and announced, "Will someone give me a few coins for a drink?"

A young man tossed a few pennies in, and she laughed. "Thank you, kind sir. What would you like to hear?"

"Can you do 'Charley, My Boy'?" the lad asked.

Years spent in speakeasies had made Teddy familiar with a great number of popular songs, so she started right up.

Afterward, more coins landed in her glass. She noticed some older listeners, and launched into "Goodbye Broadway, Hello France", a song from the Great War. This netted her a couple of bills. She played "Over There" while they sang, then realized that her fifteen minutes had passed long ago.

She took some bills from her boodle and handed them to the musicians. "Thank you for the piano rental," she said.

A gentleman from a crowded table waved to her as she waited for her next drink at the bar—another Bees' Knees, which she had decided was delicious. "Come sit with us, ma'am."

Horns announced the beginning of "Bugle Call Blues". Teddy strolled to the table, where a chair had already been stolen for her. The men and women at this table were older than most of the patrons in the club. Her host, the gentleman who had issued the invitation, had hair almost as silver as hers.

"It was a real pleasure to hear you play, Mrs....?"

"Miss. Miss ..." She shouldn't give her full name. "Call me Teddy."

"Okay, Teddy, I'm Ralph Shires. This is Miss Smith, this is Mrs. Akers, that's Mike Hill ... oh, why don't the rest of you introduce yourselves?"

The rest of the people at the table gave their names, sometimes adding compliments on the music. Teddy accepted them gratefully. From the way Ralph spoke for the group, and from the more conservative clothing they wore, she decided that they probably had come directly from a place of work.

"Are you all from the same office?" she asked.

"Yes," Ralph said. "We're having a celebration of sorts tonight."

"A profitable week?"

"Well, yes, but—you may think this is rotten of us, but the owner of our building was the fellow who died in that yacht race, the one in the papers. He was going to sell it, and we were looking for a new place we could afford. Office space downtown costs a king's ransom to rent or buy. Anyway, the son told us today that the sale is off. It's good for us, but bad the way it happened."

Teddy nodded. "They call that serendipity."

"Then let's celebrate the serendipity," Mike Hill said, and raised his glass.

There were more drinks after that, and the company was congenial. It was a shame Cornelia wasn't here with her. She would've enjoyed the war songs. Teddy couldn't go back to the hotel, though. Why was that? Her head was fuzzy.

Her reverie was interrupted by flashing lights and a scramble of customers for the exit.

Alas, there was no secret tunnel in this bar—at least not one she knew of. As the police approached, she tossed down the last of her beverage and held out her hands.

CHAPTER EIGHTEEN

The jail was packed. The surprise raid on the club had come off unusually well, which meant that at least one police employee on Charlie Wall's dole was going to feel his wrath. The patrons had been crammed into the cells with little regard for their personal comfort; the only divisions had been by race and gender.

By the time Joe Knaggs showed up to question his murder suspect, the angry voices of outraged elite and the weeping of first-timers had subsided. The grumbles of cramped prisoners and groans from the hung over had replaced them. He ignored the noises; he'd heard worse from soldiers who had a real reason to complain.

The matron for the women's cells resembled her charges: hair and clothing mussed and grumbling between yawns. Her kohl-rimmed eyes reminded him of the raccoons he'd hunted as a boy. He suspected that the woman slept at her post when the officers weren't around.

"Mrs. Reed," he said sharply, and was rewarded with increased alertness on her part. "I'm here to speak to Miss Theodora Lawless." She would probably be more tractable this morning, after spending a second night in jail. He might even get a confession.

"Miss Lawless, Miss Lawless," The matron ran a finger down the rows of the intake book. There were a great number of new entries since the bust at the club. "Prostitution or public drunkenness?"

"Neither. Murder."

"Oh. She must have come in on Elsie's shift. I'd remember murder."

"I certainly hope so."

The matron clearly remembered something; she suddenly seemed guarded. "It says here that Miss Lawless was released last night."

Knaggs' face became one huge scowl. "What do you mean, she was released? Who released her?"

Mrs. Reed flushed and flipped the book pages back and forth, barely bothering to glance at them. "She was one of Charlie Wall's working women. A guy came to bail them out."

"And you made an assumption that every female was in for one of two things?"

"No," she said. "He told me she was one of the women. A dance instructor for the showgirls."

His eyes narrowed. "One of Wall's men told you that?"

"Yeah, a Cuban guy. He paid for her bail."

"I want to see the sheet," Knaggs said. "I want his name, who else left with her, the whole shebang."

"I'm looking. Things got hot after midnight in here," she said.

"Dingbat," Knaggs muttered. He paced as he waited. This case had been a headache from the beginning. Each time he had things in order, one of them moved. Mostly that Lawless woman; she seemed to be a bundle of contradictions.

When his path took him past the cells stuffed with the no longer ossified female patrons of the Candlelight Club, a familiar voice called out.

"Good morning, Detective Knaggs! Are you here to grill me again?"

He stopped in his tracks and stared. "There you are!" How had he missed her in that crowd? She was the only woman in the cell with silver hair, and, more importantly, the only one who was smiling. If anything, she looked more cheerful than when he had put her in.

"Stop looking," he shouted to the matron. "She's in with the drunks."

"Oh, oh, yes!" the matron replied quickly. "It must have been a different lady the guy bailed out. The officers put the newcomers in her cell because we ran out of room. I must have gotten my paperwork confused. But there she is."

There she is, Knaggs thought. *Now, what to do with her?*

Percival awoke early Friday morning. He shut off all three of his alarm clocks, which were set for eight a.m. Much as he wished Saint Petersburg had provided a true vacation, it really hadn't. Yesterday's disappointing finds made today's that much more important.

During the night, the solution had come to him in a dream, like so many mechanical solutions had. Go to Sarasota and find the Rena woman. Convince her to come back with him to testify on Teddy's behalf, and set Teddy free. Cornelia would be so pleased with this, that she would surely forgive him for stealing her car.

He collected the newspaper articles he had saved concerning Teddy, and tucked a picture of Teddy and Cornelia in his pocket. These would be necessary for persuasion, since he didn't expect her to take an unknown man, however charming, at his word.

Now for the note to his niece. Whatever he wrote would infuriate her, that he knew. But how happy she would be if he returned with a witness to Teddy's innocence! Perhaps he should awaken Cornelia and invite her to come along, but she really needed to work on accruing information and evidence here, especially if he was unable to find the woman from the hat shop. No sense in wasting both their days.

Dearest Cornelia:
Please accept my apologies in advance for borrowing your car. I have left for Sarasota to search for Rena, our best witness for Teddy's time apart from us last Saturday. I'm leaving you some money

He stopped, checked his wallet, and set some bills on the table beside the couch in the sitting room.

I'm leaving you some money for the trolley, and for expenses you may incur during your investigation today. I recommend that you work backward from the incident on the yacht and focus on the captain's cap. Where did our Mystery Woman acquire it? I suggest beginning with specialty shops and men's stores. If necessary, visit the Yacht Club. Technically, I was banned, not you.

Proving our Theodora innocent is only half of the equation, of course. If you have time, look further into motives for the Stevens family members. I presume it is one of the women; neither Mac nor Mr. Downs are of proper proportion to wear such a disguise.

This note was running a little longer than he had planned, but it would provide her with multiple avenues of action.

He left it on the table next to the money and slipped out the door.

Once he was downstairs, he went to the dining room and persuaded the hostess to provide him with a cup of coffee and an egg sandwich. He dealt with the meal quickly, watching the entrances for signs of an irate Cornelia. Afterwards, he went to the valet station and requested that they bring "the family's" Dodge Touring Sedan.

His first stop was the hat shop. The Berber's sign still hung above the store, but there was a placard in the front window announcing, "Under New Management". It wasn't open yet, but he could see movement inside. A woman was putting things in order for the new day. He tapped on the window, which brought no response. He tried knocking on the door next, and then rapping on the jamb with his cane.

The woman inside realized that the man outside, who resembled Santa Claus, was not going to leave, so she came to the door and indicated the 'Closed' card.

"My dear lady, it is most urgent that I speak to someone here."

The young woman gave him a dimpled smile. "We're not open for another hour. Please come then."

His response was to take a ten-dollar bill and press it against the glass.

Her eyes widened. "Are you going to a wedding this morning or something?"

"No, but I desperately need your assistance."

She relented and opened the door.

He entered and pressed the bill into her hand. "Thank you. I'm afraid that a member of my club passed away last night, and I need to contact his niece. His name was Donnelly, but hers wasn't. I don't know what it is, but I believe she works here. She's called Rena. I don't know if that's for Irene or Renata."

"I'm afraid that Rena doesn't work here any longer, sir. My father took over the store last week from the previous owner." She rubbed the bill with her thumb. "I'm not sure I can help you. Do you want your money back?"

"If you, or your father, could help me contact the owner, you would still be of great assistance to me."

After acquiring the phone number and address for Francis Berber, previous owner of Berber's Hats, he headed there post haste. It was not necessary to crassly offer money to the newly-retired shopkeeper; the man was glad to help. The woman's name was Rena Orlov, and she had left Saint Petersburg. He didn't know exactly where she had moved to, but a shop in Sarasota had contacted him about her references. Pettijohn collected the information Berber provided, and thanked him effusively for his assistance.

Lafferty had mentioned a ferry to Bradenton. He discovered that the *Fred B. Doty* had an accommodating schedule and purchased passage for himself and the automobile on the paddlewheel steamer. Watching the flatbed barge make the crossing reminded him of younger days. It was much like the one the Army used to transport their surveillance balloon up and down the Potomac during the War Between the States.

He pushed those thoughts aside. This was no time to be drifting down a river of memories. There was a lady in need of rescue. He had to focus on Miss Teddy, who was now his fiancée, and the task at hand. During the wait for the launch, he was able to get directions to Sarasota from Piney Point, the landing dock on the other end of the trip.

The ferry ride granted a sweeping view of the bay. The waters near the shore were a rich turquoise and beryl, deepening to a sparkling cobalt when they passed the tip of Pinellas County. Pettijohn used his niece's field glasses to study what remained of Fort DeSoto in the distance. Small sailboats floated nearby, carrying fishermen and pleasure seekers alike. The breeze coming off the water was cool, but the sunshine countered it nicely. Once the mess with the deceased Mr. Stevens was straightened out, this would be a pleasant place to spend the rest of the winter.

Cornelia awoke much later than she had planned. She did her ablutions in the bathroom, got dressed, and entered the shared sitting room, ready for action. Uncle Percival wasn't there; he had probably gone to breakfast without her. How considerate of him to let her sleep a little later!

After reading the letter, she revised her opinion. Sneaky little—he'd left her to do the hard work while he took a pleasant drive in the country. And when he arrived in Sarasota, he'd have the circus to play with, too. Meanwhile, he'd left her with a chore she could do, as if she were his assistant instead of his niece. And using the term 'our' Theodora! Fuming, Cornelia went downstairs to get smaller bills than the ones her uncle had left. Then, she went to breakfast. She wasn't hungry, but she had a lot of walking ahead of her.

Evelyn circled the block, waiting for Cornelia Pettijohn to leave the hotel. The elderly uncle hadn't been with her in the dining room this morning—perhaps he was tired from yesterday's adventures, especially when they didn't end well. Lafferty had been all apologies when Evelyn showed him the photo of the arrest with the Pettijohns in the background. No, he would never have assisted the professor if he'd known he was helping her father's killer. He would definitely have words with the scheming old man that evening.

Today, she was better prepared for trailing those who would obstruct justice. Evelyn had ordered her father's car from the valet, and she'd borrowed her mother's opera glasses—was it still borrowing if she hadn't bothered to ask, but knew her mother wasn't going to be using them? She also had two pimiento cheese sandwiches in a bag in case she needed sustenance during her monitoring of the Pettijohn family.

Even better, she had a companion to pass the time. Arthur had his business to run, but Bobby Hornbuckle had nothing better to do than follow people around and gather information. Their goals weren't the same, but she was more than happy to let Bobby have the scoop in exchange for help. She had to prevent those nosy Pettijohns from muddying the waters. The Lawless woman killed her father. Evelyn was going to make sure she paid dearly for her crime.

Professor Pettijohn stopped to get gasoline at a service station near Sarasota, where bold signs informed him that he was buying Krimsun Gas, colored red for easy identification. While the attendant was busy with the Dodge, he purchased a Squeeze soda and asked the man inside if he had a map of the city for sale.

"I'm sorry that we don't, sir. Are you needing directions to a place in particular? I have a map you can look at. Are you here to see the circus?"

"Not on this visit, I'm sorry to say. But I would be most obliged if you would let me see your map."

"I should warn you," the man said, "that there's new places that aren't on here. They keep building." The man produced a well-worn map and spread it out for Pettijohn to see. The professor studied the map, memorizing it for future use. He was searching for a woman he'd never met in a city he'd never seen and needed all the information he could get.

"It's still more than I had, young man. Thank you for your assistance."

The drive into Sarasota took him past herds of cattle and sprouting farm fields. Strawberry fields and broccoli seedlings reminded him in some ways of Kentucky, but swamp land, sand pines, and cabbage palms prevented the illusion from being complete. Brackish backwater from the mouth of the Manatee River formed a birding paradise. He felt a twinge of guilt for taking both Cornelia's automobile and her field glasses. His poor niece had envisioned their Florida trip as days of birdwatching and peaceful walks on the waterfront. Her leave was near its end, and she hadn't had peace or rest.

Once he was past the river, he started seeing more farms. Before long, he began passing houses and shops, indicating his nearness to a population center. He began cross-referencing the street signs with the names from the map and found his way into downtown Sarasota.

La Mode, located on Main Street, was the milliner's shop that had checked Rena's references. With luck, she would be working there.

He was without luck. The manager told him that they had hired a different applicant. The professor considered this unfair, given the trouble he'd gone to so far.

He gave the manager the same story he'd given to Berber, about the death in Rena's family and his need to locate her.

The woman relented and located Rena Orlov's application. "She was staying with a friend at the Frances-Carlton Apartments. It's not hard to find them—head west on Main Street and turn right on Palm. You might be able to make inquiries there."

Pettijohn, who could read upside down, already had the street address and apartment number. Sadly, there was no telephone information. He offered his thanks and left.

This is a fool's errand, Cornelia thought, *and I'm just the fool to do it*. She'd visited store after store during Teddy's expedition, but now she was looking for one blade of grass in a field of feminine wheat. She started with the concierge station, where she had to plead her case to a day man that was well acquainted with the notoriety Teddy had heaped on the hotel. She explained that her uncle had tasked her with finding a captain's cap while he conducted business in Sarasota. It was close enough to the truth.

The gentleman looked skeptical, but provided her with a few suggestions, including the Yacht Club. She requested additional information about local men's stores and haberdasheries, leading to the displeasure of waiting guests who had come to the Vinoy for simple tourism. Cornelia ignored them and dutifully recorded the names and locations, giving the concierge a hefty tip afterward for his consideration.

Cornelia exited the hotel and crossed to the trolley stop. She boarded and took a seat, placing her purse in her lap. She did not hear the car start nearby and pull away from the curb. Nor did she see the Roadster that crept out of its hiding place under the trees of Vinoy Park, trailing behind her intrepid trackers.

The Frances-Carlton Apartments were built in the Mediterranean style with a Spanish flair, like most of the newer buildings he'd seen since arriving in Florida. The stucco was darker than most, though, trimmed in white. He crossed the lawn and explored until he'd figured out the numbering system. Bringing his cane had been a wise decision—he'd done a good deal of walking and standing the last few days.

He located the right apartment and knocked on the door. He waited.

No answer, but he could hear some sort of noise from inside.

Pettijohn pulled his hearing device out of his pocket and held it against the wood. A Victrola played strains of "Nobody's Sweetheart Now." The tinny recording accompanied by an off-key version of the tune emanated from the apartment. He knocked again.

Still no answer. Perhaps the gusto of the singer muffled the sound of his knock. If he could hear the music over her rendition of the song, the volume was likely set as high as the Victrola would go.

He pocketed the device and walked around the bushes to one of the arched windows. It gave him a view of a pleasant sitting room with chairs and a pink sofa. No people, though.

The professor tapped the glass, but he saw no movement in response.

The next window, around the corner of the building, was less broad and possibly belonged to a kitchen. He didn't see anyone, so he continued along the wall.

The curtains were drawn together at the next window, and the music had become louder. He might have to rap rather loudly to draw attention to himself. Then, something crunchy hit him in the back.

"I knew it!" the woman said when he turned around. She was nearly as tall as him, slightly gawky, and armed with a broom. "What are you doing peeping into my window, you degenerate lout?"

"I was not peeping!" the professor protested. "I was looking for the person who resides here!"

"And you found her, didn't you?" She swung the broom, and he blocked it with his cane. "You should be ashamed of yourself, spying on defenseless women!"

"You seem far from defenseless, madam!" the elderly professor retorted as he blocked another blow and considered making a break for it. Unfortunately, she was much younger than he was. Worse, she was driving him into a recess between the buildings.

"Please, Miss Orlov, I implore you"—he ducked—"to listen to me! I came to see you on a matter of great importance!"

She stepped back and rested the broom on her shoulder. "Miss Orlov? You came here for Rena?"

"Yes," he said, puffing. He realized that this was not the woman he was looking for and surmised she must be the friend Rena was staying with. "We desperately need her help."

"Shouldn't you know what she looks like, if you need her help?"

"It would have helped," he replied, "but I wasn't shopping for hats that day. Is she here?"

"She's working at Cecelia's on Main Street."

"My apologies, then." He bent and picked up his fedora, which had gone flying after the first blow. "Please let me leave in peace, and I shall try not to trouble you again."

She let him pass but shouted at his retreating backside. "Tell Rena that I expect a full explanation of why you came here—and I still think you were peeping!"

CHAPTER NINETEEN

Cornelia had been assigned the wrong job. She drew stares whenever she entered a men's store, even glares, as if she were a German soldier entering a Parisian shop. Most of the visits were mercifully short. The men's stores downtown tended to leave the sale of captain's caps to the Yacht Club, and she received that recommendation again and again.

Excitement stirred in her when she saw a shop window on Second Street that displayed captain's caps. She strode in, ignoring the surprise she'd become accustomed to generating.

"I'm interested in a recent sale you may have had," she said to one of the workers, indicating the window.

"Oh, the sale's still on, ma'am," the young man said. "Which hat do you think your husband would fancy?"

Cornelia tried to turn her grimace into a smile. "My niece gave my husband a captain's cap for his birthday, but it isn't in his size. I'm trying to find out where she purchased it, so we can make an exchange."

"She didn't tell you where she got it?"

"No, I'm afraid not. And she left on the train to Kentucky this morning. After she departed, my husband decided that it was too tight. We don't want to hurt her feelings by letting her know we had to exchange it."

"Oh, I see. How long ago?"

"Probably last week. I really wish she'd asked me his hat size." The lies were coming more easily now; visiting Florida was eroding her moral standards. Either that, or it was the company she was keeping these days.

"Yes, that would have been best. I don't think I've sold anything to a woman recently, but I can ask the manager. Could you describe your niece?"

No, I need you *to describe her*, she thought. "She's tall," Cornelia said, remembering the news accounts. "Fair-haired. She got a new bob last week, so I can't tell you how long it was."

The young man toddled off to speak to his superior; when he returned, the manager was with him.

"The police were in earlier this week asking about a woman who purchased a captain's hat," he said. "Their description was similar. Why are you asking?"

A word from the barracks flitted through her mind, but she didn't say it. "I'm asking on my own behalf. I would be happy to compensate you for your trouble."

"Out," he said. "Out of my shop. We have seen no such woman."

Cornelia left, cheeks reddened with humiliation.

The Pettijohn woman scrambled away from the men's store. Her face was red; something had embarrassed her. Maybe she'd learned something uncomplimentary about her aunt-to-be. Evelyn slid her remaining sandwich back into its bag.

"Those Pettijohns are a dogged pair, I have to grant them that."

"I feel sorry for the niece," Bobby said. "I learned that she served with Theodora Lawless for a long time. They must have been great friends before the engagement; otherwise, I doubt she would go to so much trouble now."

"Sweet little Teddy is using both her and the old coot to weasel out of this. She knew Daddy would set that professor straight. He's been in his ivory tower so long that anything in a dress would turn his head."

"I beg to differ," Bobby replied. "I also did a little research on Professor Pettijohn, and he's been in jail a number of times."

Evelyn lifted one carefully shaped eyebrow. "Really? Whatever for? Boring someone to death?"

"Usually for disturbing the peace. He's an inventor of sorts." Bobby leaned closer. "But he was recently released from the jail in Inverness. A land agent was killed, and he was the main suspect."

"He was suspected of murder?"

"Ab-so-lute-ly. They arrested someone else, but she was a chum of the family. Miss Cornelia even organized a letter writing effort to persuade the governor to grant clemency."

Evelyn raised the glasses to inspect their prey again. "I didn't think he had it in him. Maybe he and his fiancée kill people for fun. What about the niece?"

"She's been in the Army all this time. Awarded all sorts of medals."

"Maybe she's the white sheep," Evelyn said.

Both women giggled, hands covering their mouths.

The next shopkeeper had the impertinence to ask Cornelia why she hadn't tried the Yacht Club first, and she retorted that they didn't have all sizes in stock. He made the most useful suggestion then: why not check with the yacht dealers? A captain's cap would be a nice additional sale.

She thanked him with real gratitude and walked out.

The niece was on the street again and checking a trolley schedule. Evelyn lowered the opera glasses and restarted the car.

"Maybe she's giving up for the day; an old lady like her must be exhausted after all that walking."

"She's wearing the right shoes for it," Bobby said. "Although those Oxfords are a few years out of date."

"They go with that bag," Evelyn sneered. "It's almost big enough to be a vanity case, not that I've ever seen her made up. Her pal Teddy is the face stretcher."

Bobby took the opera glasses and peered through them. "Heavy leather; looks sturdy. I think it might be Army issue."

"She marched through Paris with that and no one said anything?"

Both women covered their mouths to muffle their laughs. A trolley rolled to the nearby stop and Cornelia

Pettijohn got on. When it began moving again, Evelyn prodded the sedan into motion. The women were too intent on their surveillance of Cornelia to notice that when they passed the Manhattan Market, the Roadster fell in behind them again.

Cornelia's trolley turned north, but she got off at the corner and walked across the street to wait for a southbound one. Evelyn turned onto a side street to keep from being spotted. The two women circled the block and found a parking spot with a clear view of the trolley stop.

"That was close," Bobby said as she fished around in the floor of the sedan to find the opera glasses. "Wonder where she's headed this time?"

Evelyn shook her head. "No men's stores this way. Maybe she's headed back to the yacht club. They'll have her ears burning if she goes there again."

They didn't have much time to speculate. Cornelia caught the next car and was headed down Bayshore.

Mitch hung back and gave his rival reporter time to trail Cornelia before pulling from the alley he'd ducked into. He still didn't know why Bobby was dogging Cornelia. He liked the strong-jawed woman, but couldn't think of anyone less interesting for the society pages. Still, if that poodle Bobby wanted to pretend to be a bloodhound, he'd better keep an eye on her.

Cornelia got off in the area near the new port. There were half a dozen businesses selling boats of one sort or another. The light had begun to slant over the waves, but she wouldn't stop until she found someone who could identify the mystery woman. Teddy's life might depend on it, even if Uncle Percival did find the woman from Berber's. She pushed open the door of the nearest dealer, took a deep breath, and walked in.

She was repeating her gift story for what seemed like the umpteenth time when she heard:

"As I live and breathe, it's the Iron Petticoat!"

Cornelia turned to see a man limping towards her. Something about him was familiar, but he was heavy-set and too gray-haired for her to place him immediately. Then, she saw the scar on his temple, and it fell into place.

She smiled for what felt like the first time in a year. "Corporal Farrell? It's been such a long time."

He grinned. "Sergeant Farrell by the time I retired. It's been a long time since I was under your care in Cuba."

"Yes, it has. You seem to have picked up a new injury when I wasn't watching."

Farrell's mouth pursed in confusion, then relaxed. "Oh, yes. I was part of the Railway Regiment at Cambrai, and we were called to the front. Got trench foot first thing and was mustered out. Are you still serving?"

"Yes, it is Captain Pettijohn these days. Now that Congress has decided to grant nurses pensions based on years of service though, I've decided to retire. I'll be mustering out myself in a few months."

"And your friend, Nurse Teddy? Did she marry that captain that was chasing her, or is she still serving, too?"

"She served through most the Great War. She was gassed at Verdun and had to retire on a disability pension."

"I'm terribly sorry. She was such a nice woman, and such gusto. Being around her cheered everybody up. How is she doing now?"

He'd given her the perfect opening. "She's here, but she's in a lot of trouble, Sergeant Farrell. I could use your help."

"She's been in there for some time," Evelyn said. "It's almost dark. Do you think there's another exit? Maybe she's tumbled onto us."

"I think one of us would have spotted her leaving," Bobby replied. "She's hard to miss. Maybe she's tumbled onto something else."

Cornelia sat in the office of the dealership while Corporal—no, Sergeant—Farrell made phone calls. She warmed her hands with a mug of coffee. It was awful enough for Army fare, which was strangely comforting.

"Hello, Tommy? This is Elmer over at Farrell Brothers' Yachts. I'm looking for a lady who bought a captain's cap maybe ten days ago. Oh, well, that woman is here. I know her, and she's jake. She's an Army nurse. Anyone you didn't mention? Thanks, I'll let you get back to it."

Wars were strange; they separated some people but drew others together. Farrell's life had been in their hands decades ago, but he hadn't forgotten. She remembered his young face, not so different from the doughboys she'd tended in the Great War, and the good heart he'd clearly never lost.

The sergeant was gesturing to her now. "When was she in? Friday before last? Wait, I want to have Captain Pettijohn speak to you."

The old nurse was at his side in seconds. He gave her the earpiece, and she leaned in to speak. "Hello, this is Cornelia Pettijohn."

"This is Ralph Mercer from Westshore Yachts. I had a woman buy a captain's cap Friday before last. She said it was a birthday gift. Knew the size and everything."

"Did it have the burgee of the Yacht Club on it?"

"Yes. We sew them on to a few of the caps we sell. Sort of a little something extra to sweeten the deal for members."

Cornelia swallowed before asking her next question. "Could you describe this woman?"

"Let's see. She was around thirty, bleached hair, dressed nice. Pretty tall."

"Anything else?"

"There was a little gap between her front teeth, but not bad. Made her look a little saucy, which she probably was going for."

Definitely *not* Evelyn. There was only one person she'd met that the man's description would fit, but Cornelia had no idea why she would want to hurt Teddy. Evelyn must have enlisted her help. Was she a knowing or unknowing accomplice? "Thank you, Mr. Mercer. You've been most helpful."

Farrell made the goodbyes.

Cornelia clasped his hand and smiled with gratitude and relief. "You've been a lifesaver, Sergeant. I don't think I could have gotten this far without you. Would you mind if I called the Vinoy?"

Farrell's cheeks pinkened. "No problem, ma'am."

Uncle Percival still wasn't back from his sojourn south. She left a message for him with the concierge, stating that she needed to speak to Miss Rivers again before returning to the hotel. Then, Cornelia filled out one of the cards on Farrell's desk and handed it to him.

"This is the number of the Vinoy. We're registered there under the name of my uncle, Percival Pettijohn. Below that is the number of Morgan Cosgrove, who is serving as Teddy's attorney. If you don't hear from me by tomorrow afternoon, please try reaching one of them."

"If I don't hear from you? Do you need for me to accompany you?" the sergeant asked.

She laughed. "No, I've spoken to this woman before. Chasing my uncle down, that's another matter."

Evelyn was relieved to see Miss Pettijohn leave the dealer's office. She and Bobby were casualties of the fading sun; day gloves were no match for the damp air near the docks.

"Finally," she said, and started the car. Their target boarded the next trolley, which was heading in the wrong direction for the hotel.

"What's she up to now?" Bobby said, rubbing her hands together.

"I don't know. Something's given her a second wind."

Cornelia disembarked at the stop near the Stevens Building, and walked briskly towards its entrance. It was twilight, and many of the nearby businesses were already closed. Luck was on Cornelia's side, though. She discovered that the entrance was still unlocked, although the lobby was quiet and dimly lit.

The blinds were drawn across the interior and exterior windows of the real estate brokerage that dominated the first floor. She peeked between two displaced slats. The flyers on display had been neatly arranged for the following day, and there were no people visible. Nearby, the card shop was also closed for the evening. She undid the flap of her military purse before venturing further into the building.

Cornelia approached the only source of light remaining: the interior of the Movie Star Gallery. The sinks were spotless and gleaming, the combs and shears were clean and organized in neat rows at each station. She didn't see anyone inside at first, but then the door to the small office opened and Lucy emerged. The younger woman carried a deposit bag and was already in her jacket.

She didn't know yet how Lucy Rivers was involved with Ansel's death, but she would find out. Perhaps Evelyn had asked Lucy to pick up the cap as a surprise for her husband-to-be. By now, though, Lucy would have deduced that she'd been used to purchase the murder weapon. Why hadn't she told the police? Did she hope to have a hold over the heirs?

It was simpler and more sensible to conclude that Lucy herself was the killer.

She regretted declining the sergeant's offer to come with her; two against one would have been much more intimidating. It couldn't be helped now, though, and the young woman inside the salon had already noticed her.

Cornelia knocked on the door.

Lucy put the day's receipts in her purse down and scowled. "The salon is closed," she said, raising her voice. "Please come tomorrow."

"It's Cornelia Pettijohn, Miss Rivers. I need to speak with you again."

The tall blonde—tall like the woman in Gene Cross' description—came to the door and gave her a pretty smile through the glass. "I really can't help you further, ma'am. And it's a little late to be calling, if I say so myself."

"I agree, but it can't be helped. Someone dear to me is in trouble, and you're the only one who can save her."

"You're talking nonsense."

"Am I? I know who bought that captain's cap. Let me in, or I'll call the police."

Lucy sighed and undid the lock. She was no longer smiling.

Cornelia entered, circling to keep a distance between them. "Thank you kindly."

Lucy moved behind the counter and began taking off her jacket. "Tell me what you mean about calling the police."

"You purchased the cap that killed Mr. Stevens. The clerk described you quite well. I also suspect that the watchman at the marina might be able to identify you as the mystery woman who put it on the Stevens' yacht."

"Maybe." Lucy laid the jacket over the chair where her open purse rested. When she turned back around, she had a Brownie pocket pistol in her hand. "But there are a number of blondes in this town."

This was what she got for pressing on instead of being sensible. She wasn't dead, though, so Lucy wasn't ready to shoot yet. Cornelia decided to draw her out. "Why did you dress like Teddy?"

"Oh. It wasn't out of personal malice. I couldn't be me, so I had to pick someone else."

"Why her? As far as I know, she's never met you."

The salon owner gave her a tight-lipped smile. "She came into the shop, and Evelyn said she'd struck Ansel. I figured she had a good reason. She was shorter, but her build wasn't that different from my own."

"Do you realize how much heartache you've caused us?" Cornelia snapped. "Teddy could easily be put to death before it's all over."

"I'm sorry, but better her than me. Besides, she could have had an alibi. I take it that she didn't have an alibi?"

"Innocent people don't work on creating alibis."

"Maybe they should. If she'd had one, we wouldn't be in this situation now."

"Yes, this is inconvenient for both of us," Cornelia said, "but more so for me than you." She dove for the corner where the counter turned at an L angle and reached into her purse for her sidearm.

"I don't understand why she'd come here," Evelyn said, staring at her father's darkened building. "It's after hours. There's no one to talk to."

Bobby Hornbuckle, face visible in the streetlights, gave her a sidelong glance. "Maybe she's searching his office."

"Oh, no, she's not!" Ansel's daughter cried, and flung the car door open. "That's going too far!"

She ran towards the double door entrance, with Bobby close behind.

They stopped short when they heard the gunshots.

Lucy sprinted around the far side of the counter. Cornelia scrambled over the closest salon chair and took cover behind the sink.

Chunks of porcelain flew when the younger woman fired the tiny pistol.

The old nurse popped up, squeezing off her own shot. It missed Lucy and hit a poster of Gloria Swanson, blacking out the front teeth in the picture.

Each woman scuttled to new positions. Cornelia crouched beside a cabinet of shampoos, and Lucy concealed herself behind an enormous hairdryer that resembled a cannon.

Cornelia waited for Lucy's next move. When she heard the clatter of heels, she lunged forward, pistol in hand, to discover that only the shoes were in the open. She instinctively dropped to the floor, toppling a permanent wave machine on top of her.

A sharp report from the Brownie cracked the window above the old nurse.

"Now look what you made me do!" an unshod Lucy cried, and advanced, pushing the dryer before her like a battering ram.

Cornelia crawled for the exit, but found her legs tangled in the wires and rollers that hung underneath the machine's frame, like tentacles under a jellyfish.

"Call the police," Bobby commanded, and sprinted for the building, pulling out her camera.

Evelyn turned, looking for the nearest café or open shop, and saw a man running across the street towards her. He was vaguely familiar; she didn't remember his name, but he was one of the reporters that had crowded around her family at the hospital. Unlike Bobby, he was armed.

"Call the police!" he also commanded, continuing his sprint towards the same entrance Bobby Hornbuckle was using.

"I got it the first time!" Evelyn cried, and headed for the Hotel Detroit.

Lucy peeked around the side of the dryer and saw Cornelia's predicament. She pointed her pistol at Cornelia, and Cornelia pointed the service weapon back at her. Instead of escaping like a sensible person, though, Lucy circled round to the electric cord of the wave machine and plugged it in.

"Now, Miss Nosy Parker, you're going to get it one way or another. Who have you been gossiping to about me?"

They continued to level their weapons at each other, but Cornelia felt the rollers touching her legs begin to warm up. She rolled on her back and tried using her free hand to pull the cords away. Her fingers met hot metal, and she jerked them away with a cry. Lucy laughed, and Cornelia glared up at her.

"The man at Westshore Yachts can identify you," the nurse said. "I told him and Sergeant—a sergeant I tended during a war. I also told my uncle who you were, and where I was going. I told all of them."

"Bushwa," Lucy said. "If any of those men had known you were coming here alone, they would have insisted on coming. And only a Dumb Dora would have come here on her own."

Then call me Dora, Cornelia thought.

CHAPTER TWENTY

Cornelia was absent when the professor returned to the hotel with the missing Miss Orlov. The message she left cheered him, though; she must have found a lead on the mystery woman. Soon Theodora would be free, and things could return to normal. In the meantime, he and his passenger needed refreshment. It had been a long trip back from Sarasota.

He took his guest to the dining room, where they demolished a tray of stuffed celery, radishes, and crab salad. Cornelia still hadn't returned when they finished, so Percival decided to contact their attorney and speed matters along. He obtained a separate room for his guest, then requested the courtesy phone.

A flash and bang echoed in the room. At first, Cornelia assumed she'd been shot, but Lucy was pointing the gun somewhere else. Bobby Hornbuckle was in the doorway, camera in hand.

Cornelia took advantage of the distraction and yanked on the device till the electric plug came loose from the wall. Pain seared through her legs where the rollers touched, and the air smelled of scorched fabric, burned flesh, and magnesium powder. She pulled the cords away, freeing herself.

The camera lay abandoned by the door. Lucy was chasing Bobby around the room. The reporter took refuge behind the counter and began flinging glass bottles from a storage cabinet. Several broke, and the stench of chemicals was added to the layers of odor already in the salon.

"Stop! Leave her alone!" Mitch Grant was in the doorway, aiming his own weapon.

The salon owner countered with her own weapon. "Get out of here!"

"Not a chance!" he said, shooting one of the sinks. Water gushed forth from a pulverized pipe. "Put down that peashooter!"

Her response was gunfire.

Mitch yelped and dropped. He dragged himself back through the doorway and behind it.

Cornelia drew a bead on Lucy, but Bobby stepped in the way. "You witch!" she cried, thumping her with one of the handheld dryers.

Lucy stumbled, stepped on glass shards with her stockinged feet, and shrieked. She spun round and went down. Bobby jumped on top of her and wrenched the Brownie away, pointing it at Lucy's face.

"Hold her there," Cornelia commanded. "I'll see to Mitch."

Mitch leaned against the wall, pressing a handkerchief against his side. "I see Bobby took care of her."

"Yes, she has. Hairdryers are more formidable than I thought. Let me examine you," she said, pulling his hand away. From what Cornelia could see through the rip in the shirt, the wound wasn't bleeding too badly, but no shot to the abdomen could be trusted.

The front entrance opened, and Evelyn entered the lobby. She saw them and rushed over. "What happened?"

"I dropped in to have my hair done," Cornelia retorted, "but the salon was closed."

If Mr. Cosgrove was unhappy to be dragged from his home on a Friday evening, he didn't show it. Detective Knaggs was slightly less enchanted. He looked as tired as the professor felt. A day of hammering iron into plow blades would have been easier.

"You couldn't have come back from Sarasota quicker?" the detective grumbled.

"My apologies, sir, but we did have to wait for the ferry," Uncle Percival replied, omitting the snack he and Rena had shared at the Vinoy. What the police didn't know wouldn't make them angry.

"Well, let's get to it," Knaggs said. "Miss Orlov, did this gentleman, Theodora Lawless, or any agents of theirs pay you to come make this statement today—tonight?"

"No," Rena said. "If you doubt that she came into the store, I'm sure Mr. Berber still has the copies of the day's receipts."

Percival suppressed a smile as Rena sweetly gave her account of Teddy's visit to the shop.

The feeling didn't last.

"Would you repeat the time at which Miss Lawless left the shop?" Knaggs asked, a light glowing behind his eyes.

The small woman blinked. "Around three. It was a slow day and the conversation was pleasant."

"And she left your shop?"

"Yes."

"Which was located where?"

"It's on First, near Central."

"Not that far from the marina," the detective mused aloud. The professor was sure it was aloud for his benefit.

Rena looked from one man to the other, confusion dawning on her elfin face. "Is there a problem?"

"Did Miss Lawless purchase any men's hats?"

"We don't sell men's hats. She purchased three ladies' hats, one of which I believe was for someone else."

"My niece, Cornelia," Percival said.

Knaggs turned and gave him the evil eye. "No comments during the statement. I believe there might still be a sufficient time gap for Miss Lawless to visit the Stevens' yacht. The watchman said he couldn't pinpoint the time."

"Theodora wasn't wearing a cloche hat when we returned from golfing," the professor pressed.

"She could have worn one of her new hats," Knaggs retorted.

"She wore the sun hat with the jacaranda blossoms out of the store," Rena said. "I wrapped up her old hat with her other purchases. She didn't buy a cloche hat."

"You should have Mr. Cross come down," Pettijohn said. "He could probably tell you that Theodora isn't the one he saw at the marina."

Knaggs pointed at the door. "Professor—please go sit in the waiting room. This is difficult enough without your interference."

The old man flushed, making him look more like Santa Claus than usual. "I need to be here to represent Theodora's interests."

"No, that's what Mr. Cosgrove is here for," Knaggs said.

Percival began to reply but was interrupted by a loud thump on the door. Duncan popped his head in.

"Joe. There's been a hullabaloo at the Stevens building, and Patrol is bringing in some of the people from our case."

One of the officers took Mitch to the hospital, over his objections. This was a big story, and now Bobby would get it instead.

Cornelia applied cool wet compresses to her burns. The stink of chemicals permeated the salon. Her eyes watered, but compared to mustard gas, it was nothing. The young officer who arrested her had been kind enough to raid the salon supplies after he saw her legs. It wasn't Dakin's Solution, but it would have to do.

The battle had dealt scars elsewhere. Cornelia had leg burns and scorch marks in several places on her dress, but Lucy had received worse. The fluids for bleaching and creating permanent waves in hair had created great welts on the salon owner's cut feet and calves. Once the police had things under control, the old nurse had quickly advised them to let both Lucy and Bobby wash their exposed skin, but nothing could be done about the back of Lucy's clothing. She had been taken to hospital wearing nothing but a beautician's smock.

"You came here because you believed she killed someone. Why didn't you call the police?" the young man asked, looking over his notes.

"Because your precious Detective Knaggs already had my companion in custody. You would have dismissed me."

"So, you decided to apprehend her yourself? With the assistance of two reporters?"

She shook her head. "I came here to interview her, not apprehend her. The reporters were not assisting me, although they have both been enthusiastically pursuing story leads. They showed up in time to save me."

"You acted alone."

"Yes. Bad planning on my part. I thought Miss Stevens was the killer at the time, and Miss Rivers was merely an accomplice. Trust me, I regret my error."

Evelyn, who was perched on one of the nearby client chairs, scowled. "You're ridiculous. Why would I kill my own father?"

Cornelia met her eyes. "Because family members often have grievances, whether known to others or not. Your sister had an obvious motive, but you were the one determined to railroad Teddy for the crime." *I was equally convinced of your guilt, and I was wrong.*

"Because she did it!" Evelyn cried. "My father had some backward ideas about Harry, but she's the one who hated him. She was going to get away with it."

"I can't argue with your assessment of Teddy's feelings," the old nurse said, "but she's had thirty years to plot a better murder than this."

I can kiss my pension goodbye.

CHAPTER TWENTY-ONE

Teddy squealed when they pushed Cornelia into the cell. "Sweetie! I'm so glad you're here. I missed you!"

"Don't call me 'sweetie' in front of the guards. They'll separate us." She sat down on the bench and groaned.

Teddy plopped down beside her and stared at the bandages on her legs. "What happened? Did you get into a catfight with that evil Evelyn?"

"No, I was almost sentenced to death by permanent wave machine. Don't touch those; I feel lucky to have received care before they hauled me off."

"I'll have my attorney see about having a doctor visit in the morning. It's so wonderful to be with you again."

Cornelia was glad that one of them was happy.

Teddy tittered.

"What's so funny?"

She pointed at the scorch marks on Cornelia's skirt. "You said you weren't going to burn that dress. So, what *did* happen?"

A familiar male voice interrupted. "That's what I'd like to know." Detective Knaggs stood outside the cell. Behind him were Officer Duncan, Uncle Percival, Mr. Cosgrove, and a strange small woman.

"I see the circus has arrived," Cornelia grumbled.

"Yes, and it's sitting in a cell," Knaggs snapped. "You trespassed in the Stevens Building after it closed and got into a shooting match with the sole person unlucky enough to still be there."

"I did not trespass—" Cornelia began, but Cosgrove stepped forward. "Miss Pettijohn, not another word. Your uncle has engaged me to represent you as well as Miss Lawless."

"You three should all be named Lawless," Knaggs muttered.

Cosgrove requested that he be left alone with his new client. At Teddy's insistence, he agreed to let her remain if she didn't interrupt. Uncle Percival, however, was shooed away. As Cornelia gave him her account of events, he began pressing his fingers to his temple. She wondered if he were prone to headaches.

"You went there to 'interview' her? For what purpose?"

"To see what she knew. I had discovered where and by whom the captain's cap was purchased. I was convinced— wrongly, I realize now—that Evelyn had killed her father and used Miss Rivers to procure the murder weapon."

"In other words, you were investigating the crime yourself. Miss Pettijohn, such matters should be left to the police or private agents."

The old nurse puffed up like a bullfrog. "The police fixed their sights on Miss Lawless immediately and stopped looking once they found a way to charge her. As for private agents, we are strangers here. My uncle has the contacts to get references for a decent attorney, but we didn't know of a local Hercules Poirot."

"I'm glad you find me decent, Miss Pettijohn. You could have requested that I find one for you."

"It was faster to do the footwork myself."

Cosgrove sighed. "Not really. You and your uncle have caused a great deal of ruckus in town. The Yacht Club has complained."

Teddy blew a raspberry. When the attorney glared at her, she covered her mouth.

Cornelia gathered herself before replying. "Mr. Cosgrove," she said, "perhaps we have caused a great deal of trouble. Perhaps it's in our blood; my uncle has been arrested several times due to the ruckus his inventions generate. In the event of this evening, however, I did not trespass. I knocked on the door and asked permission to enter. I wanted to know why she purchased and planted the hat that killed Mr. Stevens."

"So, you were angry and armed when you went to her shop. This doesn't help your case."

"But I was also not the first person to draw my weapon. Miss Rivers produced a pistol after I informed her that I knew she'd bought the cap."

"Do you always expect to get into shootouts with the local hairdresser?"

If a look of contempt could kill, her attorney would have dropped dead from the one Cornelia gave him. "I am a woman traveling around a strange city alone. I've done that many times before; I know how dangerous it can be."

"That's why you should have left it to professionals."

Cornelia almost used a word she'd learned in the barracks. "Sir, when it comes to facing danger, I am a professional. I've driven ambulances through war zones, slept in tents, abandoned buildings, and sometimes on the ground because there was no shelter. I've sliced my way through jungle with a machete, waded into swamps and climbed into muddy trenches to treat wounded soldiers. Then there were the vermin rats, lice, and flies, mosquitoes with yellow fever. Compared to those, interviewing a beautician was nothing."

The attorney leaned against the bars of the cell. He rubbed his temple again. "I can't argue with that, I guess. But this isn't a war zone or the Army. Maybe it's diplomacy or delicacy that I'm thinking of."

"I do lack those qualities," the old nurse admitted. "I can stay here for now, Mr. Cosgrove, but I do need to get back to my post in Colorado in a short time. If you could assist me with that, I would appreciate it."

"No," Detective Knaggs told Cosgrove a few minutes later. "I'm not releasing either one of them tonight. Right now, I don't have a statement from the lady in the hospital or from the three witnesses, who seem to have all coincidentally been present when the incident happened. I'll get Grant's account when I get the Rivers lady's, but I probably won't talk to the other two until morning."

"This is an outrage," the professor said, interrupting the attorney's reply. "First my fiancée, now my niece? You, sir, are allowing the true murderer to go anywhere she pleases, while these innocent women are harassed and locked up."

The detective growled, disgusted. "I've got physical evidence—your fiancée's hair comb."

Professor Pettijohn started to argue.

"She identified it, sir. And before you say anything more, let me tell you that your niece's story sounds like a lot of malarkey. She went into Miss Rivers' establishment armed and shot up a bunch of private property."

"My fiancée"—Pettijohn said firmly—"was wearing a hat, as was the 'mystery woman'. She wouldn't be wearing a decorative hair comb as well. Look at it, detective. Do you think that would fit under a woman's hat? Someone put that comb on the *Nittany Nob* on purpose."

"Perhaps she did, as some sort of statement. You ever think of that?"

"Now you're insulting her. I've a mind to speak to your chief."

"He'll be here in the morning, like everyone else important. Unless he decides to run for election, too," Knaggs said. "You can come back then. If you prefer to stay, I can probably find you a billet in the men's jail."

"I'd prefer not to have a third client in jail," Cosgrove said, tapping Professor Pettijohn's arm. "Come with me, sir. We need to get Miss Orlov to her lodgings for the night. It's become rather late."

The elfin woman straightened at the sound of her name. "I'm so sorry I couldn't be of more help, Professor. I'm sure she's innocent."

"It is I who should apologize to you," Pettijohn said. "I've left you to fend for yourself instead of seeing to your needs. I am sincerely sorry."

There was a chill in the air when they exited the police station and walked to the nearby parking area. The professor offered Miss Orlov his coat, but she declined.

"Where do you suggest we go from here, Cosgrove?" the professor asked. "Detective Knaggs is proving rather obstinate."

"We need to account for that short time during which our good man assumes Miss Lawless sprinted to the waterfront, shopping bags and all. The trolley wouldn't have been fast enough, and a taxi would give them a witness." The attorney opened the door for the professor's birdlike guest, then hesitated. "Miss Orlov," he asked, "May I inquire further about the hats you sold my client?"

"Yes, you may," she replied. "What do you need to know?"

"Did any of them have a decorative piece, perhaps one with rhinestones?"

"No, sir," she said. "These were hats for daywear; a sparkly item would be more appropriate for evening wear."

"And the one she wore into the shop?"

"A straw sun hat with a spray of tiny silk roses. I'd say it was a Marie Louise creation or inspired by one."

Cosgrove smiled. "You know your hats."

Rena made a tiny curtsy.

"So, then ..." the attorney said, glancing over at the professor, "for Miss Lawless to have left this hair clip on the yacht, on purpose or not, she would either be carrying it in her purse, or need to run back to the hotel."

"Excuse me, Mr. Cosgrove, but she couldn't have had it in her bag," Rena said. "Miss Lawless was carrying a small straw bag that day. I admired the way it matched her hat. But the size was all wrong. It was the kind of bag designed for a lipstick, a compact, a lady's handkerchief, and a little mad money. She would have never put a dressy comb in a bag like that. It would have been ruined."

"Besides, she didn't have it any more." Professor Pettijohn added. "She lost it the first evening we were in Saint Petersburg, along with her temper. Cornelia told me it came free of her hair and slid under the Stevens' table."

Cosgrove pulled his coat collar more tightly around his neck. "Then there are two avenues to pursue. When I can meet with the ladies again, I'll see if I can get more information about where the captain's cap was purchased. The salesman would be a good witness to call."

"I presume the other is to find out who picked up the hair comb and how it got aboard Mr. Stevens' vessel."

"Yes. But please don't go off investigating on your own again, Mr. Pettijohn. There is a lot of bad association between your family and the Stevens family. I cannot emphasize enough the necessity of avoiding another altercation. Whoever picked up that comb was at that dinner table the night this all began. I'll get a private investigator on it first thing tomorrow."

CHAPTER TWENTY-TWO

Saturday morning's *Saint Petersburg Times* bore a banner headline: "Shooting at the Stevens Building". Below it, in smaller type, was the subheading "Times Reporter Wounded". Patrons at every table of the Vinoy dining room were reading the article.

At the Stevens' table, the reading was over, and the discussion had begun. Florence was having an intense conversation with her eldest daughter.

"You could have been killed! What would Grandpa McKinley say about your taking the law into your own hands?"

Evelyn, face pinker than the façade of the hotel, dabbed at her eyes with her napkin. "Mother, please lower your voice. People are staring."

Which was true, except for one retired professor. The young man attending Pettijohn asked him if he desired coffee, orange juice, or both, but was ignored. The old man did not have his hearing device in his ear and was too busy reading the continuation of the article on Page Two to notice the waiter.

Miss Orlov, also seated at the table, gave the youth an embarrassed smile.

"I'd appreciate a coffee," she said. "Perhaps when you come back, the gentleman will be ready to order."

A few minutes later, Pettijohn folded the paper and set it down long enough to turn on his hearing device. "Mr. Grant is dedicated to his craft. He phoned the article in to the *Times* from his hospital bed."

The attendant returned with Rena's coffee and he requested a cup for himself. "Please bring me an Eggs Benedict with a side of toast and some jelly. And bring my guest whatever she desires." His blue eyes were brilliant with anticipation. "This is going to be a busy day."

"Is it good news, then?"

"Mr. Grant reports that when he entered the salon, the owner was attempting to perforate Miss Hornbuckle with her pistol. I'm certain Miss Rivers had a good reason to be aggrieved. Miss Hornbuckle has that effect on people."

"Does your Mr. Grant say why the salon owner brandished a pistol?"

Professor Pettijohn looked thoughtful. "No, he doesn't. In his telling, Mitch makes it clear that Miss Rivers—the salon owner, that is—was the threat and not my niece."

"That is good news." The elfin woman peered closer. "I still don't understand why the press was there in the first place. Does he explain that?"

"I presume they were both there to be nosy," Pettijohn opined. "He doesn't delve into that, but perhaps he was short on time. The article was completed by his editor, who states that Mitch Grant was taken to surgery. Since the headline says 'wounded' rather than 'killed', I would venture that the surgery was a success."

Rena nodded. "I suppose our next stop is the hospital."

Professor Pettijohn's eyebrows rose. He hadn't expected Miss Orlov to take such a keen interest in joining the investigation. "Are you sure you wouldn't rather enjoy the amenities of the hotel? There is quite an assortment of amusements you can charge to the room."

"I came to help Miss Lawless," she replied. "It wouldn't be right to indulge in luxury while she's locked in that awful cell."

"In that case, I'll have the car brought round after we eat."

Detective Knaggs was at the hospital before breakfast. If the interference of the Pettijohns wasn't bad enough, Grant had managed to get his hands on a telephone and call in his story in time to make the morning news. His murder case was being overrun by amateur detectives who didn't have the good sense to leave police work to the police. He had a good mind to lock the lot of them up until that Lawless woman's case went to trial. The statements he'd received from patrol had the earmarks of an argument gone wrong, but Grant had made the incident sound like an armed killer was on the loose, and the Pettijohn woman was some sort of hero.

He found Grant's ward without much trouble. The curtain hooks rattled a good deal more than he expected. In his peripheral vision was a nurse headed his direction, but he was too intent on giving the crime reporter a piece of his mind to acknowledge her.

Knaggs stopped mid-growl when he caught sight of Mitch. The reporter was as pale as wood ash. Bottles hung on both sides of his bed and were attached to tubes on his arms. If not for the slight rise and fall of Mitch's chest, the detective would have taken him for dead.

"You're going to have to come back later if you want to speak to my patient," a middle-aged nurse who bore an uncomfortable resemblance to the Pettijohn woman announced. "The doctor left strict orders that he was not to be disturbed."

"What happened? The officer that accompanied Mr. Grant said he wasn't hurt bad. He walked in under his own steam." Knaggs fiddled with his hat, not looking at the nurse or Mitch. "Shucks, the man even called his newspaper from the hospital."

"Abdominal wounds are like that. It may look innocent enough at first sight, but inside there's almost always damage to the hollow organs. Mr. Grant was a lucky man to have a military nurse there when he was shot. If she hadn't applied pressure to that wound, he would probably have lost too much blood to survive surgery."

"But he is going to be all right?" Knaggs couldn't believe he was worried about a crime reporter. Mitch was a pain in his backside. He wasn't a bad sort though, for a reporter.

"Why don't you check back in tomorrow?" the nurse said. "We're giving him enough morphine to sleep through today."

"What about the woman who was brought in with him?"

"Woman? Oh, the blonde with all those chemical burns. Ward four. That's where all the burn cases go."

Knaggs put his hat back on his head and headed the direction Grant's nurse had pointed. He wondered if he was going to find her drugged to the gills and out cold, too.

The nurses in the burn ward went about their duties in somber silence. Cries of pain came from behind curtains, and Knaggs felt the hairs on his neck prickle. He'd landed in one of the hospitals for a bullet wound during the war, but felt fortunate when he heard the shrieks and moans of dying men scalded by mustard gas. The survivors were often scarred for life, inside and out.

It did no good to dwell on that; he had a woman to interview, whether victim or murderess. Knaggs softly asked to see Miss Rivers, and a nurse led him to a curtained area removed from the other patient berths.

"Sorry for the walk, but our other patients are all male at the moment. We wanted to offer her privacy."

Knaggs steeled himself as the plump woman pulled the curtain back. He hoped Miss Rivers would be decently covered.

Instead, he saw an empty bed.

Professor Pettijohn arrived at the hospital. He stopped at the front entrance to let Rena out. A taxi driver was busy assisting a bandaged woman wearing a smock into a taxicab, so he parked behind him and went around to open the door for his guest.

Rena stood near the doors until the professor returned from parking the sedan. "That poor woman who just left," she said. "Bandaged from head to toe. Each movement caused her great pain, you could tell."

"You would think that a reputable hospital would have kept her abed longer."

"Perhaps it was an issue of money. They charge quite a bit these days."

The professor held the entrance door open for Rena. "Where do you think we should begin, Miss Orlov?" Pettijohn asked. "With Mr. Grant, or Miss Rivers?"

"I believe we've already read the best portions of Mr. Grant's account," Rena said. "So, I would suggest visiting Lucy Rivers."

"Very astute of you." Pettijohn approached the patient information counter. "Pardon me, ma'am," he said to one of the women there. "Could you advise us how to get to the burn ward? My niece was brought in last night."

The receptionist peered at him through thick glasses. "That would be Ward Four," she said. "If she's bad off, though, you may not be able to see her."

"Oh, I pray that is not the case. My dear darling niece. Even speaking to her nurses would be a relief. Her mother in Kentucky is frantic for news."

Pity crossed the woman's face. "Perhaps I could have one of them come down."

"Oh, I don't want to take them that far away from their patients. Could you give me directions?"

Soon, the pair were standing in front of the elevators.

Rena leaned close to Percival. "Are you going to tell the nurses she's your niece?"

"Perhaps," the professor ventured, studying the hospital directory. "Although I haven't tried impersonating a physician yet. There was a doctor I knew in—"

Detective Knaggs burst through the door of the stairwell. He charged in their direction, then stopped short. "What are you doing here, Professor Pettijohn?"

Percival gave him an innocent smile. "We're here to visit Mitch Grant, of course. He's a friend."

Rena quickly fell in with the ruse. "We read this morning that he'd had been shot. What a brave man."

"Did you see a woman come this way? Possibly in a wheelchair?"

"There was a woman getting into a taxicab when we came in," Rena said.

"What did she look like?"

"I couldn't tell you much outside of her being slender," the hat lady replied. "She had bandages around her head, much like one of those Egyptian mummies."

"D—drat!" Knaggs said, and bolted off.

"I think that our plans have been preempted," Pettijohn said.

Mr. Cosgrove arrived at the jail early, but not entirely bright. Cornelia thought he looked tired, which was no surprise given the hours he'd kept last night. Under other circumstances, she would have felt sorry for him. Today, she took some pleasure in knowing he'd had a bad night. It served him right for his abysmal treatment of Teddy. Any attorney worth his salt would have exonerated her by now.

"Good morning, Miss Pettijohn," Cosgrove said. "I am told that Detective Knaggs went to the hospital and is not expected to return for some time."

He took a copy of the morning paper from his briefcase and handed it through the bars. "It is rumored that the mayor was not favorably impressed with his investigation once Mr. Grant's story hit the press."

Cornelia took slow steps toward the newspaper. "Mitch is back at work?"

"No, he is still in the hospital under heavy sedation."

"Then how did he ..."

Cosgrove held up a hand. "Your Mr. Grant is a determined man. The hospital staff left him and the emergency room desk unattended for a few moments to tend another patient. My sources tell me he got out of bed to commandeer the phone before they returned."

He chuckled. "I also hear Miss Hornbuckle is livid that he scooped her."

She scanned the front page, then turned to Page Two. "It says here that he was taken to surgery."

"The bullet hit a rib and nicked his small intestine, but please don't fret. Surgery went well. They tell me the damage is minor. The nurses will keep him sedated today because they don't want him to undo last night's work. If he can behave, Dr. Bishop expects him to make a full recovery."

Cornelia's voice was gruff. "Abdominal injuries are never minor. He has a serious risk of infection."

"I think the same thing could be said of your injuries." Mr. Cosgrove pointed to the bandages on her legs. "I've requested permission to have a doctor examine those burns. You should have been taken to the hospital with the others."

"I've been checking them," Teddy said, "but I fully agree with you. They should be disinfected with Dakin's Solution and covered more securely. This is not the most hygienic environment."

"No. I hope that I can get both of you released, although they may let Miss Pettijohn go first."

"That's not fair," Teddy protested, "I've been here longer."

"You have the more serious charge. Despite Miss Orlov's statement yesterday, which I believe should have absolved you, Detective Knaggs still believes he has cause to take you to trial."

"Of course he does. He's been set against me from the start."

"Then we will have to change his mind. Let's start with the hair comb. I know we've been over this before ..."

"I lost it over a week ago," Teddy said. "Well before the murder."

"At the Stevens' table?"

Cornelia puffed. "Once again, I saw it hit the floor. It went under the tablecloth."

"Did you buy it here in town?"

"No," Teddy said. "I hadn't had time to shop yet."

Cosgrove nodded. "Perhaps from a nearby town?"

"Not unless you count Lexington as nearby."

"Kentucky," Cornelia clarified.

"So, it is unlikely that someone purchased a duplicate here to plant on the yacht."

Teddy smiled. "Oh, that would be so clever! I hadn't thought of that."

"It doesn't do us much good, I fear," the attorney said. "If you had to guess, who do you think picked the comb up?"

"I don't know," Teddy said. "I was too upset at the time."

"I believed it was Evelyn until yesterday," Cornelia said.

Cosgrove turned to her with interest. "Why?"

"Because she was dead set on convicting Teddy. The papers said nothing about whether family members visited the yacht before the race."

"She is rather the witch," Teddy added.

Their visitor didn't seem impressed. "What changed your mind?"

"The gentleman from Westshore Yachts described the woman who purchased the yacht cap. I had recently met Lucy Rivers, and it was a good fit. She also matches the description in the newspapers of the mystery woman—perhaps more so, since they said she was tall. After I returned to the salon to ask questions, Miss Rivers' behavior spoke for itself."

Rena and the professor went to visit Mitch next, but received the same rebuff from the nurse as Knaggs had.

She looked up at Pettijohn after they exited the hospital. "Are we going to the jail again?"

"Not yet," he said. "I think a trip to the airfield might prove more advantageous."

Her brows, carefully plucked into delicate arches, wrinkled. "The airfield?"

"Stevens' son, Mac, has offices there."

"Wouldn't he be spending the day with his mother, or at the business office at a time like this?"

"He wasn't at the table, and if he is a wise lad, he will steer clear of his mother and sister for the time being. Reporters will be swarming the Stevens building, so that would also be an undesirable location for him."

"What about his home?"

"That would be the next place the press would check. Fewer of them will know where his hangar at the airfield is, and it has guards."

"How smart of you," Rena commented. "What do you plan to talk to him about?"

"As the only living eyewitness on the yacht, he may have information he doesn't know he possesses."

"Didn't Mr. Cosgrove advise us to stay away from the family?"

Percival helped Rena into the passenger seat of Cornelia's car. "He meant the distaff side."

"I don't recall him being that specific."

He shrugged. "If we learn something useful, he will forgive us. If not—well, we simply won't mention the visit. It will be faster for us to go now than to wait while Cosgrove engages an agent of inquiry and explains the circumstances to him."

His argument was dubious. She doubted that he believed it himself. Still, the day was bright and warm, perfect for a lengthy drive across the county. Rena removed her sunhat and opened the window. "This was farmland the last time I came through here. Progress has certainly been at work."

"Yes, although Progress should stick to the hammock land and leave the marshes alone. They're not suitable for construction."

"That doesn't stop them here," Rena said. "Beach Drive was on the bay when I moved to the Berg. All that land between the road and waterfront was created from swamp. In Tampa, a developer took two tiny keys and made them into islands by dredging up mud from the Bay. They're going to build a resort with three hotels on it."

"These developers are too eager for their own good," Pettijohn opined. "Too many of them want to build luxury hotels or houses that are cheek to jowl so they can crowd as many customers in as possible. The coastline here is prone to hurricanes. They could lose their investments in one fell swoop. Then, there's the potential for flooding—"

"But I thought you and Miss Teddy were going to make a home here."

Her companion hesitated briefly. "Well, we heard sweet promises and saw beautiful pictures of the ocean before we arrived. Now that we're here, I've seen too many houses lined up like kernels on an ear of corn. A man deserves some space, and to see something other than the walls of his neighbors' houses."

"So does a woman," she said.

"What? Oh, yes, so does a woman."

Rena pointed ahead. "Watch out, sir!"

"What's this?" The professor slowed the sedan to a near-stop. They were at the end of a line of vehicles creeping at the speed of gopher turtles.

"It's a beautiful Saturday, so you're caught in beach traffic. Some of it will turn off at the Jungle Prada."

"That's where we will be turning off, too," Pettijohn grumbled.

"Oh," the elfish woman said. "At least it is a nice day."

The professor gave her a sidelong look, but kept further opinions to himself.

Cosgrove left when the physician arrived, a Dr. Urich. He winced after he uncovered the burns.

"What an odd pattern. How did you get these?"

"I got tangled in a medieval torture device at the salon."

"A what?"

"A permanent wave machine with hot curlers," Teddy said.

"Same thing," Cornelia grumbled.

"Sounds like a dangerous place." After his inspection, Dr. Urich cleaned the lesser burns with hypochlorite solution and applied gauze with salve to the more serious ones. After the standard admonition to keep the area clean, he left.

Once he was out the door, Shirley and her mother entered and approached their cell.

"Teddy! Miss Cornelia!" the young woman cried. "I'm so sorry you're here!"

"It's nice to know someone agrees with us," Teddy said. "Detective Knaggs is convinced that this is where we belong."

"He's wrong," Shirley said. "I think the morning paper completely vindicates you."

"The detective doesn't believe everything he reads." Cornelia nodded to Anna Wheeler, who was carrying a basket. "Do you have a file in there?"

Anna laughed. "No, but they checked." She opened the lid and brought out biscuits wrapped in wax paper. "I didn't know what they were feeding you in here," she said, handing one to each woman.

Cornelia eyes pricked with moisture. It was a simple gesture, but so touching. "You're so kind," she managed to say before taking a bite. The biscuit was light and flaky, the way it should be, with a slice of ham between the halves. For a moment, she was back in Kentucky, at her mother's breakfast table.

Anna produced a bottle of milk next, but the matron came over. "They can't have the bottle. It has to go into cups."

"We're public enemies," Teddy said, fetching the cups left from their first breakfast.

They each had a second ham biscuit, washing it down with cool milk.

"Thank you both so much," Teddy said afterward. "I feel quite fortified."

Percival's impatience faded when they finally arrived at the airfield. The young man he'd seen before opened the gate.

"Nice day to fly," he said. "You have another gal with you today. I didn't know you were such a sheik."

"My previous companion was my niece," the professor said. "This is Miss Orlov, a friend."

"If you say so," he said, and winked.

They rolled past the jokester and entered the property.

"You're going to get a reputation." Rena glanced around with interest. "I've never seen an airplane up close before."

"If young Mac is on the ground, you may have the opportunity."

Mac Stevens was not only on the ground, but in his office. He was on the telephone, surrounded by stacks of notes and telegrams. "Yes, you can make delivery on Monday. The regular staff will be in. Yes … yes … oh, and Mother says thank you for the flowers."

He rang off and stood. "Professor, what brings you here? Are Nurse Teddy and Nurse Cornelia out of jail yet?"

"I fear they are not," Pettijohn said. "This is Miss Orlov. She came from Sarasota to make a statement on Teddy's behalf. She's helping me."

"Pleased to make your acquaintance," Mac said. "I assume this is not a social call."

"No, we both have straits to navigate," the professor replied. "We may yet prevail in freeing my niece, but the authorities won't budge where Theodora is concerned."

"I'm sorry," Mac said. "I'm sure she'll be freed. I read in the papers that you were engaged to her. My congratulations for that."

"Thank you." The professor looked doleful. "If we had wed in Midway, it would have saved us a great deal of grief. Instead, I have been forced into making my own investigation. Mr. Cosgrove is hiring an agent of inquiry, but I would like to spare the women of your family if I could. Would you be willing to answer a few questions?"

The phone rang; Mac ignored it. "Sure. Let's go outside; I've been stuck in here all morning."

They entered the hangar first. After allowing Rena a few minutes to walk around Mac's Jenny and express her admiration, they stepped back into the sunlight.

"My apologies in advance," Pettijohn warned, "but I'm interested in getting an account of what happened on the boat that day. I'm certain the police questioned you *ad nauseam* about it, but they haven't seen fit to share their information with the defense."

Mac drew in a deep breath. "Where should I start?"

"When you boarded the yacht. Did you board at the same time? Was anyone else there?"

"No one else was there. Father was already on board, admiring his new cap. If only I'd known ... but how could I?"

"No one would have suspected," the professor reassured him. "Did you see the interior of the box, or the card?"

"I didn't really look at either long," Mac replied. "Dad was pleased the Yacht Club had chosen sides. He put his old cap in the box with the card and stowed it away. After that, we prepared to launch."

"So, there was nothing else in the box?"

"Not that I saw, but as I said, I wasn't really paying attention. I was more concerned about the race and what would happen if Dad won. Harry is a friend, and Violet adores him."

"Were you thinking of slowing the vessel down?" Rena asked, and they both stared at her. "To help them, I mean."

Mac managed a smile. "I toyed with the idea. I mean, they were entitled to their share of happiness. There's not enough of that in the world."

"No, there's not." The professor stroked his beard, which was brilliant white in the sun. "Anything unusual or remarkable during the launch?"

"No, the weather was good and the wind was with us. The only thing that startled me was seeing Violet on the *Silver Breeze*. She was dressed like a boy and had her hair tucked under her cap, but it was her. I don't think Dad spotted her—at least, he didn't let on if he had. He was watching for the flag."

"When did you first realize something was wrong?"

Mac drew in another breath. "Dad was fine for the first half of the race. We were on the way back when I noticed how hard he was breathing. At first, I thought maybe it was because we'd fallen behind. Then he started swaying, and I heard him … heard him gasping for air. I tried to take control, but he wouldn't let go of the helm. He was determined to catch up with Harry's vessel."

Rena took the young man's hand and patted it. "You poor boy."

Mac absent-mindedly put his hand over hers. "I was at the boom when he collapsed. I rushed over to help him instead of taking control of the vessel. Then I heard the penalty alarm and looked up. The penalty flag was waving, and we were headed for the pier." He winced. "I couldn't get the ship turned in time."

"You were trying to help your father," Rena said in soothing tones.

"I had hold of the wheel, but Dad almost went into the water. Probably would have if the front of the ship hadn't crumpled. I dragged him back and looked for a safe way off.

Then the marina crew showed up to help. We both went to the hospital. I was okay outside of some bruises, but Dad wasn't."

"My apologies for making you recall it again," the professor said. "What happened to the *Nittany Nob* afterward? The authorities towed it away."

"They took it to an impound area," Mac said. "Not that it's liable to get stolen."

"Have you had access to the vessel since?"

Mac shook his head. "I haven't wanted access. I'd be happy to never see it again."

"Understandable," Pettijohn replied. "What about your family? Or young Mr. Brockman?"

Mac frowned. "Why are you asking?"

"Miss Orlov here has been an excellent witness for our defense, but we cannot account for an item that was found on the *Nittany Nob* by the police."

"An item? Besides the cap?"

"A decorative hair comb," Pettijohn said. "It belongs to Theodora. She lost it on our first night at the Vinoy, and my niece is convinced she saw it slide under ..." He stopped speaking when he saw Mac's flush.

"I picked it up," he said. "I meant to return it to Miss Teddy, and I've been carrying it in my jacket ever since. You were always out of the hotel when I dropped by, though, and then—well, I took it off after the crash because I thought I'd have to swim for it with Dad. It must have fallen out."

Rena cried out with joy.

Pettijohn's eyes had become radiant sapphires. "The police found the comb on the yacht. It's their one piece of physical proof connecting Theodora with the cap."

"Oh, my lord," Mac said. "I forgot all about it after Dad died. What an idiot I was for not leaving it at the hotel desk in the first place!"

"Nonsense. The police are the idiots for not asking the entire family about what they'd found."

"We need to tell them straightaway," Mac said. "Let's go back in and I'll contact them now."

"What happened last night with Lucy?" Shirley asked. "I thought you were going to see her the other day, not last night."

"I did," Cornelia said, "but I went back after I got a description of the woman who bought the captain's cap. I meant to question her, but she decided to put up a fight instead."

"She might have been involved with Ansel," Shirley said. "I mentioned her once to him, since we were both in the same business, and he said something about her looking like a vixen but being a harpy in disguise."

"Familiarity breeds contempt, where he's concerned," Teddy said. "Did you know he was going to sell the building out from under his tenants?"

Cornelia nearly dropped her cup, which she had been holding out for more milk. "He what?"

"When I went to The Candlelight Club, I met a group of people who were celebrating their continued residence in the Stevens Building," Teddy said. "I don't know the details, but Ansel was selling the building and told everyone they had to move."

Shirley pursed her too-red lips. "Ooh! That would have put Lucy out on her ear, along with her staff."

Cornelia was puzzled. "When did we visit The Candlelight Club, dear?"

"Oh, I found it on my own one afternoon when you were out," her companion replied quickly. "The people I met said it was a real hardship to afford a new place downtown."

"I can see why, with all the business in town," Cornelia mused. "What would have happened to the Movie Star Gallery?"

"I have a good idea," Anna Wheeler said. "I've wanted to move into downtown for quite a while, but we can't afford it. Miss Rivers offers prices we couldn't compete with for the cost of the location. She must have been a *very* special friend of Ansel Stevens to have a salon and staff that large."

"How disappointing," Teddy said.

"Disappointing?" Anna asked.

"That I went through all this because of money. So pedestrian."

"You're still going through it," Cornelia reminded her. "Detective Knaggs says you have time you can't account for."

The other woman shifted, shuffling her feet. "I can account for it, but I don't think Mr. Cosgrove would be pleased with how. Neither would young Violet nor Harry."

CHAPTER TWENTY-THREE

Tenants of the Vinoy nodded at Knaggs as he passed them in the lobby. He'd visited the hotel so many times in the past week, he should have booked a room there. The Stevens family wouldn't be happy to see him again, but he needed all the information he could muster to find Miss Rivers. The single hairdresser he'd been able to find at home didn't know much about her employer's personal life. Her landlords might know more.

Evelyn Stevens' fiancé answered the door. "Detective."

"Mr. Downs," Knaggs said. "May I come in?"

Downs looked behind him and, after a nod from Florence Stevens, let him into the suite.

"I apologize for troubling you again, ma'am," the detective said, "but it is urgent that I locate a tenant of the Stevens Building."

Florence glanced at her elder daughter, who said, "Lucy Rivers? We read about her in the paper this morning. Isn't she in the hospital?"

"She was," Knaggs said, "but she's taken a powder. We were unable to question her last night, and we need to find her. I hoped you might have information in your files."

"I don't understand why you're here," Florence said. "Shouldn't you have called my son? He's at the airfield today."

"I tried," the detective confessed, "but no one is picking up the line."

"She has an apartment near Mirror Lake," Evelyn said. "I can get you the address from the office."

The professor and Rena followed Mac's car back to St. Petersburg in the sedan. It was a much faster trip when one was headed away from the beach.

Pettijohn's blue eyes sparkled; he was all smiles. "Soon, we'll have the ladies out, and we can put this terrible business behind us. I'm grateful that you came back with me, Miss Orlov; your testimony and Mac's should be sufficient to end the matter."

"I was glad to help," she said. "So, when and where are you and Miss Teddy getting married?"

The car swerved. "Sorry, madam; a rabbit crossed our path. I'm afraid we haven't set the date yet. We wanted to choose our home and, of course, find the right church to join."

Rena slanted her eyes in his direction. "That makes sense," she said. "I don't remember seeing an engagement ring when I met her. Does she have one yet?"

"Do you know a good jeweler?"

When they arrived at the Stevens Building, Knaggs asked Evelyn and Arthur if Lucy's car was among the ones parked in the lot or on the street.

"No, I don't see it," Evelyn said. "She usually parks somewhere along that wall, but her car isn't here."

"What sort of car does she drive?"

"A blue Oldsmobile," she replied. "It's rather new and smart-looking."

"We'd better get that address," the detective said.

Evelyn unlocked the side entrance of the building. The elevator was off, so they took the stairs to the second floor. After she located Lucy's address, she and Arthur cooled their heels while Knaggs called the station with Lucy's address and requested that officers be dispatched. "Call me back at—what is the number here, ma'am?"

A short time after, the phone rang. Knaggs answered, and frowned moments later. "Thank you. Tell Patrol they should start looking for a blue Oldsmobile with a young blonde woman at the wheel."

He turned to the pair. "Miss Rivers isn't at the apartment, but Sergeant Duncan believes someone was there and left in a hurry. The door was unlocked, and the closets were open. She needed fresh clothing, if nothing else. Oh, and"—he tugged his collar—"they found a can of Black Leaf 40 on the kitchen counter."

"So, what happens now?" Evelyn asked.

Knaggs sighed. "Now, I take you back to the Vinoy."

Evelyn relocked the office and they went back down to the car.

As they headed towards Beach Drive, Knaggs asked, "Do you have any idea where she might seek help, Miss Stevens? Friends, family?"

"I really didn't know her that well," Evelyn said. "I've only come down for a few months at a time for the past four or five years. Violet or Mac might know better, but he's at the airfield, and Violet ... she might be at home or somewhere at the marina." She blushed.

"Lucy has no living relatives left," Arthur said. "Her brother was killed in the Great War, and her mother died of the Spanish flu, like mine."

Knaggs said, surprised, "You know Miss Rivers?"

"We both grew up in Oldsmar."

"Well, why didn't you say so?" Knaggs snapped. "We could have saved a lot of time."

"You wanted to know where she lived now," Arthur said. "I didn't know she lived here; I hadn't seen her in years. I only met her again last week."

"No father?"

"Died in a farm accident when I was a kid."

"Is there somewhere in Oldsmar she might go? Did she have close friends there?"

"I don't know her current friends," Arthur said, brow wrinkling, "but she might have gone to the family farm. She sold it some years back, but there are several outbuildings we kids used to play in."

Knaggs dropped Evelyn off at the Vinoy, over her protests. Arthur stayed in the vehicle, writing down directions to the farm.

"We're going to the station first," the detective said after they left the hotel. Evelyn glared at their car from the curb. "I need to contact the sheriff's office and request that deputies be sent to the farm before I head out. I'd like to take you along, Mr. Downs. Tell me about the farm."

"The current owner, a Mr. Wilcox, rebuilt the main barn where the old one stood. There's a smaller barn by the grain silos." Arthur said. He paused for a moment and closed his eyes. "There's a tool shed, the chicken coop, and a smokehouse. Oh, there are also a couple of cabins that the seasonal workers—and the occasional tramp—use. Those're down by the tree line."

They arrived at the station and found Knaggs' office in an uproar. Mac Stevens, Professor Pettijohn, and the hat lady were there, all talking to Sergeant Duncan at the same time.

"Quiet, all of you!" Knaggs shouted. "Duncan, what's going on?"

"Mr. Stevens came in to provide exonerating evidence in his father's murder," the slightly bewildered sergeant said. "Then, these other two came in and decided to help."

The detective scowled at the older pair. "Well, stop helping! The man is old enough to speak for himself."

"Yes, he is," Rena said. "We're sorry."

"I'm not," the professor grumbled.

Knaggs looked daggers at him.

The professor wasn't at all repentant. "I'm not sorry," he repeated. "Mac, tell this so-called detective what you told me."

Mac repeated the story of how Nurse Teddy's hair comb ended up on the boat for the third time.

Knaggs ordered them all out of his office. He picked up the phone and called the sheriff's office to alert them about the fugitive. Next, he contacted the district attorney's office. It was a short but loud conversation. Finally, Knaggs called the jail.

When he opened his office door, Professor Pettijohn's piercing blue eyes met his. "Well?"

"The DA says there is nothing he can do until Monday."

He didn't give the professor time to voice yet another opinion. "If you're ready, Mr. Downs ..."

Detective Knaggs arrived in Oldsmar with Sergeant Duncan in the front seat and Arthur Downs in the back. His call to the sheriff's office had been brief but effective. If luck was with them, the Rivers woman would already be in custody. If it weren't, things would get ugly quickly. The idea of dragging a woman from her hiding place, even a murderess, made his skin prickle.

They rolled down State Street, passing broad cross streets lined with palms. When they arrived at the Wayside Inn, he leaned back to speak to his passenger. "Where do we go from here?"

"Keep going. Ahead is a left turn towards the racetrack they're building. The road also goes by the farm."

Out in the middle of nowhere. Knaggs hoped the sheriff's department would already be on the scene. If not, they were likely to miss the farm entrance in the gathering dusk, even with Downs as a guide.

The streetlamps ended after the turnoff, and shortly thereafter the paving did, too. Oyster shells crunched under the car tires as they headed into the darkness. Wooden fences reflected the headlights in spots, forming welcome guiding lines for staying on the road. A handwritten sign for fresh strawberries, "Picked Today", was briefly in view, then another one for tomatoes.

The landmarks became fewer, and Knaggs drove more slowly, eyes fixed on the path of shells in front of him. "Let me know when we're getting close, Downs."

The younger man had unrolled his window. "I'm looking, sir. It's been a while."

Calling ahead had been Knaggs' smartest move; they saw the headlights of the deputies' cars before finding the turnoff. The farmhouse's lights were also on, but merely formed a small oval of light in the darkness. The flashlights of the deputies were bobbing brilliant points in the distance, like fireflies in summer.

Knaggs walked to the farmhouse, flashlight in hand. Duncan and Downs followed. A deputy was waiting there with the landowner. Swarms of gnats swirled around them.

"I'm Detective Knaggs of St. Petersburg. Any luck so far?" he asked.

The young officer nodded. "A little. I'm Deputy Rankey, sir. We found a car hidden in the underbrush near the trees. It was still light enough then to spot the color, and it's her vehicle. No sign of the woman so far. We've checked the tool shed and the outbuildings, and now the men are going over the fields. If we don't find her tonight, the sheriff said he would bring dogs in the morning."

Downs broke in. "The cabins for the seasonal workers will be in the trees to the south. Near the corn field."

"It's not a corn field no more," the landowner stated. "I planted oranges."

"Where did you buy the saplings?" Downs asked, scowling. "It wasn't from me. Who'd you use, that cheapskate Perkins?"

Knaggs broke in. "Thank you for letting us know, sir. Deputy Rankey, gather the other men and let's concentrate on finding those cabins."

"Don't you be knocking those trees over!" the landowner shouted after them. "They haven't been up that long!"

"Bad root development," Downs snapped. "You get what you pay for!"

The detective dragged him away.

Picking their way over the fields had its challenges, especially with a quarter moon. Rocks, mounds of soil from pocket gophers, and the occasional pile of cattle droppings provided the three men with plenty of reasons to be cautious. When they reached the trees, darkness quickly robbed them of any distance vision. Knaggs scanned the undergrowth with the flashlight, looking for a way through the brush and vines.

Downs tapped his shoulder. "There's a path. Let me have that, and I'll see if I can find it."

The exchange was made, and the nursery owner proceeded ahead of them. His memory served him well; they walked on a trail that, while overgrown, provided passage through the jungle. Wet fronds of palmettos slapped them as they passed.

When they came to a fork, Downs stopped and pointed. "The first cabin is that way, not far from here."

"Thank you," Knaggs said. "Give me the light. I suggest that you stay behind us for your own safety."

What Downs referred to as a 'cabin' was little more than a shack of warped boards and tar paper. Knaggs motioned with the flash to Duncan, and the sergeant sidled up to the door and shoved it open. A moment later, he jumped back with a shout.

An opossum bolted from the opening and disappeared into the brush.

Both officers chuckled too heartily and peered into the structure. Duncan entered, but came back out quickly.

"No sign of anyone bunking here with the critter," he said.

The second cabin was deeper in the trees but had a broader clearing around it. Knaggs suspected it had been built before the one they'd just seen; the path ended here, and the cabin was larger, with a little stoop at the door.

Duncan circled behind the building. Knaggs headed for the door, reached out for the latch, but was stopped by a cry behind them. He turned, leveling the flashlight at where they'd been.

Lucy Rivers stood behind Downs, pressing a small pistol to his head.

Knaggs took a deep breath before speaking. "Miss Rivers, please put that away. We don't want to harm you."

"I can see that," the woman crooned. Her face and form were dark, but a shimmer of pale fabric in the beam of light revealed that she'd traded the soiled smock for a robe. "That's why your guns are out. I think you should put those away."

"We only want to talk right now," Knaggs said. "Things will go better if you release Mr. Downs."

"Talk? That's hooey. You don't have all those bulls tromping up and down the fields because you want a chat." She tugged at Downs, pulling him backward, away from the officers. "C'mon, Artie, we're going to the car."

Knaggs gritted his teeth. If she took Downs with her, there was a good chance he'd wind up dead. Controlling him in the car would be too risky. Either she would shoot him, or he would try doing something foolish. He made up his mind.

"Deputies! Deputies!" he bellowed. "She's over here! Come here!"

"You're a stupid man," Rivers hissed, and the gun moved from Downs' head. Knaggs and Duncan both dropped to the ground as she fired.

Downs jerked away and flung himself into the brush.

The Rivers woman fled into the darkness. Ears ringing, Knaggs scrambled to his feet and gave chase.

The trip back on the path was short, much shorter than it had seemed going in. Knaggs carried the only light they had, but the flutter of silk was easy to spot among the leaves and hanging moss. Lucy burst out of the forest, a white shape running across the silvered fields. She ran for her car, then stopped.

A deputy stationed at the car shouted a warning and pointed his gun. In the distance, Knaggs saw the sheriff's vehicle rumbling over the grass in their direction, headlamps making it much easier to see the slender woman who had brought them all here.

Lucy Rivers turned around, now staring at the fields. The points of light that dotted them were moving in her direction, bouncing over the pasture and through the orchard.

She stood tall in the light, raising her gun to her head.

Knaggs believed he heard a sob before she fired, but he might have imagined it.

Bobby Hornbuckle's account of the battle at the Stevens Building splashed across the front page of the *Evening Independent*, with a dramatic photo of Cornelia at Lucy Rivers' mercy. When she arrived at the hospital, Mitch Grant was awake and surrounded by members of the press. For once, the crime reporter was the subject of the story.

"Glad to see you're doing better, Mitch." Bobby shoved a man from Citrus County aside and presented Grant with a vase of roses. Flashes went off as she did so, and then again when she handed him a copy of the *Independent*. "I thought you might appreciate flowers and some reading material. You know, so you won't get bored."

The following morning, the *St. Petersburg Times* featured the picture of Bobby offering Mitch the flowers under the headline "Rival Reporter Does Role Reversal". Below it was another headline: "Salon Owner Dies; Believed to Be Murderer of Local Developer." Nearby was the smallest, but most satisfying headline for Cornelia: "Case Collapses Against Pennsylvania Socialite."

CHAPTER TWENTY-FOUR

Even with the press—all of it—on their side, the ladies weren't released until Monday morning. As always, bureaucracy came before justice.

The first thing they did was bathe. Well, *Teddy* bathed. Cornelia took a sponge bath and washed her hair in the sink. Uncle Percival and Rena were sent to purchase saline and ointment, so she could clean and dress her burns afterward.

Later in the day, they sat on the veranda, enjoying the sun.

"I like what you've done with your hair," Teddy said. "It's different, but that twist suits you much better than a bob would."

"Someone reminded me that there's life outside the Army," Cornelia said. "I'll be retired soon, and I'll have to figure out what to do with myself."

"I have some ideas," her companion said, "but they're for later. We need to get back to our vacation. I'm sorry my being arrested took so much of your leave."

"I'm sorry, too," Cornelia replied. "I expected this trip to have its complications, but so far, it's gone over the top."

"I'll do my best to make the rest of your time pleasant." Teddy sat up in her rocking chair, and then stood. "Look! There's a good omen for the future."

Cornelia stood up and lifted her field glasses. The *Silver Breeze* was gliding out of the marina and into the bay. Young Harry steered the vessel while Violet adjusted the sails. Both were smiling and waving towards the dock, although Cornelia would have sworn she saw a glimmer of tears on Violet's face.

They watched as the yacht headed into deeper waters, then shifted course to the south, towards the Gulf and into an unknown future. Cornelia didn't know where life would take them, but they would face it together.

THE BEE'S KNEES

In 1920's "the bee's knees" was slang that meant 'the best.' The Prohibition-era cocktail was a gin sour blend of lemon juice and honey that was created to mask the harsh "bathtub gin" smell. The earliest book to publish the recipe was the 1930 edition of San Francisco bartender and author Bill Boothby's cocktail compendium *World Drinks and How to Mix Them*. However, the drink is believed to be from Post World War I Paris, where sugar was in short supply. The true origin of the drink is the subject of much debate and so far, there is no definitive answer.

There are several existing versions of The Bees Knees, including one that is still served at the Vinoy Park Hotel. They differ in some ways, but all of them agree on three basic ingredients: honey syrup, gin, and lemon juice. Instead of bathtub gin, I recommend you experiment with more modern and palatable versions until you find a favorite.

The Bee's Knees

1 Cocktail shaker of crushed ice.
2 oz. gin
1 oz. honey syrup
1 oz. fresh squeezed lemon juice
Shake the liquids with crushed ice and strain the drink into a cocktail glass. Garnish with a lemon or orange twist and/or a sprig of fresh basil.
(Honey syrup is made by thinning honey with hot water. I recommend every 3 ounces of honey be thinned with one ounce of hot water. If you prefer a less sweet drink use honey and hot water in a 1 to 1 ratio.)

AUTHORS' NOTES

Saint Petersburg, Florida is known as "The Berg" to locals. The city's history begins with the story of a coin toss between two men who shared a vision. In 1888, General John C. Williams bought the land and traded some of it to Peter Demens in exchange for bringing the Orange Belt Railroad to the area. Demens won the famous coin toss and the right to name the city. He chose to name it after his hometown, Saint Petersburg, Russia. As Demens laid tracks for his railroad, Williams constructed the first hotel in the new city and named it after his hometown. The Detroit Hotel still stands but has been converted to condominiums. Renovations have changed the Queen Anne's façade, but the old lobby was preserved as part of the Garden Restaurant.

At the end of World War I, the City of St. Petersburg saw a golden opportunity to attract wealthy tourists who usually wintered abroad to a warm climate closer to home. John Lodwick, an ambitious young newspaper man, was hired as the first municipal public relations director ever employed in the United States. Soon, smiling pictures of Florida visitors appeared in newspapers and magazines across the country, promoting St. Petersburg as "The Sunshine City."

The land boom of the 1920s had a huge impact on St. Petersburg, which was already billing itself as a tourist town. The Gandy Bridge, opened in 1924, cut travel time across Tampa Bay and helped grow the city. Tourists came from all over by automobile, yacht, and railroad. The population growth turned St. Petersburg into the largest city in Pinellas County. The city also adopted the Mediterranean-style architecture brought by Snell Isles founder Perry Snell. Snell's influence on the city's architecture can still be seen in its historic buildings.

The Berg suffered major setbacks in growth and tourism when the land boom went bust, throwing Florida into depression long before the rest of the country. Growth didn't resume until the Public Works Administration invested some ten million dollars in improvements that included construction of a new city hall.

The Million Dollar Pier was the brainchild of Lew Brown, editor of the *Evening Independent*. When both the popular municipal pier and the railroad pier were destroyed in the hurricane of 1921, Brown challenged the city to build a "Million Dollar Pier" and used his paper to raise funds for the project. The campaign quickly collected some three hundred thousand dollars. Brown used the success of his campaign and his editorial power to pressure City Hall into floating a bond issue for the remaining funds.

The pier was an engineering marvel of the time. Over ten thousand visitors were present when it opened on Thanksgiving Day in 1926. The 1400-foot-long pier led to a spectacular Mediterranean Revival-style casino. The St. Petersburg Pier boasted a swimming area called Spa Beach, a solarium in which to sunbathe in private, a bait-house for fishermen, a streetcar line, an observation deck, and the studios of a popular radio station, WSUN. It was an instant success and quickly became the most recognizable landmark in the city.

St. Petersburg's pier was the focal point of social life in the city for the next forty-six years. It hosted regattas, speedboat races, water skiing exhibitions, dances, fishing competitions, and numerous other events. The shift in America's perception of St. Petersburg in the 1960s from tourist destination to a city of old people, coupled with the city's failure to properly maintain the pier, led to its demolition in 1967.

The Vinoy Park Hotel opened with a grand ball on New Year's Eve 1925, but its story began in 1923 with an expensive pocket watch and a wager. Aymer Vinoy Laughner, a wealthy Pennsylvania oilman, hosted a party at his winter home in St. Petersburg. Famed golfer Walter Hagen was among the guests.

Laughner boasted that Hagen, who was known for his powerful drives, couldn't drive a golf ball hard enough to break the crystal of his watch. The watch was set up on the lawn and Hagen bounced several golf balls off the face of it, doing no damage. The balls landed on a vacant waterfront lot across the street from Laughner's house. While they were retrieving them, Hagen suggested Laughner buy the property and build a grand hotel.

Laughner purchased the property for 170,000 dollars, and then hired architect Henry L. Taylor and contractor George A. Miller to build his namesake hotel. Construction began February 25, 1925. Miller and his construction crew set a record in building the hotel in just ten months.

The Vinoy Park was probably the most opulent of St. Petersburg's boom-era hotels, a sprawling assemblage of Mediterranean Revival splendor. The hotel was built on a twelve-acre site in the heart of the waterfront park area. The architectural embodiment of the Florida boom, the Vinoy Park had everything: Moorish arches and tile-lined cupolas, elegant Georgian-style ballrooms with leaded glass windows and carved beam ceilings, scores of crystal chandeliers and ornamental urns, and 367 lavishly appointed rooms. A single room went for twenty dollars a night during the mid-1920s, the highest rate in town, but it was a bargain considering that the hotel promised to surround its customers with the "quintessence of beauty" including "the blue sea and the sapphire sky and the same profusion of vivid flowers as greeted the earliest Spanish explorers on Florida shores."

The hefty price of a room didn't stop the rich and famous from spending the winter months at the lavish resort. During the 1920s and 30s, the Vinoy hosted businessmen, athletes, movie stars, and presidents. Just about anyone who could afford it stayed at the Vinoy sooner or later: Calvin Coolidge, H. L. Mencken, Babe Ruth—heroes and antiheroes alike—all came to sample the decadent pleasures of St. Petersburg's grand hotel.

In the 1940s, the hotel joined the war effort. On July 3, 1942, the Vinoy ceased operation as a hotel and was leased to the U.S. Army Air Force, and subsequently to the United States

Maritime Service, as a training center and housing for military cooks and bakers. By the time the training center was closed, more than 100,000 trainees had passed through the city of St. Petersburg.

The hotel underwent extensive repairs after the war and reopened to the public. For a few seasons, the *grande dame* of St. Petersburg regained its prewar preeminence as a go-to destination for the rich and famous. However, the popularity of air conditioning, and the Vinoy's resistance to it, ushered in an era of decline. In 1974 the hotel closed, and its trademarked china, crystal, and other items were sold at public auction.

Despite its declining condition, the community petitioned to have the hotel added to the National Register of Historic Places. At its lowest point, the landmark hotel was used as a training ground for SWAT teams. But there was still a soft spot in the heart of the Berg for the Vinoy. Citizens came together again in 1987, and a public referendum saved the hotel from the wrecking ball.

After seventeen years of being unoccupied and misused, the Vinoy was reborn. Two years and over ninety-three million dollars went into the restoration and expansion of the grand hotel. In 1992, the Vinoy reopened and again became *the* place to stay in downtown St. Petersburg.

The Bee Line Ferry made its first public crossing of Tampa Bay on Valentine's Day in 1926, although the regular schedule did not begin until March 7. On calm waters the eleven-mile trip took 45 minutes. Crossing time extended to a one-hour ride on a choppy day. Sea spray soaked the cars at the front of the boat, and sometimes the drivers as well. Still, with road conditions nearly as bad as the rubber tires rolling on them, the saltwater shower was much better than having to circle back through Tampa or Oldsmar to travel south.

The ferry service crossed the bay from Pinellas Point at the south end of St. Petersburg to Piney Point in Bradenton. This shortened the trip from Pinellas to Manatee County from 69 miles to 22, and shaved two hours off the travel time. Even so, the ferry did not make money in its first two years of operations. Real estate agent J.G. Foley, civic booster Charles

R Carter, and attorney James E. Bussey expected to lose money on the service when they founded the Bee Line Ferry. They first considered a bridge, but that proved too difficult and expensive for the time. Their purpose for creating the enterprise was to sell homes on the south end of St. Petersburg. In that respect, the Bee Line was an instant success. With the completion of the Tamiami Trail in 1928, the ferry service began turning a profit. In 1929, the state of Florida granted Bee Line a 50-year franchise on the bay crossing. Their franchise was purchased in 1944 in order to begin construction on the first Skyway Bridge.

St. Petersburg's Green Benches are an icon dating back to 1906, when real estate salesman Noel Mitchell decided he could improve his business by providing people a place to sit. He ordered fifty bright orange benches and placed them outside his business at Central Avenue and Fourth Street. They were an instant hit. Soon, there were thousands of benches in different colors all over the city.

In 1917, Mayor Al Lang got the city to pass an ordinance that the benches all be one style, one height, and one color: hunter green. There was some grumbling from business owners, but they grudgingly accepted the ordinance and over seven thousand St. Petersburg green benches became part of the city landscape.

The popularity of the benches had an unintended consequence after World War II. Retirees began settling in St. Petersburg in large numbers. The benches were very popular with the retirees, at least with white retirees. The benches, like many other amenities in the Segregated South, are tainted by the injustice of racism. The 1960s brought two changes: an end to the 'whites only' laws and a change in how the city saw the green benches. The number of retirees enjoying watching life in Sunshine City from the benches earned the Berg a new and less welcome nickname as "God's Waiting Room." The city quietly began removing the green benches. By 1970, the benches were gone.

In 2002, the city's famous green benches once again made news when the K.C. Brady sculpture of a Dali-style melting clock opened at the Dali Museum, draped over the back of a green bench melting into the earth.

Thankfully, the garden is no longer the only place to find the city's green benches. They are making a comeback along the waterfront in St. Petersburg. While the style is different, the purpose is the same. The benches are there to allow residents and tourists to relax, enjoy looking at the Gulf, or do a little people watching in a vibrant downtown. The big difference today is that everyone is welcome to have a seat and enjoy the beauty of the city.

St Petersburg Police Detectives must have been hard pressed to know who was in charge from day to day at the time of this book. St. Petersburg had a small plainclothes detective unit, but the department was plagued with corruption and conflict. They had thankfully gotten past the 1923 problems that gave them two chiefs of police: one chosen by the mayor, and the other by the city council. But divisions and conflict still reigned in the ranks.

On February 15th Chief of Detectives GC Rodes resigned after only one month on the job. He had taken the job after Chief of Detectives John Trotter was forced to resign over corruption charges. Howard Smith was promoted to the position the following day. During his first weeks on the job, he was embroiled in a sheriff's department investigation over the lynching of a black prisoner being transported to the county jail in Clearwater.

The Klan played a large role in the department's troubles, even after black officers were added to the force. It would take until the 1960s and a lawsuit in the federal courts to resolve the legal conflicts in the St. Petersburg police. The dozen black officers that brought that suit were men of remarkable courage and determination. Their actions paved the way for black police officers all over the country to gain career advancement and equal treatment.

The Gangplank Night Club was located in the exclusive Jungle Prada neighborhood on the eastern shore of Boca Ciega Bay. The Spanish Caribbean building was built in 1924 and was the first nightclub in St. Petersburg. The club was rumored to be partly owned by Al Capone. Capone's "business partner," Johnny Torrio, wintered in St. Petersburg—his wife's family lived there—and engaged in land speculation. He and Capone were shareholders in the Manro Corporation, which bought up approximately 50 acres all over the city. The extent of Capone's involvement is hard to say; in 1926, he spent a grand total of two days in St. Petersburg.

What we do know is that during Prohibition, the club was a hotspot of activity. Rumrunners' boats would dock at the small pier a short distance from the building. From there, the booze was taken through a tunnel that opened in the fireplace of the club, keeping the Gangplank well supplied with high quality alcohol from the Caribbean and avoiding any attention from the police.

The Gangplank was the first, but not the only, club in town. Despite the efforts of teetotaling ministers and other moralistic crusaders, St. Petersburg had more than its share of bootleggers, speakeasies, and nightclubs. Local enforcement of Prohibition laws tended to be extremely lax, and liquor was sold by the truckload within the neighborhood of police headquarters. To the delight of most tourists, city officials rarely levied serious punishment to the pursuers of pleasure. Drunk or sober, those in search of the high life could drive out to the Jungle area to visit Walter Fuller's Gangplank Night Club.

Today, it is still worth driving to the Jungle Prada to see the club. The area has changed, but the feel of the 1920s speakeasy is still there. You can see the remnants of the bandstand and the dance floor shaped like the prow of a ship. In the 1920s, bright striped canvas awnings covered the open-air dance floor.

Opening the door to the bar is like stepping into a time machine. The bar where Babe Ruth was married, and countless illegal bottles of rum were consumed, is much the same, though the fireplace is gone. I don't know about the tunnel.

While we were working on the book, we were able to visit and take some photos of the ship prow rising out of the sandy ground. We ordered drinks and food at a bar that took us back to the age of flappers and gangsters. Around us were graceful archways, beautiful stained-glass windows, and dark wood paneling that were all original to the building.

If you are a history junkie like me, you'll appreciate that across the street from the Gangplank is a park with several ancient Indian Mounds erected by the ancient Tocobaga Tribe. Historians believe that this is the spot where Europeans first set foot on the North American Continent in 1528.

A 1920s beauty parlor might easily be confused with the lair of a mad scientist. Women in long white smocks worked on women draped in beauty capes. Along with the scissors, combs, razors, and clippers, the shops had early and sometimes dangerous versions of curling irons and hair removal treatments. One particularly noteworthy one is the x-ray hair remover. Yes, until many women started showing up in hospitals with radiation sickness, the x-ray hair removal machine was the height of fashion.

Shop walls were lined with bottles of chemicals for bleaching and coloring hair, hair sprays and gels, nail enamels, and polish removers. The makeup counter included everything from bow-shaped stencils for perfectly shaped lips to fat-removing soaps. Yes, the flapper clothing was designed for thin boyish figures, so the beauty industry responded with soaps promising to wash the fat away like dirt.

Shop equipment included shiny chrome dryers shaped like cannons, mounted on tall metal posts and attached to wheels. These were rolled from station to station. For customers with thick long hair, as many as three dryers could be arranged to blow from all sides. The permanent wave was accomplished by the use of strange metal machines with long black electrical wires. These electric tentacles were fastened to women's hair with metal clips. Last, and perhaps the strangest of devices, was the nose shaper. This was a device designed on the battlefield for use in plastic surgery. Post-war, they found their way into the beauty parlor for reshaping women's noses to resemble those of their favorite Hollywood stars.

Roser Park is one of the more unusual developments in St. Petersburg. Charles Roser, the developer, was a baker before he entered the Florida real estate business. He perfected a method of creating a very popular fig-filled bar that was the signature product of his bakery business. He is believed to be the inventor of the Fig Newton, though the National Biscuit Company refuses to comment on the recipes gained from the many mergers and acquisitions they were engaged in at the time. The sale of his company to Nabisco provided Roser with a considerable fortune.

Roser's first entry into Florida land development was the purchase of a hotel and the construction of a second one. He sold both in 1914 because his wife was unhappy with their new lifestyle. She enjoyed the sunshine of their new hometown, but missed the suburban neighborhood they left behind in Ohio.

Roser Park is the result of his attempt to create that kind of neighborhood. It is a small residential community built on an orange grove he purchased in the south end of St. Petersburg. The result of his efforts to please his wife is a streetcar suburb of eclectic houses and lush landscape. Unlike most of the city, the neighborhood is built on hilly land around Booker Creek. A major landscape feature of the Park is a narrow green space along the steep creek banks. Roser walled the ravine banks along the creek in 1914. In some places, the walls reach a height of five to six feet to prevent the banks below the residences from becoming unstable.

His neighborhood included expensive brick streets, rough carved granite curbs, a public school, and land he donated to the city for public parks. Unlike the developers who dredged new land from the floor of Tampa Bay, he preserved the natural contours of the area and built the kind of houses suited to small business owners and local professionals. Streetcar lines were extended to allow easy commutes into the downtown area. He added a nurse's residence to the nearby Mound Park Hospital and contributed to improvements to the hospital. Roser also donated funds for the construction of the only colored hospital in the county.

St. Petersburg Newspapers: the *St. Petersburg Times* and the *Evening Independent* mentioned in the book were not the only two newspapers in St. Petersburg, but they were the most widely read. The *Evening Independent* was the first daily newspaper in St. Petersburg. It opened as a weekly in 1906 and became a daily by November of 1907. It was best known for its "Sunshine Offer." The paper was free for the day after the sun did not shine in St. Petersburg. They made good on that offer 296 times between 1910 and 1986. If you're wondering, that means that the sun shone 96% of the time in St. Petersburg.

The rival *St. Petersburg Times*, now known as the *Tampa Bay Times*, started as the *West Hillsboro Times* in 1884 Dunedin as a weekly. By the end of that year, it moved to Clearwater. In 1892 the paper moved to St. Petersburg and was renamed the *St. Petersburg Times* by the end of the century. It became a daily in 1912.

At the time of this book, there was a big rivalry between the two papers and reporters went to great lengths to scoop the competing daily paper. One of the key reasons for this ongoing fight for readers was the number of real estate ads at stake. More than 80 developments vied for ad space in the papers and provided a steady source of income to both presses.

The rivalry continued until November of 1986, when the *Evening Independent* was merged with the *St. Petersburg Times* and in 2012 the paper was renamed the *Tampa Bay Times*.

Nicotine is best known as an addictive ingredient in tobacco products, but it is also poisonous in larger amounts. Nicotine poisoning can happen when a child ingests cigarette butts, but it is best known as the cause of 'green tobacco sickness' in farm workers. The symptoms are nausea, vomiting, headaches, and dizziness. It can be fatal if the victim isn't removed from the source of poisoning and doesn't receive medical aid. Handling tobacco, especially when the clothes become wet, can lead to nicotine being absorbed through the skin. Gloves help prevent this, as does water-resistant clothing.

It also has a long-term history as a pesticide. Nicotine's earliest known use as an insecticide dates from 1690, and accidents do happen. Poisoning can happen through inhalation, ingestion, direct contact on the skin, and even indirect exposure through fabric. An article in the May 27, 1933 edition of the *Journal of the American Medical Association* recounted several cases of nicotine poisoning via clothing, including ones where the patient became (re)contaminated after putting exposed clothing back on without washing it first.

At the time of this book, Black Leaf 40 was one of the most popular pesticides, consisting of 40% nicotine sulphate. It was so potent that, in the 1960s, Black Leaf 40 was rumored to have been in the "poison pen" the CIA agent tried to use on Fidel Castro. It was banned by the EPA in the 1990s.

ABOUT THE AUTHORS

Hair and Photo by Jay Martello

Gwen Mayo is passionate about blending her loves of history and mystery fiction. She currently lives and writes in Safety Harbor, Florida, but grew up in a large Irish family in the hills of Eastern Kentucky. She is the author of the Nessa Donnelly Mysteries and co-author of the Three Snowbirds stories with Sarah Glenn. Her stories appear in A Whodunit Halloween, Decades of Dirt, Halloween Frights (Volume I), and several flash fiction collections. She belongs to Sisters in Crime, SinC Guppies, the Short Mystery Fiction Society, and the Independent Book Publishers Association.

Gwen has a bachelor's degree in political science from the University of Kentucky. Her most interesting job, though, was as a brakeman and railroad engineer from 1983-1987. She was one of the last engineers to be certified on steam locomotives.

Sarah E. Glenn is a Jane-of-all-trades. She has a B.S. in Journalism, mostly because she'd rather write about stuff than do it. She also spent time as a grad student in classical languages, boning up on her crossword skills. Past occupations include: interning at a billboard company, helping doctors navigate a continuing education website, and updating listings in telephone books. Her most interesting job was working the reports desk for the police, where she learned that criminals really are dumb. Sarah loves mystery and horror stories, usually with a sidecar of humor. Her baby is the *Strangely Funny* series, an annual anthology of comedy horror tales by talented authors. Sarah's great-great aunt served as a nurse in WWI, and she was injured by poison gas during the fighting. After being mustered out, she traveled widely. A hundred years later, 'Aunt Dess' would inspire Sarah to write stories she would likely disapprove of.